PLAYMAKER: A SAPPHIC HOCKEY ROMANCE

LARGE PRINT EDITION

LAUREN GALLAGHER

Copyright Information

Playmaker

First large print edition

Copyright © 2024 Lauren Gallagher

Edited by Cecily Green

Cover Art by Lori Witt

Large Print ISBN: 978-1-64230-278-3

eBook ISBN: 978-1-64230-214-1

Paperback ISBN: 979-8-33257-343-9

Hardcover ISBN: 979-8-33257-354-5

 Created with Vellum

ARTIFICIAL INTELLIGENCE

 HUMAN POWERED CREATOR

No artificial intelligence was used in the making of this book or any of my books. This includes writing, co-writing, cover artwork, translation, and audiobook narration.

I do not consent to any Artificial Intelligence (AI), generative AI, large language model, machine learning, chatbot, or other automated analysis, generative process, or replication program to reproduce, mimic, remix, summarize, train from, or otherwise replicate any part of this creative work, via any means: print, graphic, sculpture, multimedia, audio, or other medium. This applies to all existing AI technology and any that comes into existence in the future.

I support the right of humans to control their artistic works.

PLAYMAKER

Lila Hamilton is thrilled to be joining the Pittsburgh Bearcats, the League's latest expansion team. She's rehabbed from her knee injury and ready for a fresh start in a new city.

But did Pittsburgh *have* to sign Sabrina McAvoy?

Lila's played with and against Sabrina before. She's hot and she's exactly Lila's type, but she's also hockey royalty—her father was a generational talent, and her brother is a star in the men's league. Players, coaches, and sports commentators fawn all over her because of her family name, and Sabrina *shamelessly* exploits that.

Lila doesn't care how attractive she is—*no*, thanks.

But there's more to Sabrina's story than Lila realizes.

Sabrina knows what people say. That her journey to professional hockey was an easy one thanks to her dad. That she left her ex-husband and reverted back to her maiden name so she could leverage her family's dynasty to sign with a team. That she's nothing more than a nepo baby on skates.

But she knows the truth, and this is her chance to prove she deserves to play at this level on her own merits. Prove it to the haters. Prove it to her father.

And absolutely prove it to Lila Hamilton.

CHAPTER 1

LILA

Pittsburgh Signs Team USA Stars, UFAs for Inaugural Women's Hockey Season

PITTSBURGH – The Women's Hockey Professional League expansion is well underway, with all six new teams adding headliner players to their rosters alongside an outstanding draft class from Europe and North America.

In addition to collecting exceptional talent via the League's expansion draft, the Pittsburgh Bearcats have fared incredibly well in the free agent market.

General Manager Chloe Morin announced last week that the organization had agreed to terms with unrestricted free agent Lila Hamilton, an Olympic medalist and World Junior Women's gold and silver medalist. Though Hamilton's three lackluster seasons in Omaha were plagued with injuries—she only played seventeen games last season—Morin stated that the defender's knee has recovered, and she will go into this season with a clean bill of health.

"It's impossible to play at your best with an injury," Pittsburgh Head Coach Hannah Reilly said during yesterday's media availability. "Her knee is back to 100% after surgery and rehab, and we are fully confident that her hockey will follow suit."

Yesterday, Morin told reporters that the Bearcats had also signed Sabrina McAvoy to a four-year deal. The decorated forward is a member of the McAvoy hockey dynasty—daughter of legendary Buffalo centerman Doran McAvoy and sister of two-time Cup winner Mark McAvoy, who currently plays for St. Louis. She disappeared from hockey after marrying Houston goalie Ty Caufield, re-emerging last year on a professional tryout contract with the Seattle Winterhawks following her divorce. The PTO turned into a one-year deal, with McAvoy putting up 79 points in 72 games.

"We're thrilled to have a McAvoy on our team," Bearcats co-owner Wendy Trusch told a press conference. "Her father and brother are extraordinary players, and so is she. I have no doubt the family's legacy will continue in Pittsburgh."

McAvoy is a two-time World Junior Women's gold medalist. She has played together with Hamilton on Team USA at the Olympic Games, earning silver and bronze medals, and both are thought to be strong contenders for the next team selection.

Pittsburgh, Cleveland, and Nashville are the newest additions to the League's Eastern Conference, with Anaheim, Albuquerque, and Denver joining the Western Conference. The WHPL—once thought to be a pipe dream destined for disappointment—now boasts twenty-four teams across the U.S. and Canada, with several rivaling the men's hockey league for ratings and game attendance.

Training camps begin later this month, and the regular season commences in October.

I rolled my eyes and shoved my phone in my pocket. I needed to finish packing, not grind my teeth over my new team gleefully announcing that they'd signed my *favorite* player.

I muttered a few choice curses as I opened the curio case to start wrapping up my trophies and medals. The movers would be here later, but there were things I only trusted myself to pack. Lesson learned the hard way after some movers broke my MVP trophy from my junior division finals. At least I'd been able to repair that.

As I carefully slid one of my medals into its box, then started wrapping it in bubble wrap, I couldn't help thinking about the article I'd just read.

I knew I should've felt better than this after reading the article. I was excited to play in Pittsburgh. I'd been frustrated from the start with my team here in Nebraska, and I looked forward to the change of scenery, not to mention playing for

Hannah Reilly, who'd been an assistant coach at my first World Junior Women's. She'd been a great mentor back then; seeing her in a head coach position was no surprise at all, and I was thrilled to be playing for her now.

But did Pittsburgh *have* to sign Sabrina McAvoy?

My shoulders sagged, and I pushed out a tired, frustrated sigh as I carefully placed the wrapped box inside the larger crate. There were so many top tier players up for grabs right now. As far as I knew, Ella Chambers was still unsigned, and she'd been the League's top scorer two seasons in a row. Why in God's name would our GM grab Sabrina while Ella was *right there?*

Yeah, I knew it was more complicated than that. There were likely other teams vying for Ella, and cap space was an issue, especially for someone who commanded the salary she did. But come on. Sign her along with a bunch of prospects and college players, and build a team around her.

For whatever reason, though, we now had Sabrina. Suddenly Pittsburgh didn't feel like the breath of fresh air I'd imagined.

And the article itself just pissed me off. I knew better than to read articles mentioning her because they were always stupid and irritating. Of course, the reporter had to talk about both of us. And of course, they had to harp on my knee and how my performance had taken a dive because of it, and like, let's all hope Lila Hamilton gets her shit together because she can't use her knee as an excuse anymore.

Did they talk about Sabrina's injuries? Or how her stats were down last season after she, you know, took four whole years away from hockey? Of course not. But they sure took the time to name drop her dad, her brother, and even her ex-husband. They just rolled right on past the part where she stopped playing for *four years* and then picked it up again like it was nothing. She didn't even have to go into the minors. Just strolled on in, got a PTO, and scored a one-year deal as a second line center as if she'd never been gone.

Ugh. Typical. Sabrina'd had injuries too, but she could probably have a shattered knee and be one concussion away from being barred from the ice, and reporters would *still* ignore all that to talk about her family. The rest of us had to bust our asses to get to and stay at this level, but all Princess Hockey had to do was wave around her family name. She knew it, too; why else had she been so quick to change back to it after the divorce when she wanted to play hockey again?

I'd gritted my teeth through playing with her on the Olympic and World Junior teams because those had been short term. There were practices and all, but it wasn't protracted like playing a full regular season together. Now we were stuck on the same team for at least two years. Well, unless my knee gave out, one of us got traded, or Sabrina found another sugar daddy from the men's league and "retired" again. I wondered which of those three was most likely.

I pulled another medal from the case and paused, running my thumb over the cool edge. It was the gold I'd brought home from my second World Junior Women's. Sabrina had been on my team—it was her first time, since I was a year ahead of her—and I honestly didn't remember much about her. I didn't remember much of anything, really. It was all such a chaotic blur of pressure and travel and hockey and adrenaline, and sometimes when I got nostalgic and watched the highlights and recaps, I couldn't actually remember being there for certain moments.

I remembered Sabrina scoring the game-winning goal. Double overtime against Finland. Clear as day, I remembered watching from the bench as she stole the puck off a forward's blade. The instant she'd started toward the offensive zone with no one between her and the net except the goalie, we'd been on our feet. I remembered screaming her name, screaming "Go! *Go!*", my heart pounding and my head spinning because the defender was coming up on her heels and that netminder had been a brick wall all night, and then—

To this day, I could feel the surge of euphoria that hit me when I'd watched Sabrina tap it in. The red light had come on, the crowd had gone wild, and we'd flown over the boards to celebrate.

And to this day, I vividly recalled the way my heart had sunk a little deeper every time a reporter had asked us a question about what it was like to play alongside a McAvoy. They'd all acted like she'd singlehandedly hauled us all the way through the tournament, as if this *same* team—*minus* Sabrina—hadn't silvered the previous year. Never mind that the reason we'd wound up in overtime in the first place was because of a disastrous turnover from Sabrina that had resulted in a buzzer beater goal against. Or that she'd taken a costly penalty in the quarterfinals that had given Denmark the chance to expand their lead to two goals. Or that it had taken some highlight-reel worthy magic from some of our teammates *not* named Sabrina to overcome that deficit and pull off a win.

I sighed and closed the box with the medal in it. That was how it was, playing on the same team as Sabrina. All her mistakes and injuries were glossed over. Meanwhile, I would always be defined by my inability to play at my usual level after a torn ACL.

Footsteps thumping down the stairs pulled my focus back to the present, and I turned to see my dad coming into the living room with a box in his arms. He rested it on the back of the couch, letting it lean against his hip while the couch took most of the weight.

Gesturing back the way he'd come, he said, "Your mother's almost done packing up your jerseys." He tapped the top of the box he'd been carrying. "This has a few, too—we might need another box for them."

I laughed. "Guess I held on to more of them than I thought."

He smiled brightly, a hint of that proud look he'd given me after the medal ceremony at my second Olympics. "Of course you did. They're important." He tapped the box again. "I'm going to stick this in the garage with the others, but then how about we figure out lunch?"

My stomach grumbled; apparently I was hungrier than I'd realized. "Lunch sounds good. Do you want me to order something?"

"Nah." He hoisted the box back into his arms. "I'll throw together some sandwiches for everyone."

"Sounds perfect. Thanks, Dad."

He flashed me another smile, then disappeared into the garage to add the boxes to the small pile in there. As I watched him go, I managed a smile of my own. At least Pittsburgh meant I'd be closer to home; Bethesda was only about a four-hour drive, so it would be a lot easier for my parents to come to games.

I hadn't wanted them to come all the way to Nebraska to help me move, but they'd insisted. Tomorrow, the movers would come for everything we *hadn't* put into the U-Haul. Then Mom would ride in my car while Dad drove the U-Haul, and we'd make the trek to my new city. While I felt a little guilty that they were going to all this trouble, I was grateful for the help and the company. I was grateful my parents understood that I didn't trust the movers with certain things, like my hockey stuff and some antique furniture they'd given me. And what could I say? Packing and moving were a lot less boring when I had my parents to chat with, or when they started pretending to have a light saber fight with some of my old hockey sticks before taking them down to the garage.

It was good to have them here, and it would be good to be able to see them more often.

As a bonus, maybe that would distract me from the fact that I'd be wearing the same sweater as Sabrina McAvoy for the foreseeable future.

The thought made me groan, and I swore as I continued packing up my medals.

Too bad there was no way in hell I'd be lucky enough for Pittsburgh to trade her. They wanted the prestige of a McAvoy on the roster, and they wanted the hockey magic they assumed was a guarantee from someone who shared DNA with two generational talents. Maybe they would trade me if I gave them a disappointing season, but there was no guarantee any other team would take me. I was as likely to wind up on waivers or in the minors.

Like it or not, I was stuck with Sabrina for as long as we were both in Pittsburgh.

I glanced down at the black brace around my left knee. At the tiny scar peeking out beneath one edge.

I sighed.

I'd try this season. I'd try to keep skating even when my knee ached like it did right now. I'd try not to lose my mind sharing the ice with Sabrina McAvoy. I'd try to pretend that I could cope with skating in someone else's shadow. That hockey didn't hurt.

And maybe after this contract was up...

Maybe after this year, if my knee demanded it...

Maybe it would finally be time to hang up my skates for good.

CHAPTER 2

SABRINA

Today was stressful enough without the sight of that familiar black Ferrari parked beside the moving van in my driveway.

I swore at my steering wheel and seriously debated finding a reason to not be here for a few hours, but I pulled up behind the car anyway. After all, I'd left my sister in charge of the move while I was at a doctor's appointment, and while she was reasonably assertive with the movers, she was an absolute doormat for our father. Most people were. The last thing I needed was for Dad to take over and tell the movers to unpack and leave, and he was not above that.

I shut off the engine, paused for a moment to steel myself, and then got out and headed inside. I'd known when I'd come back to Buffalo after my contract ended in Seattle that it would suck living this close to my dad, and I'd been right. Good thing I was getting the hell out of here again.

Two movers were carefully maneuvering a desk through

the kitchen toward the garage, so Dad hadn't called off the move. Yet. I gave them a smile and a quick nod, then hurried past them to find Dad and Zoe.

As I came up the stairs to the second floor, Dad's voice filtered down the hall, and I followed the sound.

"This is ridiculous," he was saying. "It's a waste of time, money, and my hard-earned reputation."

"She's earned her spot," Zoe replied weakly. "Give her a chance. She'll—"

"It's women's hockey." Dad's laugh was full of derision. "There's nothing to 'earn'."

I rolled my eyes. Then I stepped into the main bedroom, where I found my sister and father standing amidst a sea of boxes. Zoe jumped, her face suddenly coloring as if she hadn't been defending me. Dad turned to me, and his expression hardened. He was about to say something, but I spoke first.

"It's not wasting your time or your money," I said coldly. "And it's *my* reputation at play here, not yours."

Dad tsked. "You have no reputation without mine."

Anger surged in my chest, but I kept it down where it belonged. The last thing I needed was him telling me I was too emotional, which was exactly what he would do the second I let the cracks show.

Keeping my tone even—something I'd perfected over a lifetime of going toe-to-toe with him—I said, "Your reputation didn't score those goals or—"

"Neither did you," he snapped.

I had to fight hard not to grind my teeth or lash out at him.

Dad *hated* the way I played. He'd been the leading goal scorer in the men's league for multiple seasons. I racked up points that kept me well within the upper ranks of my own leagues—whether the pro one I was in now or major juniors before—but I had far more assists than goals. Always had. Yes, I absolutely could and did score, but I'd been a playmaker since my youth days. I was the one who'd fight through the other skaters, get the puck into the offensive zone, win the board battles, and send it to the person who was in a better position to shoot, whether she was at the blue line or on the edge of the crease. I was faster than most of my teammates, more agile in maneuvering around and between opposing players, and I used that speed and agility to get the puck where we needed it before letting a sniper finish the job.

My dad was convinced that I was just compensating for being a weak shot. My coaches, teammates, and fans knew better—that I absolutely could make the shots when I needed to, and they didn't give a damn either way when my playmaking ultimately resulted in goals. I didn't care who got the puck in the net and who got the A as long as it meant a point for the team, and even my dad couldn't deny that my assists were frequently the reason my teams won by multiple goals.

But he didn't like my style of play, and he didn't like women's hockey being a thing in the first place, so what was the point in arguing?

"It doesn't matter how good a female hockey player is," he'd told me once when I'd been begging to sign up for youth hockey. "There's nothing more useless than being good at something worthless."

Thank God my mother had secretly signed me up, and since Dad had still been an active player back then, he'd been gone too much to notice.

Here in the bedroom of the rental house I was moving out of, I steeled myself and, once again, kept my voice mellow and even. "No one's asking you to come to the games. But I'm doing this, and the contract is signed." I shook my head. "So there's nothing to argue about."

His lips pulled tight as he crossed his arms and glared down at me. "Hockey is a *men's* sport, Sabrina. This women's nonsense will never be taken seriously, and neither will the girls who play it."

I gritted my teeth. And people wondered why our mom had left him. "The League has twenty-four teams now and plays for sellout crowds."

Dad huffed with annoyance and rolled his eyes. "Sellout crowds of little girls and people who want to gawk at women who think their sports matter."

It was all I could do not to let a sly smile come to life. "The ticket sellers don't care who's buying the tickets and filling the seats."

"They should," he muttered.

Yeah, yeah. I'd heard it before. As far as he was concerned, ten little girls in a crowd were worth less than one adult man, and if men and boys weren't going to games, then no one who mattered was. Sometimes I wondered if he was one of those nameless, faceless assholes who littered the comments on articles or posts about women's hockey, announcing that "no one cares about women's sports" and "beer leagues are better than this bullshit." I didn't read the comments anymore, though, so I wouldn't be able to comb them for turns of phrase that would give him away.

Right now, I just wished he would *go* away.

I pushed my shoulders back and turned to my sister, who looked like she wanted to crawl into a hole instead of stand here listening to us argue. "We should load up the cars while we still have daylight."

That brought her to life. She perked up and quickly said, "Good idea. I'll pull mine up behind yours."

Then she hurried past me and down the hall, probably relieved to be escaping from the never-ending headbutting between Dad and me.

As coolly as I could, I faced my father. "The contracts are signed. The movers are here." I shrugged. "There's no point in arguing over any of this."

"There is, though." He tightened his arms across his chest. "There's the matter of my name on your jersey."

That fury again tried to surge to the surface, but once again, I tamped it down. "It's my name, too."

His laugh was full of derision. "And you were certainly quick to change it back when it came time for you to start this"—he made air quotes—"'professional hockey' nonsense. Weren't you?"

I very nearly lost control of my temper. Even two years later, that wound was still far too raw, and I was pretty sure he knew it. Some aggravation slipped into my voice as I said, "I didn't change back to my maiden name so I could play hockey. I changed it back to *my* name because I didn't want *his* anymore."

He laughed again, sounding more patronizing than before. "Of course, it was just convenient that you left him and took back my name right when the girls' league took an interest in you."

Before I could respond, he brushed past me and strode out of the room.

I stood there for a moment, eyes closed as I took in a few slow, deep breaths. The press had floated that same theory about why I'd reclaimed the McAvoy name shortly before signing my PTO with Seattle. So many people were convinced my name took me farther than my talent or hockey IQ, and yeah, changing it back right before I came out of retirement did raise some eyebrows. I just had to wonder if, much like I suspected he was a misogynistic internet troll, Dad was the reason that particular theory had gotten so damn much mileage.

I rolled my stiff shoulders and looked around my mostly empty bedroom. I knew the truth. I knew that I hadn't cared about reclaiming my name nearly as much as I had about shedding my ex-husband's. Getting this far away from him had been well worth it, even if it had given my dad and the media rumor fodder.

I'd proven in Seattle that I could still play hockey even after I'd retired from competition. My dad's name hadn't racked up those points or defended our zone. I had, and I would again.

Hockey mattered to me. Women's hockey mattered to me and to the fans. For the next four years and hopefully longer, I would play like I was worth the contract I'd signed. Because I *was*.

My dad would just have to make peace with that.

"Did you kick this Hamilton chick's puppy or something?" Zoe called out from the couch in our barely unpacked Pittsburgh condo.

I looked up from making myself a protein shake. "Huh?"

She held up her phone. "Lila Hamilton. She just did an interview, and... meow."

"Seriously?" I picked up my shake and moved into the living room. I eased myself onto the couch, legs still aching from this morning's workout and from moving boxes and furniture around. Zoe scooted closer to me, and she restarted the video as she held up her phone so I could see.

In front of a Pittsburgh Bearcats backdrop, Lila Hamilton stood in a team hoodie and a backwards baseball cap.

My first thought was... Wow. Someone had a glow-up since Juniors. I mean, I'd played with her at the Olympics and I'd seen her around the League. I'd played against her last season. But that didn't mean I'd stopped to look at her or anyone else. The regular season and playoffs were absolute chaos. I'd gone to the gym in mismatched socks like three times during the postseason. When I was focused on hockey, I missed things.

And apparently one of the things I missed was that Lila Hamilton was seriously hot now. She'd been cute back in Juniors and the times I'd seen her since. Today, though? Whoa. Her blond hair, which she used to wear in a single long braid during games, was shorter now, the ends just brushing past her collar. Her sleeves were rolled up enough to reveal the elaborate tattoos covering her forearms. Long, dark eyelashes framed intense blue eyes above skate-sharp cheekbones, and she had those slim, perfect lips I could just stare at for ages.

Playing alongside her, you'd think I would've figured out sooner that I was a lesbian. That came with the territory, though, of not only hyper-focusing on hockey, but of being told all my life only lesbians played hockey. Years of defensively telling everyone *"I am* not *a lesbian!"* had convinced myself for a good long time.

I sure knew now, though, and that woman was just... wow.

Until she started talking, anyway.

Her first few answers were benign and pleasant enough. She was excited to be in Pittsburgh. Her knee was much better now. She was happy to be playing with some of her previous teammates.

That last question prompted a reporter to ask, "What are your thoughts on Sabrina McAvoy as an addition to the team?"

Lila's media training slipped for a second, her neutral expression allowing disgust and annoyance through, but she quickly schooled it away. "I've only played with her a few times, so I don't really know what she's like as a teammate. She's good, though." Lila half-shrugged. "Hopefully she'll bring what she did in Seattle to Pittsburgh." Her smile was frosty. "At the end of the day, I don't care what name is on someone's jersey. I care how they handle the puck and work with the team."

Zoe whistled even though she'd already watched it once. "Damn. You think the PR team is going to let that slide?"

"Probably," I muttered into my protein shake. Truth was, the comment *could* be interpreted as a dig, but it could also just be read as someone saying the most important thing was a cohesive team that worked together. Which was true; few things threw off a team like one person trying to be the solo star.

But on the heels of her mask slipping... I suspected it was a dig.

I just rolled my eyes. "Well, this will be a fun season."

"At least she won't be on your line."

There was that. Lila played defense and I played offense. Though she would probably be on the top D pair and I would most likely be a top six forward, which meant a lot of minutes per game for both of us, and a lot of overlapping shifts. And Lila was almost always on her team's top power play unit. So was I. So... yeah, we'd be playing a *lot* of the same minutes.

Still, that only meant interacting on the ice. We didn't have to be friends the rest of the time. There'd be plenty of other teammates I could hang out with, including a few I'd played with in the past.

If Lila didn't like me or had some kind of issue with me—if she bought into the idea that my name was the only reason I wore any team's jersey—fine. She wouldn't be any worse than my dad when it came to accusing me of nepotism, and at least she took women's hockey seriously.

At the end of the day, I knew I was good. I had the stats and the accolades to prove it. Hannah and Chloe also knew I was good. They'd both pursued me from the moment they'd been hired on in Pittsburgh.

It didn't matter if I was a McAvoy. I was a hockey player, and I was a damn good one.

Lila Hamilton could die mad about it.

CHAPTER 3

LILA

Two weeks before training camp started, the Pittsburgh Bear-cats ownership threw a party for players and their families. They'd rented out one of the most exclusive restaurants in the city, and by the time I arrived, there were already three news vans parked outside.

That part wasn't a surprise. This city took its sports seriously, and everyone was excited as hell to have a WHPL team. Pittsburgh had been putting in bids to the League since the inaugural year, and they'd finally been selected during the most recent expansion. I'd heard some of the other cities had been a bit more tepid in their receptions; the teams had played in front of near-sellout crowds, but the local media and sports culture just pretended they didn't exist.

Not Pittsburgh. I'd come here during my first season for an exhibition game when the League was still feeling out cities for upcoming expansions. The crowd had been huge and *wild*, the hunger for women's hockey palpable in ways it hadn't been in other cities. When the League announced Pittsburgh would be part of the most recent expansion, I didn't imagine anyone was surprised.

So no, it wasn't a shock to see the local news here. I kind of hoped they weren't on the guest list, though. I was looking forward to spending time with my new teammates and coaching staff without camera lenses and microphones in our faces. There'd be plenty of that once training camp started, and even more during the season. Not my favorite part of being a pro, but if that was the price of admission—and it was —I'd take it with a smile.

As I stepped into the restaurant, I was pleased to see that there weren't any giant cameras or blinding lights set up. I recognized Tanya Jackson, who I was pretty sure was the Bearcats' team reporter, but she didn't have a microphone in her hand or a camera nearby. Probably just here to meet the team like everyone else. After all, she'd be traveling with us, interviewing us in locker rooms, and basically our shadow for the duration; made sense for her to make introductions now.

Since she was a familiar face and didn't seem to be busy, I made my way over to her. I was two steps away when she turned, and her face lit up.

"Hams!" She opened her arms. "I was so excited when I saw you were coming to Pittsburgh!"

I smiled and accepted the brief hug. "I'm looking forward to playing here." As I released her, I kept my smile in place. "Better weather than Omaha, right?"

Tanya laughed and rolled her eyes. "That's a low bar. But after a couple of winters in Minneapolis"—she grimaced—"I won't complain about the weather *anywhere*."

"Pfft." Marci, the team's PR director, appeared beside us, handing one of two glasses in her hands to Tanya. "Blah, blah, blah, horrible winters." She took a sip from the other glass. "Get back to me about bad weather when you've spent a summer in New Orleans."

I wrinkled my nose. "Eww. No thanks."

"Uh-huh." She tipped her drink toward me. "Exactly."

With the weather small talk having broken the ice, we chatted about the trials and tribulations of moving, what we liked about Pittsburgh so far, and the neighborhoods we were living in. Marci and her husband had been here for years— she'd been working for the men's team up through last season —and they'd bought a house near Cranberry. Like me, Tanya had found a nice rental in the North Hills, about halfway between Cranberry (where the team practiced) and downtown (where we played).

"How are you handling the hills?" Tanya asked with a playful smirk. "I feel like after Nebraska, you'd get altitude sickness stepping onto a curb."

I laughed. "Hey, you joke, but after a year there, my ears pop driving up hills that I wouldn't have even noticed before. That place is *flat*. But it's nice having some actual hills here. And trees. God, I love the *trees*."

For a second, I was afraid they'd think I'd lost my mind, being so happy about stupid trees, but they both nodded.

"I went to college in New Mexico," Marci said. "I'm all about trees now."

"New Mexico, huh?" I arched an eyebrow. "But you didn't want to take the job with the Albuquerque team?"

That team had made me an offer as well, and I'd gone back and forth for a while before settling on Pittsburgh.

"Ugh. *No*," Marci said. "Don't get me wrong—I liked it there. I really did. But that dry climate and I do *not* get along." She made a face and lowered her voice a little. "There was also no way in hell I was working with Vanessa Barkley."

Tanya and I both leaned in, eager for the gossip.

There wasn't anything scandalous—and like everyone in this room, Marci was way too media-trained to tell us if there was—but apparently Marci and Vanessa had played hockey together in college, and they hadn't gotten along well.

"Too much alike," Marci admitted. "We're both happy being chefs in our own kitchens, but neither of us wants to be the other's line cook, if that makes sense."

Oh, it did. There was nothing worse than two people trying to lead the same group in opposite directions, especially when they were trying to lead each other as well. From the sound of it, Marci and Vanessa were perfectly friendly as long as they were just colleagues. Put one in charge of the other? Well... I could see why Marci hadn't taken the offered position.

I chatted with Marci and Tanya for another ten or fifteen minutes, and then we all drifted in different directions to mingle with everyone else from the team.

There were a lot of familiar faces in this room, which didn't surprise me. Hockey was a small sport, and most of us had crossed paths at one time or another, whether in our youth days, major juniors, college, or international competition. At the very least, I could put names with faces even if we didn't know each other personally.

I got a little thrill at the sight of Val—Jenny Valentine. We'd played together for a season in major juniors, and she was a power forward. She was five-foot-nothing, so she didn't have much reach, but she had speed to burn and could maneuver both herself and a puck through people in ways that seemed to defy physics. I couldn't wait to see her play at this level.

Talking to her—and towering over her because she was like six-two—was Anastasia Ilyasov. When her name had been called during the expansion draft, I'd shouted so loud I'd startled my roommate. What could I say? I was thrilled to be playing alongside the woman who held our major junior league's records for both hat tricks *and* shorthanded goals.

Not far from Anastasia and Val, Simone Yates had her toddler on her hip and a glass of wine in her other hand. I was thrilled to have her here, too. Sims and I had been D partners at one World Junior Women's and at the Olympics, and I had my fingers crossed the coaches paired us up again. She was a solid stay-at-home defender, which gave me the freedom to play more offensively without worrying I was leaving our zone unprotected. We were a perfect match. I hoped the powers that be agreed.

I wanted to go say hello, but she was chatting with her wife and a couple of women I didn't recognize. I thought one of them might be Euli Eskola, an amazing defender from Finland who I'd played against once or twice. The other looked like Nora Bille, a defender from Denmark who I'd almost gotten into a fight with at junior worlds. There was no bad blood there—it was hockey, and despite the sexist rules, fights *did* happen sometimes—but I didn't know either of them personally yet.

I didn't want to interrupt their conversation, so I kept wandering the room in search of familiar faces.

I locked on to one such familiar face, and my mood dipped a little. Colin Harvey. *Anyone* who knew hockey would've recognized him in an instant. He was a great guy from all accounts, but the fact that he was here bugged me. They'd invited players from the men's league? Probably to give us some more legitimacy. Ugh. As if we needed that endorsement. I mean, don't get me wrong—I appreciated that the men's league had been so enthusiastic and supportive, and they'd played a huge role in getting our league off the ground. I wasn't oblivious to that. But couldn't we stand on our own now? Did we *need* the guys at our events to make them real?

Apparently so. Yay.

But... then I recognized the woman standing beside him— Anya Apalkov. Also known as... our star goalie.

I turned away and took a long drink. Wow. I had completely forgotten they were a couple. Colin wasn't here to endorse women's hockey—he was here to support his *wife*.

Some warmth rose in my face, and I silently chastised myself. Why was I so damn prickly about everything? I'd been cynical for a long time—hard not to be when I was part of a women's league breaking into a male-dominated sport— but lately I'd just been... I didn't even know. On edge. More pessimistic than usual. Looking for every reason imaginable to throw up my hands and yell "Fuck!"

Could've been the long recovery on my knee. Missing most of last season and spending so many months rehabbing hadn't done great things to my optimism or positivity about much of anything. That came with the territory sometimes.

Getting signed with Pittsburgh had been a bright spot for a little while, but even that had dimmed pretty quickly. Like the shine wearing off a cheap, badly-plated medal, it had gone from gleaming and exciting to... not.

What is wrong *with me?*

But then my gaze snagged on another teammate, and it all started to make sense.

Sabrina McAvoy.

She was near the edge of the room, talking with Chloe Morin and Hannah Reilly, our GM and head coach, respectively. She was listening to something Chloe was saying, smiling in a way that seemed genuine.

I didn't want to admit it, but she looked good tonight. She always had—hockey players were my catnip anyway, and she had the audacity to be *seriously* hot. In a tailored sapphire blue suit with her dark hair tumbling loose over her shoulders, she was... God, she was *criminally* attractive.

Like me, she was on the taller end for players; I was a hair under six foot, and if I recalled from her stats, she was about five ten. She had that slim but powerful hockey build that made my mouth water—hips and thighs for days, arms and shoulders that made me glad she was wearing a jacket right now so I didn't start openly drooling.

I took refuge in my drink again and pulled my attention away from her. She was, fortunately, still talking to our head coach and GM, so she hopefully hadn't noticed me staring at her. I was grateful she hadn't looked my way, both so she didn't bust me and because for all I disliked her, I found those dark eyes absolutely mesmerizing.

Maybe it was just as well that I couldn't stand her. If I actually liked her as much as I was attracted to her, I probably wouldn't be able to skate around her.

Why can't I be attracted to someone I like?

Ah well. I'd only been in Pittsburgh for a little while. I had plenty of time to meet women who weren't insufferable and unavoidable like my teammate.

Teammate. Ugh. Great. That meant that for the next few seasons, none of us would be able to do anything without commentators and reporters bringing Sabrina into the equation. I *hated* that no one could talk about Anastasia's accomplishments and records without also mentioning that Sabrina had the primary or secondary assist on most of her goals. It was like no one could exist in the same place as her without being described as if they were in *her* orbit. All roads led to Rome, and all scoring titles and achievements in women's hockey somehow led back to Sabrina McAvoy.

I could grudgingly admit she also received a lot of praise she deserved. Watching her play sometimes filled me with envy. Her strong but seemingly effortless skating—the speed, the agility, the way she could maneuver while also protecting the puck—I'd have killed to be half that good. She also saw the ice in ways so many people didn't; it was like she was always three steps ahead of everyone and knew exactly where to be or where to send the puck. There were moments when everyone from the commentators on down wondered what in the world she was doing, but then the puck would suddenly be in the back of the net, leaving us all wondering what just happened.

Imagine how many other players would be that good if they'd had access to all the training and resources she did.

Okay, I needed another drink. Maybe a stronger one this time. Sabrina was here, I was here, and I wasn't going to let her presence sour this whole experience—both the party and playing for Pittsburgh. I just needed to get the hell over it, focus on hockey, and ignore the talking heads who screeched her name like trained parrots.

I took a deep breath, rolled my shoulders, and headed for the bar. As the bartender poured me a beer, someone appeared beside me, and I had a split second to worry that Sabrina wanted to talk to me for some reason. Just what I needed.

Then I realized who it was—Faith Adamo, my best friend. She was my roommate here in Pittsburgh, too, and she'd been hired as the team's skills coach.

"Hey." She nudged my elbow and said in a stage whisper, "We're at a party, not a game."

"Not a—I know." I eyed her. The bartender handed me my drink, so I paused to thank him, then turned to Faith as we stepped away from the bar. "I know we're at a party. That's why I'm in this." I gestured at my suit.

"Mmhmm." She cocked her head. "But you have your murder face on."

"My—" Oh. Crap. I cleared my throat and schooled my expression. Media-trained as I was, I could still forget myself sometimes and let my mood show through. "Better?"

She giggled. "You don't look like you're about to dump your drink on someone, so... yes."

I managed a laugh, which made the less hostile expression easier to maintain. "I'm fine. I'm just—"

"Hams!" a voice broke through the noise. "Oh my God!"

I turned toward the sound, and my mood brightened a little as Joanna Lawson—Laws, as she was called—crossed the room. She was tiny, not even five feet tall, and there was a reason she was described as "sunshine off the ice and a fireball on it." She was an absolute menace out there—a lightning fast skater, a wicked sniper, and a fearless fighter if she was pushed far enough—but once the buzzer went off, she was the sweetest person in the world. We'd played together in major juniors and against each other at the Olympics.

When she was close enough, she squealed, "Hey!" Then she pulled me down into a tight hug. "I was so excited when I saw that you were signed here too!" Releasing me, she met my gaze with a huge grin on her face. "I can't believe we get to play together again!"

"I know, right?" I couldn't help smiling, my irritation fleeing in the light of my teammate's smile. Gesturing at Faith, I added, "You remember Faith, don't you?"

Laws's eyes lit up, and she hugged Faith, too. "Of course I do." She scowled playfully at my roommate. "I'll never forget you mugging me at the Olympics."

Faith laughed and shrugged. "It isn't like it made a big impact on the game or anything. Ooh, waaait..."

Laws rolled her eyes and tsked as Faith and I shared a fist bump. "Too bad we beat you in overtime, eh?"

We all chuckled. That gold medal final between Team USA and Team Canada had been intense, and Canada had finally beaten us in triple overtime. Disappointing, sure, but we'd earned the hell out of our silver medals, so I had no complaints.

Well, aside from everyone acting like we'd only made it that far in the first place because we'd been blessed with the Goddess McAvoy's talent and—

I dismissed those thoughts and took another swallow of beer.

Fortunately, Laws's wife joined us right then with their three-year-old perched on her hip. Introductions were made, and we all fawned over Reagan; who wouldn't? The kid was adorable.

Naturally, though, the conversation quickly shifted back to hockey.

Laws looked at me. "So how's your knee doing?" She grimaced. "I was so scared you wouldn't be able to come back after what happened last season."

I suppressed a shudder. I still had nightmares about that game. That awful moment when I'd realized something in my knee had moved in a way it shouldn't have. That pop. The way my knee had been an explosion of both pain and instability. The panic, the certainty my career had just ended—it was burned into my memory in the most visceral way.

"I was worried myself," I admitted. "But it wasn't as bad as everyone made it out to be."

"A torn ACL wasn't that bad?" She gaped. "I'd have been freaking out!"

"Oh, I was. But honestly, the doctors told me pretty early on that I'd recover. They always recommend sitting out most of the season after that just to make sure it heals right. And they figured as long as they were going in to fix the ACL, they might as well clean up some of the other issues, so..." I half-shrugged to mask another shudder. "It wasn't fun, but my leg is a lot better now." I bent and straightened it as if to emphasize my point. "I'm good!"

"That's great!" Laws sounded genuinely relieved. "I'd bet money you'll be on the first power play unit."

I smiled. "Well, let's hope I impress the coaches."

Faith and Laws both scoffed, and I laughed. I was proud of what I brought to a team's power play. Omaha had had the number three power play in the League the season before last, and I had no qualms about acknowledging my part in that. This was a sport that had taken a long time to get the respect it demanded, and I wasn't about to shy away from the respect I'd earned on that ice.

Laws dropped her voice a little. "Can you believe they signed Sabrina McAvoy? What a score!"

Annnd... there went my brighter mood.

Struggling to keep my media smile in place, I said, "Yeah. That was... We're definitely lucky to have her."

"We are! I mean, we have Sabrina McAvoy, and we have a healthy Lila Hamilton." She clapped her hands and bounced on her feet. "This season is going to be amazing!"

Of course there was always that qualifier—a *healthy* Lila Hamilton. Because everyone knew I was an asset as long as my knee was cooperating. The instant it was out of whack, I was a liability who needed to either retire or be launched into the sun. Yeah, I read the comments on articles and social media. I knew how people felt about me.

But hey, if my knee decided to be stupid, maybe no one would notice this time because the spotlight would be so focused on the dynastic generational talent we were so blessed to have.

I sipped my drink but didn't really taste it.

Maybe I should've accepted that offer to play in Albuquerque after all.

CHAPTER 4

SABRINA

Back when my dad had still been a pro, I'd gone with my mom and siblings to watch training camp. I'd dreamed of being out there someday myself—skating with the prospects and veterans, playing my butt off so I'd be noticed by the coaches and wouldn't get cut.

A vivid memory from my childhood was Dad's training camp the year I turned nine. He'd always shit on the idea of me playing hockey. He'd humored my mom letting me play as a little kid, thinking I'd grow out of it before long. He never went to any of my games, though, and he was never interested in talking about hockey with me like he was with my brother. Mom had always tried to dismiss it as him being busy—the regular season was, we all knew, incredibly intense—and she just told me to let it go.

That year, a week or so before training camp, I'd stubbornly decided that he *would* finally acknowledge me and my hockey. Bad idea, and Mom had tried to gently dissuade me, but I'd finally commanded his attention at dinner one night and boldly announced that my U10 team was going to win our division's trophy that year.

For the couple of seconds he'd stared at me in surprise, I'd been sure I'd finally gotten through. He'd finally noticed me.

But then he'd exhaled hard and turned his scowl on my mother. "What is she still doing playing hockey? It's not a sport for girls."

"I'm good at it!" I'd shot back. "I'm the second line center on a boys' team!"

That had *infuriated* my father. He'd been enraged that I was taking a coveted space that would be better suited for a boy who had potential to go somewhere in the sport. When I'd refused to back down—when I'd shouted at him because I'd been so mad—he'd sent me to my room.

I hadn't even made it out of the kitchen before he told my mother, "She's not playing any more hockey and that's final."

I'd gone to my room and cried until I almost threw up. Some time later, Mom came in with the reheated remains of my dinner.

"Eat," she'd gently told me. "You've got practice coming up."

"Dad says I have to quit."

"I know." She'd stroked my hair. "But you're not going to quit. Dad doesn't want you to play, and that's not fair, so it's going to be our secret."

It was the most defiant thing I'd ever heard my mother say up until that point. She never told us to keep secrets, and she'd always told us that if a grownup said "this is our secret," that was our cue to come straight to her or Dad and tell them.

Somehow, even at that age, I'd known this was different. That this was her pushing back against my father in a way that kept my dream alive and kept a roof over our heads. My siblings and I weren't stupid—we'd heard him threaten to make her and us homeless if she stepped out of line. While defying him by keeping me registered for hockey probably sounded trivial to most people, Mom knew—and nine-year-old me knew—that it was dangerous.

But she did it anyway.

All these years later, I still wondered sometimes if that was the night she'd finally started gathering up the courage to leave. If she'd begun forming her escape plan during that fraught dinner, or if it had already been in the works by that point. For some reason, I never wanted to ask.

Whatever the case, training camp happened while Mom and Dad were still married and I was still secretly playing for the Orchard Park Tigers. After the first day, while we were having lunch with Dad and some of his teammates, he'd laughed about how I'd taken up hockey.

"There's no point," he'd chuckled. "Piss away money on gear for a few years, maybe get a pitiful scholarship to a college with a women's team, and then never even make a beer league." He'd scoffed. "What a waste."

In the moment, as rage had boiled quietly behind my ribs, I'd hated his teammates for laughing along. Years later, Mom had told me they'd been visibly uncomfortable, but they obviously hadn't wanted to get their captain fired up.

"You didn't notice how they felt," she'd said. "But I did. It gave me a lot of courage that I needed a few months later."

No, I hadn't noticed. It had, however, fueled that fire

that made me want to prove myself on the ice. The next two days of training camp, I'd fumed as I'd watched Dad and his team and the prospects through the puck-scuffed glass. I'd vowed to be there one day. To prove to him that I was just as worthy of a place on a professional team as he and my brother were.

Someday, I'd told myself over and over, *I'll be on the ice while he's behind the glass. If there isn't a team for me to play on, I'll fucking* make *one, damn it.*

Yeah, I'd cursed even to myself. I was nine, but I was a hockey player. My vocabulary was what it was.

And now, almost two decades later, with a lot of the anger cooled but the determination still burning fiercely in my belly...

I skated out onto the ice to join the Pittsburgh Bearcats for training camp.

I smiled to myself as I glided between players I'd known since my youth and major junior days, and as I watched the young prospects and their awestruck faces. This wasn't my first professional training camp, but I doubted the novelty would ever wear off.

I'd made it. Despite every obstacle that had been laid out in front of me, I'd made it. The pro women's hockey league I'd helped get off the ground was thriving, playing in front of sellout crowds all over North America while multiple cities clamored to be part of the next expansion.

Reporters were crowded in at one end of the rink. Along the side with stands for the spectators, dozens of kids—especially little girls—pressed their faces and signs to the glass, wearing huge grins beneath Bearcat beanies. Several had on jerseys from the team; I'd heard those had all but sold out the minute they'd gone on sale.

Nine-year-old me had imagined breaking into the men's league and finding a place there, but this was even better. We had our own place. Our own teams. Our own fans who were here to see *us*.

Maybe someday the novelty would wear off, but I hoped it didn't.

And maybe someday, it wouldn't sting so much to remember the one face that would never be in that crowd, cheering me on with all the pride he brought to his son's games.

That thought threatened to sour my mood, so I shook it away. I grabbed a couple of pucks on my stick and tossed them over the glass. There was nothing in the world better than the way a kid's eyes lit up when they caught a puck. I loved how they'd hold it up triumphantly and squeal with joy while snow still tumbled down on them from the puck in their hand.

It just didn't get any better than this.

You don't know what you're missing, Dad.

I wished I didn't care so much that he didn't care. I wished I didn't miss him. Or, well, it wasn't that I missed him. I missed the *idea* of him. The idea of a supportive dad cheering me on from the stands. I'd had teammates whose dads were so loud, you could sometimes pick out their voices even over the glass.

That would never be my dad. It was a sad, heavy thing to accept, but it was reality. Sometimes I imagined looking over and being startled to see him sitting there after all, beaming with pride. I didn't know what I'd do if that ever happened. Cry? Forget how to play hockey?

It wasn't going to happen, though, so I didn't dwell on it.

Fortunately, hockey was always a good distraction from just about anything, and right then, Coach Reilly blew the whistle. I grinned as I skated over to join my teammates.

Training camp. Here we go.

We were divided into three teams based on our jersey colors—black, white, and gold. For today, the gold team would be on the other rink while black and white stayed in this one and practiced together. Tomorrow, my team—black—would be separated while gold and white were together. Over the next three days, the coaches would put all of us through drills, conditioning exercises, and scrimmages, and from there, the team would be whittled down to twenty: two goalies, twelve forwards, and six defenders.

A lot of the prospects would be heading back to their college or major junior teams, and this was mostly an opportunity for development. They weren't likely to make the roster yet, but there was nothing quite like training with the pros to develop their skills. I envied them that chance; there hadn't been a pro league during my major junior days.

Of the rest of us, some would be sent to the minors while others made the roster. There were a few who were essentially shoo-ins for the roster—especially for the top lines. I'd been told in no uncertain terms that I was on that list, but as far as I was concerned, I was here to prove myself just like everyone else. Nothing bred resentment more than someone who half-assed camp and practice because they knew they were guaranteed a spot. I'd earned my place with the front office and coaching staff, but this was where I had to earn it with my teammates.

And besides, what good did it do for the prospects to practice with veterans who weren't giving their all?

It didn't hurt that I thought practice was fun as hell, even during the chaos that was training camp. The drills were intense and the coaches were demanding, but I enjoyed it. Probably because even after all this time, I still loved playing hockey.

"Mac!" Nora called out to me during a battle drill. I turned toward the sound of her voice, and she fired the puck right onto my tape. One of the opposing players tried to body me around and separate me from the puck, but I shouldered her off me and passed the puck to Nora.

A heartbeat later, someone else checked me into the boards. *Hard.*

I recovered quickly—it wasn't fun, but she hadn't hit me at full speed, and I was decked out in protective gear—but irritation flared in my chest. What the hell? This was a drill, not a game. Yeah, we were supposed to get physical, but checking like that seemed unnecessary, especially when I didn't have possession.

I looked up as the other player skated off, and my temper surged as I read the name across her lower back.

Hamilton.

Of course it was Lila fucking Hamilton.

I rolled my eyes and continued with the drill. My momentary distraction had only cost me a handful of seconds, but every heartbeat counted in hockey.

And when I found the right second, I was going to pay

Hamilton back. This was the third time she'd messed with me since practice had started. Earlier, it had been an unnecessary hip check during a defensive drill. After that, stealing the puck from me when we were supposed to be playing on the same side.

"Oops," she'd said with a smirk after I'd called her out on it.

I'd just rolled my eyes and gritted my teeth, but now I was pissed. First chance I had, it was payback time.

That opportunity came during the next battle drill, and I shamelessly took it. Hamilton had the puck. I could've easily poke-checked it away, but screw that—I slammed her into the glass, *then* stole the puck.

The muttered "bitch" barely registered because I was halfway across the ice by then, and I just grinned behind my visor as I continued through the drill. I passed the puck to Laws, who shot it into the net behind Anya. Laws and I shared a fist bump, and then we both tapped Anya's pads because this was a drill, we were teammates, and there were no hard feelings.

"I hate you both," she said, laughing behind her mask.

"Nah, you don't." I grinned, skating backwards away from her. "We're just sharpening your skills for the real thing!"

She rolled her eyes and held up her blocker. "You can't see it, but I'm giving you the bird."

I returned the gesture, confident that my bulky glove hid my upraised middle finger from the fans watching us behind the glass.

Coach Reilly blew the whistle, and we all headed to the bench for some water. After we'd caught our breath as much as anyone ever did during hockey practice, Coach called out, "Hams. Mac." She beckoned to Lila and me. "The rest of you..." She nodded toward Lynnie, the offensive coach, who was standing at the whiteboard beside the bench. While our teammates skated over to listen to her lay out the next drill, Lila and I exchanged caustic looks, then skated over to our coach.

A safe distance away from the rest of the team, Coach lowered her voice to an irritated growl. "Is there something going on here that I need to know about?" She flicked her eyes back and forth between us. "Or was that just some overly enthusiastic checking for training camp?"

"Nothing going on," I said with a grin. "Just showing the prospects how we play at this level."

Coach was unamused. "Whatever this is"—she pointed to each of us—"unfuck it, or else one of you is going to be playing someplace else."

Then she skated away to join the rest of the team by the whiteboard, leaving me alone with Lila. I wasn't sure what Coach meant by "someplace else"—if that was a threat to send one of us to the minors or to trade us out of Pittsburgh. Whatever the case, I wasn't interested in going anywhere else, least of all because Lila Hamilton had her nose out of joint over something.

I turned to Lila and asked under my breath, "You have a problem, Hams?"

"No problem at all," she growled back.

"Oh, yeah?" I nodded toward the boards where she'd checked me. "So what was that all about?"

"Exactly what you said." She smirked and shrugged.

"Showing the prospects how we play at this level." Then she added a more acidic, "And making sure they know we don't handle the nepotism babies with kid gloves."

Before my jaw had finished falling open, she was skating away, leaving me standing there with white hot anger roiling in my chest.

That was what this was all about? Seriously? Ugh. For God's sake. It was bad enough everyone and their goddamned mother in the media thought I was only here because of nepotism. I didn't need one of my own teammates fueling that bullshit.

A knot wound beneath my ribs as I scanned the ice, taking in the sight of my teammates, from those I'd played with before to the ones I'd only recently met.

How many of them agreed with Lila and the press?

How many of them thought I didn't actually belong here? Goddammit.

And how many of them would turn on me once Lila and the reporters dripped enough poison in their ears?

Renewed fury surged inside me. I'd already been less than thrilled with Lila's frosty attitude toward me. Now I was pissed that her bullshit might infect the rest of the team, and even more so when I realized my focus was gone. She was screwing with my concentration. She had no right to live rent-free in my head, and I wasn't going to put up with it.

I joined my teammates and took a knee in the back row, and I fumed throughout the offensive coach's explanation of our next drill and its objectives. When she dismissed us to set up for the drill, a few players did some slow skating around the ice just to keep their legs loose. Not unusual.

While they did that, I found a puck and headed for the untended goal, and I slapped that puck hard into the back of the net.

Fuck Lila Hamilton. I'd *earned* my place here, and I was going to earn my place on the roster. On the top six. Hell, I wanted the top *line*. I was going to prove to Lila Hamilton, to my father, to my ex-husband, and to everyone else who thought I'd come here on Easy Street that I *deserved* to wear this sweater.

Nepotism my ass.

CHAPTER 5

LILA

"There has to be something in the Geneva Conventions about this," I gritted out as I gingerly bent and straightened my knee. "I feel like I should report you to the Hague."

Collette, my physical therapist, snorted. "You'll feel better tomorrow and you know it."

I huffed. She had a point, no matter how much I wanted to argue that she was *mean* and *evil* and just enjoyed sadistically manipulating my poor knee. But... yeah... it usually felt better the next day. And if not, the day after that.

It just sucked in the moment, sort of like how blocking a puck with my body hurt like hell, but it was sure worth it when it kept the other team from scoring.

"So what do you think?" I rubbed the side of my knee. "Am I getting better?"

I didn't like the way she quirked her lips and skimmed over her notes. I knew physical therapists and doctors didn't have instant answers, and there were often a lot of layers to whether something was improving or not. But my gut said she was avoiding my gaze.

I could've been wrong. I'd started working with Collette when I'd first arrived in Pittsburgh, and that had only been a few weeks. Long enough to figure out someone's tells, but maybe not all of them.

Frowning, she met my eyes. "I do think it's improving, but I also think you're pushing yourself too hard if you want to continue on that trajectory."

My stomach somersaulted, and I forced a laugh. "I'm a hockey player. That comes with the territory."

Her frown deepened. "I understand that. But if you'd like to *stay* a hockey player, you might want to go a little easy on your knee, at least for a while."

"During training camp?" I laughed again, sounding almost as panicked as I felt. "There's no going easy on anything."

She eyed me, and I could tell she was losing her patience.

Sighing, I said, "I know. Trust me—I get it. But I have to push hard if I want to make the roster this season. If I baby my knee right now, I'm going to end up in the minors."

"And if you don't baby it," she countered, "you're going to end up on the bench in a brace. And that's best-case scenario."

My stomach flipped again. She was right and I knew it, but it was still tough to hear.

Apparently reading my unease, she gently said, "I was an athlete too, you know. Never went pro, but I was at the top of my game in college." She tipped her head toward some framed photos on the wall from her basketball years. "When I say I know how hard it is to find that balance between babying an injury enough to heal and pushing yourself enough to succeed, I'm not blowing smoke."

I swallowed. "I know. And I... I mean, I get it." My shoulders dropped. "It *is* hard."

"Yeah. It sucks."

I managed a quiet laugh. "Seriously." Then I met her gaze and sobered. "So how do I do this?"

Collette gnawed her lip. "You're not going to like my answer."

"Probably not, but let's hear it anyway."

She straightened a little. "The *best* thing you can do is take a few more months off from hockey. Keep conditioning and training, but focus on strengthening your knee and allowing everything to really finish healing rather than subjecting it to the strain of hockey."

"Well, you're not wrong. I don't like that answer." I tapped my fingertips on top of my uninjured knee. "What's my next best option?"

"You take extra time to warm up before *every* practice and every game," she said sternly. "You keep your legs in absolute *peak* physical condition so the muscles can support the joint and the damaged tissue. And if it hurts... rest it. Even if that means sitting out a game now and then. Your coaches and trainers will understand."

I nodded as she spoke. Yeah, they'd understand. They all knew how taxing this sport was on the body, and that it was better to err on the side of taking care of an injury before it turned into a major one.

They also knew—as did Collette—that hockey players

would play through anything short of a shattered spine. I'd played in the postseason in major juniors with a hairline fracture in my hand. At the Olympics, Sims had taken a puck to the face, been stitched up, and returned for the next period. One of the goalies I'd played with in U16 was now in the men's league, and two years ago, he'd refused to have hip flexor surgery until the season was over. The dude could barely walk, but he'd made it all the way to the Cup finals and had two shutouts during that seven-game stretch.

Suffice it to say, hockey players were not known for taking it easy when something hurt. Sometimes that was just because we were too stubborn to stop playing hockey for any reason. Other times... Well, there were people who theorized that hockey players weren't quite sane, so there was that.

But there was also that very real fear of becoming a liability. A precautionary stint on the bench could become protracted, not because the injury got worse, but because the player who'd come up from the minors to fill in went on a hot streak. They were under a ton of pressure to shine when they came up to the majors, and sometimes they did exactly that. What coach would send them back down when they were killing it out there, just to reactivate a player who probably wasn't 100% yet and likely needed some time to find their timing again? Why not keep the young talent on the roster? And then when free agency came up, suddenly that injured player's cap space could be better suited toward signing one, two, or even three talented prospects.

So that precautionary couple of games on the bench could turn into weeks off the ice, which could turn into the team letting her walk—or limp—out the door at the end of her contract so someone young, talented, and healthy could take her place.

Collette nudged my arm. "Wherever you're going in your head—don't. You have to listen to your body, Lila."

Swallowing, I nodded again. "I know. But the media can't stop talking about me like a liability because of my knee. I have to take care of my body, but I also have to hold my position as a professional."

She sighed. "I get that. But having that position as a professional won't do you any good if you've broken your body beyond repair."

I winced.

She was right. I knew she was right.

But I was pretty sure we both knew I was going to keep pushing. This sport was my life. It was my job now.

I'd come too far to let anything derail me.

CHAPTER 6

SABRINA

Training camp finally came to an end, but that meant the real work was just beginning. With the roster established, the focus was now on the season ahead. Practices and off-ice workouts filled our calendars alongside media availabilities and the media days where we did photos and videos for hype montages. The first preseason games were just a couple of weeks away.

It was a ton of work, and the schedule was demanding as hell, but I loved every minute of it. After taking the long, bumpy way to get this career, I was determined to savor all of it, even the tedious and exhausting parts.

Today, we'd had a great on-ice practice, and now everyone was stripping off gear, showering, and dressing. Then we'd go eat before joining our coaches in the auditorium for a team meeting.

After my shower, I pulled on a T-shirt and gym shorts. Then I wiped the towel over my face before tying my hair back into an unruly ponytail. Even now, almost two years after my divorce, I sometimes got a little rush of rebelliousness when I put my hair up like that.

"Would it kill you to just put it back in a normal ponytail?" Ty had groused one morning. "Like, a tidy one instead of... *that?*"

"It's just to keep it out of my face," I'd replied. "I don't need to look put together while I'm doing housework."

The way he'd rolled his eyes had made my stomach turn. So did his remark of, "Then let's just hire a damn housekeeper. I shouldn't have to trade my wife's appearance for a clean house."

I'd decided I was too tired to fight with him, so I'd switched to tidier ponytails after that. And we'd hired a housekeeper. And I'd kept doing my hair the way he wanted to because it just wasn't worth the attitude I'd get if I didn't.

Now Ty was gone and I could do whatever I damn well pleased with my own hair. It was a minor thing—a petty one, really—but it felt good, so... fuck it.

"I thought guys *liked* messy ponytails," my sister had mused a few weeks after I'd left his ass and moved in with her. "What was his damage about it?"

"What was his damage about anything?" I'd muttered. "He didn't like it braided, either. Probably because that was how I used to wear it when I played hockey."

These days, with some time and distance to cool my emotions, I thought that might've been close to the truth. Ty had always resented any reminders that I'd ever played hockey—he hadn't even liked my trophies being on display— and I'd eventually sussed out that it was because those often segued into the fact that I'd played hockey *well*. He'd barely made it into major juniors, and he'd been undrafted into the men's league. Though he'd eventually been signed and made a name for himself, especially in recent years, his lackluster professional start still bugged him. Sometimes I thought it grated on him to be around or even hear about my dad or brother, because they'd both been first overall draft picks for major juniors *and* the pros.

Being married to a woman who'd also been selected first overall to her major juniors? Even if women's hockey was barely above beer league? Yeah, I was pretty sure that stung.

In my pettiest moments, I wondered if it bothered him that I was playing at this level now. Maybe I hadn't been drafted—over his dead body would I have declared myself for the draft when the WHPL started—but I'd eventually made it here and was making a name for myself.

Bet that just eats at you, doesn't it, Ty?

The thought made me chuckle. I tried not to dwell on my divorce, and those petty moments of *"fuck you, Ty"* were less and less common as time went on. But what could I say? They were *so* satisfying sometimes. And apparently today I was feeling extra catty for some reason.

I let my gaze drift across the locker room, and it landed right on Hamilton, who was pulling on a hoodie.

Ah. Right. That *explains my uptick in cattiness.*

Meh. Whatever. She and Ty could both eat a dick. I had a life to live and a career to enjoy, and I didn't have time for either of their bullshit.

As we all finished getting dressed, Coach Reilly stood in the middle of the room at the edge of the Pittsburgh Bearcats logo. "Great practice today, ladies. You've got ten minutes before the press comes in. Before we let them in, though..." She smiled. "We've got a little announcement about your team's leadership going forward. Your alternate captains for our inaugural season are Jenny Valentine and Joanna Lawson." She nodded toward me. "And your captain is Sabrina McAvoy."

Some heat bloomed in my face for some reason as my teammates applauded, and someone called out, "Captain Mac!" I'd known about the captaincy already—Coach had told me last night to make sure I was willing to take it on—but it always felt more real when the team knew. I'd worn a C on my jersey before, and I was thrilled to be wearing one again. Especially at this level.

As our teammates congratulated me and our two alternate captains, I *wanted* to not notice Hamilton's reaction. I *wanted* to be completely oblivious to her and the subtle eyeroll that the towel she was using on her hair didn't quite hide.

No luck, unfortunately.

Eh. She could live with it. If she couldn't, she could always ask the GM to send her someplace else. Sure wouldn't break my heart if that happened.

Minutes after Coach's announcement, the press descended on the room. Since we were a new team, there was a lot of interest in us from both local networks and the larger syndicated sports networks. I wondered if there would be this much press after this season.

Secretly, behind my media-trained smile, I hoped at least *some* of them would lose interest. It was no secret that some sports reporters thought about as highly of women's hockey as my father did, and at best, their reporting was laced with the usual misogyny. Asking some players about juggling hockey and motherhood. Zeroing in on stats about our bodies instead of our performance. Even getting our thoughts on the aesthetics of our jerseys and team colors. It was tiresome to say the least, and I was pretty sure that while many were well-meaning, there were a few who were subtly trying to delegitimize the sport.

Like the asshat who started asking Anya Apalkov questions as she toweled off her hair at the stall next to mine.

"Are you concerned about the effect this is going to have on your children?" the guy asked with a perfectly straight face. "With the amount of traveling you'll be doing?"

Anya shrugged, tossing the towel onto the bench behind her. "Of course no one wants to be away from their kids, but it's strange how no one asks my husband the same questions." She looked the reporter right in the eyes. "Colin and the kids will manage while I'm on the road the same way they and I manage when he's on the road."

"So you don't think it's concerning for children to be separated from their mothers as often as players in this league have to travel?"

Laws and I exchanged incredulous looks.

Anya didn't even flinch. "It's no more ideal than it is for the kids of players in the men's league to be separated from their fathers. But it's only for half the year, and we spend extra time with them during the off season." She smiled sweetly, which made her eyes frostier. "And since our teams are very rarely on the road at the same time, they'll have time to spend with just their father." She inclined her head. "That's a good thing, isn't it? Children having time with their dad? At least, when their father is as loving and involved as Colin is?"

The reporter made a sour face, which only made Anya grin.

Laws and I both suppressed snickers. Everyone knew he had kids he rarely saw, so it took some serious audacity to throw stones. Especially at Anya, who didn't have time for anyone's bullshit.

Unsurprisingly, he didn't have any more questions for Anya.

Unfortunately, he turned his sights on me. After the usual questions about how I liked the city, how I was playing, what I thought of my team, and all of that, he said, "Sabrina, walk us through how your family helped you get to where you are now."

I froze, barely keeping my practiced neutral expression in place. "I'm sorry?"

His smile was insincere. "You come from a spectacular hockey dynasty. You had far more opportunities and connections than most in this league or even the men's league. Tell us how your family got you here."

I sensed Laws watching us, but I didn't look to see if she was gaping at his brazenness or keeping an eye on me in case I decided to drop gloves. Anya had exited stage left as soon as he'd moved on to me, which was probably a good thing; she'd have reamed him out over that question, media training be damned.

I did the best I could to pretend this jackass wasn't getting under my skin, and I gave a quiet and hopefully convincing laugh. "The League is pretty strict about how many people can be on the ice at a given time." I gestured at the hallway leading out to the rink. "My family isn't out there practicing, skating, passing, and scoring. I am."

"Of course." The reporter's chuckle was patronizing at best. "But the road to this locker room was certainly different for you than it was for your teammates." He made a sweeping gesture around the locker room. "What was that like?"

The way I was gritting my teeth just then, I wondered if I needed to start wearing my mouthguard during interviews.

Calling on all the media training and rehearsed bullshit answers I possessed, I looked him right in the eye. I smiled just enough to keep the peanut gallery from describing me as "unfriendly" and "prickly" (since they couldn't actually *say* "bitchy" on most media outlets). "A name might open some doors in this sport—I won't deny that—but open doors don't move pucks. This is a sport where people don't last long if they aren't playing well because one player can drag a whole team down. My name might've put me on some radars, but the way I play hockey is what keeps me here."

From the subtle twist of his lips, he didn't like that answer. And I wasn't entirely happy with it either, mostly because I knew my words would be contorted against me somehow. They always were.

"What about the coaches and training your father was able to help you access?" he asked. "Those obviously took you to a much higher level than if you hadn't had those opportunities."

"The coaches I had were amazing," I said with complete

honesty. "My mom also got me some private lessons when I was struggling with skating and stick handling, and those instructors made a world of difference. Without them, and without her driving me to a million practices, lessons, games, and tournaments, I definitely wouldn't be standing here."

I could tell he didn't like that answer any better than the previous one. He wanted me to drop names and gush about everything my father had done to further my career. He wanted a sound bite with Doran McAvoy's name in it.

Sorry, pal, I didn't say out loud. *Ask my brother if that's what you want.*

"Thank you, Sabrina." The man flashed an irritated smile, then stalked away to pester another of my teammates.

As soon as he was gone, I released a long breath.

Ugh. Couldn't wait to see how *that* interview came back to bite me in the ass.

CHAPTER 7

LILA

"How's your knee?" Faith grimaced as she watched me settling onto the couch with a pile of icepacks. "Are you going to be okay for the game?"

"I'll be fine." I started arranging icepacks over, under, and around my knee. "It's just sore."

She scowled but didn't say anything further, and she went into the kitchen while I continued getting situated.

Truth was, my knee was bothering the hell out of me today. And yes, I was worried about how it was going to affect me on the ice. What I should've done was grab one of the trainers after practice this morning and get their input. Maybe I needed some more PT. Or maybe some more anti-inflammatories.

But I was afraid to ask the trainers or even hint that there was any discomfort because I was afraid of getting benched. Sometimes trainers could err on the side of too much caution, and they'd park my ass on the sidelines just because there were some aches and twinges.

I wasn't letting them bench me this time. Our home opener was tomorrow. I didn't care what my knee had to say about it—there was no way in hell I was missing that game. I wasn't giving anyone any more reason to insist I needed to hang it up or that I was dead weight to my team.

If I had to grit my teeth through the game... fine. But I was playing.

And if you push it too hard and mess up your knee again, then what?

Closing my eyes, I exhaled. That was the balance I was still learning to strike—pushing hard because I was a professional athlete while not pushing so hard that I caused more damage. Especially damage that couldn't be repaired.

"Your knee is only going to tolerate so much surgery," the orthopedic surgeon in Omaha had warned. "I can keep fixing it until we're blue in the face, but there will come a point where it won't heal well enough."

"Well enough to play hockey?"

He'd scowled. "There will come a point where you will always have some pain and some mobility issues. The point at which you can no longer play hockey will come much, *much* sooner."

I wasn't at that point now. I couldn't be.

At least training camp was over. It was always a grueling week, and I was never sad to see it end. Since then, we'd been ramping up through the preseason. Going forward, my life would be dominated by hours of intense practice, off-ice workouts, and all after a summer spent training, but none of that was as demanding as training camp. So that was all it was; my body was tired from that hellish week. I was still getting back into the groove after rehab, and ever since my injury, my knee had always taken a little longer to get with the program.

I'll be fine. I nudged one of the icepacks against an especially achy spot right along my meniscus. *Just need to do some more stretching and baby it a little more. I'll be fine.*

As the ice did its thing along with the anti-inflammatories I'd taken earlier, I tried to focus on anything but the annoyingly persistent aches and pains. The best distraction? My phone, of course.

I checked my various socials and responded to some emails and DMs. A lot of my hockey friends were in preseason right now too, same as me, so there weren't as many messages or posts from them. As energized as we all were about the new season—especially those of us on newly-minted expansion teams—everyone was tired, too. Or spending time with their families, since there would be a lot of long hours and traveling over the next several months.

After I'd gone through socials and messages, I flipped over to some sports news sites. I was curious if anything had come of the allegations against one of the head coaches in the men's league; he'd been accused of bribing and even blackmailing officials last season. Two officials had already been barred from the League, banned from any games or events, and fined within an inch of their lives, so they'd sung like canaries about who they'd been taking bribes from. A GM and two owners had already confessed. The head coach was the last holdout, insisting he was innocent and would never do such a thing.

According to the first article that popped up, though, he'd not only been busted, he'd been stupid enough to commit his bribery via emails and texts. Yeah. He was *done*. What a dumbass.

I was about to close the app when another headline caught my eye.

In an instant, my stomach curdled with irritation. I should've continued closing the app, but I couldn't stop myself, and I tapped the link.

Daughter of Hockey Legend Balks at Questions About Nepotism

Bearcats' center reluctant to acknowledge role of legendary father in pro hockey comeback

PITTSBURGH – The daughter of Buffalo superstar Doran McAvoy appeared to shy away from questions regarding her father's influence on her own hockey career.

With the sport all but baked into her DNA, questions about the McAvoy legacy are certainly inevitable. Her elder brother, St. Louis winger Mark McAvoy, is regularly effusive about his father's support, expressing gratitude for access to the best coaches, trainers, players, and equipment from the time he was small.

Sabrina McAvoy, captain and star center of the WHPL expansion team in Pittsburgh, is far less willing to gush about the influence of Doran McAvoy.

I stopped reading there. I wasn't at all surprised she didn't want to talk about it. Who wanted to admit out loud that they'd had an escalator while the rest of us had to crawl up the stairs? Yeah, Sabrina was good, but she wouldn't be *half* the player she was without all the advantages her father and her name had bestowed upon her. She knew it, her teammates knew it, the *fans* knew it, but God forbid she admit it out loud.

Maybe she just didn't understand how much other people had to struggle. I couldn't imagine being that oblivious, though. Even the most privileged players had to at least notice some of their teammates wearing gear held together by duct tape and prayers. Or all the fundraisers for those of us whose families couldn't afford gear or fees. Or how many of us squeezed in part-time jobs because no matter how much our parents tried, there was only so much money to dog-ear for hockey. The rich and middle class kids may not have fully grasped how hard that was. They may not have understood just how much some of us had struggled to hold on to hockey, or realized that some incredibly talented players had been forced to quit hockey for reasons that had nothing to do with injuries or talent.

But they had to at least have *noticed* that some of us weren't playing on Easy mode. Right?

Or maybe they just thought riding Daddy's money and influence to the top was their birthright, and that they'd earned their spot by being lucky enough to be born into that kind of family. While the rest of us were so grateful for our parents' sacrifices we could cry, maybe the genetic elite were satisfied that they *deserved* to be where they were. Who knew?

Well, whatever the case... Must be nice.

I shook myself and refocused on my phone, and that was when I realized there was a video embedded in the article, and from the thumbnail, I recognized Sabrina. She was still in her gear, dark hair swept up into a messy ponytail, and I refused to dwell on how unreasonably attractive she was like that.

I was curious about the interplay with the reporter, though, so I tapped Play.

"Sabrina," the reporter said, "walk us through how your family helped you get to where you are now."

Ooh, yes, I thought. *Do tell.*

It was hard to miss the moment Sabrina went on the defensive. The faint twitch of her lips, the subtle tightness in her jaw, the slight narrowing of her eyes—they weren't super obvious, but they were there, as was the note of irritation in her voice.

I didn't keep watching, though. I just rolled my eyes, shut off the video, dropped my phone on the end table, and sighed as I adjusted the icepacks on my knee.

Cry me a fucking river, Princess. How dare anyone call you out for riding Daddy's name to the top.

I didn't know why she bothered denying it. The way she'd jettisoned her ex's name and slapped her dad's back on when she decided to come out of retirement? Yeah, that wasn't obvious or anything.

"Ooh, I know that face." Faith came into the room, and

she watched me as she settled on the other end of the couch with a mug of coffee between her hands. "You're pissed about something."

I didn't know if that was the right word, but I didn't gainsay her. "There's an article about Sabrina on one of the sports sites." I rolled my eyes. "Something about how she refuses to acknowledge how her dad helped her get where she is."

"Ooh." Faith put her coffee on a coaster and picked up her phone. "Which site?"

I sent her the link. She opened it, and after a couple of taps, she was peering at her screen with a furrowed brow, her eyes flicking back and forth as she read the text. When she'd finished, she made a disgusted face. The words, "I know, right?" were on the tip of my tongue, but what Faith said caught me by surprise: "Did you notice how long it took for the reporter to actually mention her by name?"

I blinked. "What?"

She gestured at my phone. "Read it again. The article is about her, but her name doesn't actually appear until—what? The third paragraph?"

That couldn't be right.

I opened the article again and reread it. Sure enough, Sabrina was referred to by everything except her own name until the third paragraph. "Wow." I put the phone aside again. "That's... weird."

"I know, right?" Faith rolled her eyes. "Can't imagine why she doesn't like talking about her dad's impact on her career."

"But... he did have an impact on it."

"Sure, but like, your parents helped you a lot, right? They

scrimped and saved and sacrificed so you could play hockey. You probably wouldn't have been able to learn the sport, never mind get here, if they hadn't done any of that."

"Right. And I never miss an opportunity to show them and everyone else how grateful I am for that."

"Of course. But imagine if everyone talked about them instead of you. Like if every article about you was focused on them."

I made a face. "Eww."

"Right? So she probably gets tired of that, too." Faith held up her phone again. "Especially when reporters write articles that make it sound like they're writing about her dad while she's an afterthought."

"Damn. Yeah, that would probably make me feel scummy too."

"But you still don't like her."

"No, I don't," I admitted without hesitation. "I get it if she doesn't like reporters using stories about her as a chance to kiss her dad's ass. But I mean, the least she can do is own the advantages she's had."

"Maybe." Faith didn't sound convinced.

"Like, yes, she's a great player," I went on. "No one can deny that."

"You'd like to, though." My friend's comment was a prod, but not quite an accusation. "Wouldn't you?"

I had to think about that for a moment. I couldn't really argue with her. I *wanted* Sabrina to be a great player because she was one of my teammates, but I also *hated* that she was a great player because everyone acted like the rest of us were just extras in a show about her. Was I jealous of all the advantages she'd had, from mountains of money and access to the cream of the coaching crop right on down to her literal DNA? Yeah. I was. And maybe if she'd just own that, I'd...

Probably not feel any different.

I sagged against the couch. "Am I... Am I *wrong* about her?"

Faith pursed her lips. "Maybe?" She fixed her bright blue eyes on me. "But maybe that's not the question you should be asking yourself."

"Oh yeah?"

"Mmhmm." She studied me, then gently asked, "Why are you so determined to hate her?"

I pushed out a harsh breath. "I don't know. Maybe I just hate feeling like a superstar diva's backup dancer."

Faith laughed softly. "Yeah, that would suck. But it kind of seems like that's an issue with how everyone else regards her. You haven't said anything about how *she* acts."

"Besides the part where she refuses to own where she came from?" I asked dryly. "I don't know. It's just—whenever they talk about her, it's all about her dad, her brother, and her ex, and she just avoids it or glares at them. Then they gush about everything she does on the ice, but no one says shit about her mistakes, and she doesn't exactly argue with them."

"They *do* talk about her mistakes, though."

I eyed her. "Where?"

She shrugged. "Anyone who doesn't like Doran McAvoy, his team, or the existence of professional women's hockey."

Exhaling hard, I leaned back against the couch cushions. "Okay, but even then, they're just hating on her because they hate someone else. Women's hockey commentators and reporters love the sport, but they'll criticize any of us. Like, *how* many times did they show the replay of me crashing into Anaheim's net last season?" I flailed a hand at my phone. "But when she fucks up and costs her team a critical game—crickets."

Faith seemed to consider that. "I mean, maybe they're just afraid to cross Doran McAvoy."

"I guess? He *is* kind of a dick."

"Understatement," she muttered.

God, wasn't that the truth. There were generational talents in this sport who were startlingly humble and kind people. It barely even seemed to register with them that they were superstars. They were the players who happily and patiently signed things and took photos with fans, even when it was pouring down rain after practice or when they were feeling like shit after a bad game.

One megastar had been asked to grant a wish for a Make-A-Wish kid. All the kid wanted was a chance to skate with him. The star had pulled out all the stops, getting the entire team to stay after practice for a scrimmage where she was his linemate. Whenever the star was in the kid's hometown after that, he'd take the family out to dinner or to an amusement park, and he'd made two trips out to visit her in the hospital.

That was just how a lot of players were—they loved hockey, they loved fans, and they were genuinely kind, down-to-earth people. Even the guys who were absolute thugs on the ice could turn around and be near saints in their daily lives.

Doran McAvoy was a spectacularly talented hockey player, but he was also a notorious bag of dicks both on and off the ice. He was one of those talents who *knew* he was gifted and *knew* he was a star, and he didn't let anyone forget it.

A former teammate of his had once made a comment to a reporter that their embarrassing loss that night had been as much a team effort as their wins. "We all fell apart," I remembered him saying. "All of us. It just wasn't a good game for anyone in a Buffalo jersey."

Somehow, Doran had taken that personally, interpreting it as a cowardly, underhanded swipe. As if the player had been specifically calling him out for singlehandedly losing the game. To this day, people whispered that Doran was the reason that player had been traded to Los Angeles a month later. Depending on who you asked, that was either because the front office had wanted to separate them, or because Doran had stomped into his GM's office and demanded it.

So, hell. Maybe Faith was on to something when it came to the press treading lightly about his daughter's play.

"Hmm. You could be right." I played with the edge of one of the icepacks on my knee. "Maybe all the reporters are afraid to say anything negative about Doran McAvoy's daughter."

"Wouldn't *you* be?" Faith asked. "I'd be terrified to let a hot mic catch me even suggesting she was having a bad hair day."

"Yeah. I get that. I still don't like it. Nobody in this league or any other should be immune to criticism because they or their famous daddy might throw a fit." I shook my head and looked at Faith. "The commentators and reporters should be able to talk about her as much as they talk about the rest of us. Good *and* bad."

"No argument there." She inclined her head. "But is it her fault if they won't?"

I bristled. "No. But she benefits from it, and she doesn't push back against it at all. She's just like him—he refused to credit his teammates for anything, and she refuses to credit *him.* "

"She *does* push back, though." Faith gestured with her own phone. "Because that interview didn't sound like—"

"Of course she pushes back against the nepotism rumors," I grumbled. "But does she lift a single finger about them talking about her like she's God's gift to hockey?" I snorted derisively. "She doesn't seem to mind that part."

Faith studied me silently.

I fidgeted. "What?"

"Still just trying to figure out why you're so bound and determined to hate her. I mean, even if nepotism got her in the door, you can't argue with her ability on the ice."

"I can resent the shit out of her for having access to every imaginable advantage to *getting* that good." I huffed a bitter laugh. "Bet she never had to work at a rink's concession stand just to earn enough to buy thirdhand gear."

Faith quirked her lips, then shrugged. "Okay, sure, I guess. But however she got here, she plays her ass off and she's earned the right to *stay* here."

I couldn't argue with that. I really couldn't. But I also couldn't deny how much it still irked me that Sabrina McAvoy was here at all.

Apparently sensing that I was still annoyed, Faith

reached over and patted my arm. "I know you're not her biggest fan. But you two *are* teammates."

"Is it wrong to hope the trade deadline resolves that?"

She laughed dryly. "I mean, maybe? But that's not until March. That's a long time to be hissing and spitting with someone on your team."

Closing my eyes, I groaned. "I know. I know. And I... God, I guess I should just be thankful she's a forward. If we had to be D partners..."

"I don't think any defensive coach worth her salt would put you two on the same pair."

"No," I muttered. "They'd put her on the top pair and drop me down to the second." I rolled my eyes. "That's what happened on my last team, remember?"

"Oh, I remember."

I kind of felt bad for the amount of time I'd spent texting Faith to vent about the situation in Omaha. It hadn't been the same as with Sabrina, but it was similar enough to make my teeth grind. I was a *way* better defender than Amy Voorhees, but much like Sabrina, she came from hockey royalty. No one dared put her on the second or third pair, not even when her stats barely warranted a place above the minors. And since she and I both played left-handed, we couldn't be paired together, so I was bumped down to the number two spot despite *earning* that top billing.

Not that I was even a little bit bitter. Especially since it had *also* happened in major juniors. And in U16. All through my hockey years, there had always been either someone's princess or a coach's "rising star" son taking a slot that should've gone to a player with better stats, not the one with the impressive pedigree.

Faith glanced at me again. "Look, I know you're frustrated. After all the crap with Amy, and getting passed over on your other teams, anyone would be. But Sabrina didn't do any of that to you, and she *is* a good player. She's incredible. And she's not knocking you down on the roster."

"I know." I dragged my fingers through my hair and sighed again. "It's not her fault. And I won't pretend she's not a great player." I paused. "Sometimes I think that makes it worse."

"How so?"

"Because how much better would so many *other* players be if they'd had access to everything she did?" I threw up my hand. "You know, if they didn't have to play in secondhand gear that didn't fit and spend their youth days hearing that they shouldn't be playing on the boys' team?"

"You're not wrong," Faith said. "I always envied the kids —the boys *and* the girls—who could get the good gear and didn't have people trying to chase them out." She glanced at me again. "But the ones who did have the good gear and the great coaches—it's not their fault, you know?"

"Yeah, I know," I whispered. "It just sucks seeing them take all the top spots when there are so many players out there with raw talent and drive who just didn't have the support they needed."

"I get that. I do. But you did get to this level. You did overcome everything and earn your spot." She shot me a look. "Don't let someone else ruin it just by being here. She's on your team, but so are you, you know?"

I nodded. She didn't keep pushing; she knew me well enough to know when she'd made her point. She was right, too, but man, it was going to be a struggle. It was hard not to resent someone who took the easy road to the top of the game, especially while the rest of us were hidden away in her shadow.

Still, I had to get it together. As much as I hated the idea, I would have to figure out how to get along with Sabrina. Or at the very least, coexist with her. That honestly didn't sound too hard. For as much as her very presence irritated me, I'd had teammates in the past who I didn't get along with, and the nature of the sport meant all our animosity stayed off the ice. We had to concentrate on too many things happening at once—too many bodies and sticks moving too fast in too many directions—to devote more than one or two brain cells to rivalries.

Even rivalries between opposing players faded somewhat while the clock was running. We might grab an opportunity to check someone harder than necessary, and there'd be some aggressive chirping, but hockey moved too fast for more than fleeting bumps and snark.

Unless of course someone took a cheap shot at a team-mate. Then all bets were off, and that was usually when fights broke out.

If someone took a cheap shot at Sabrina—a trip, a dirty check, an uncalled high stick—I'd probably answer the bell. I'd either check the offending player hard enough to make her rethink her life choices or, if things got really heated, drop gloves with her. As much as Sabrina pissed me off, she was still my teammate, and nobody played dirty against someone wearing my team's sweater. Not even if that someone was Sabrina.

And hey, the WHPL allowed both checking and fighting, unlike our youth and major junior leagues. No more of this "checking is a penalty" and "no fighting ever for any reason" garbage that the men's league never had to worry about. We could throw gloves just like they could. Fighting was still a penalty, same as it was for the guys, but it wasn't an automatic ejection or suspension anymore.

As frustrated as I'd been before training camp had even ended, I could see myself taking out some aggression once the season started. I was a defender, after all.

Maybe this would be the season I got into my first professional fight.

I just hoped it wasn't because I was coming to Sabrina McAvoy's defense.

CHAPTER 8

SABRINA

I was right that the interview came back to bite me. Sooo shocking. Everyone in this sport was determined to kiss my dad's ass, and they hated that I didn't partake.

Daughter of Hockey Legend Balks at Questions About Nepotism.

McAvoy Dynasty Hockey Talent may be Generational, but Humility is Not

Is McAvoy's Daughter Good Enough to be this Arrogant?

The words "ungrateful" and "spoiled brat" had made it into a few articles, and I'd had plenty of DMs and social media comments putting me in my place. Everyone was committed to the narrative that I was nothing more than an extension of my dad's legacy, and they were determined to make me acknowledge that. Whenever I pushed back or refused to fawn all over good old Dad, it rubbed a lot of people the wrong way.

Fortunately, the Bearcats' PR department didn't give me any grief for it.

"No one would bat an eye if someone from the men's league said the same damn thing." Marci, our PR director, rolled her eyes. "The minute our players are anything other than cheerful and ladylike, they lose their minds. Like, have they never met hockey players?"

I laughed, relieved that she got it. "Right? I'm, uh..." I cleared my throat. "Sorry for the extra headache, though."

Marci waved her hand. "Trust me—this is nothing. And I mean, aside from the people who have to give you crap, I think most people probably watched that interview and thought the same thing I did—you're an athlete who's busted your ass, and you're over people trying to give that credit to someone else."

I let my shoulders sag a little, and I exhaled. "God, I hope you're right. There's just always so much..." I shook my head.

"Oh, I know. But put it in perspective. Any time the League announces an exhibition game in a city that might be getting an expansion team, there are dozens—hell, *hundreds*—of comments from people about how stupid it is. Women's hockey is too slow. Nobody cares about women's sports. All the comparisons about how their bottom-tier beer league team could easily beat them." She made another dismissive gesture. "You get the idea. Read all that shit, and it's really demoralizing, you know? Sounds like nobody wants us. But then game day comes, and the stands are packed."

"Huh. I hadn't thought about that, but you're right."

Marci smiled. "Trust me. You're just hearing a lot of noise from trolls and from journalists who are desperate to be relevant. Meanwhile..." She picked up her tablet and thumbed to a spreadsheet, then showed it to me. "McAvoy jerseys are flying off the rack so fast, the team store can't keep them in stock. And I don't mean the Doran McAvoy jerseys."

"The Doran—" I craned my neck at the tablet. "We're selling my *dad's* jersey?"

She rolled her eyes. "Someone in marketing thought it would be a good idea."

"Of course they did," I muttered.

"But I don't think they're going to keep stocking them." Marci pointed to a line on the spreadsheet. "Only four have sold. Meanwhile, *yours* are backordered in all but two sizes."

I peered at the screen, and sure enough, all but one child size and one adult size were backordered, and the two sizes still in stock had fewer than ten available. Dad's jersey, on the other hand, still had ample inventory in every size.

I laughed quietly as I handed back the tablet. "Don't tell my dad."

"Oh, no one is going to say a word." She tucked the tablet under her arm. "But I'll be very surprised if we're still carrying Doran McAvoy jerseys come Christmas."

It was probably petty as hell to be this satisfied about that.

Oh well. Apparently I was that petty.

"All right, ladies." Coach Reilly scanned the room, locking eyes with each of us in turn. "This is an historic evening for Pittsburgh and for women's hockey. We've got a packed house. This is a sports town, and they're turning out in droves for us just like they have for the men's football, baseball, and hockey teams." She smiled broadly. "So let's give them the level of hockey they came to see."

Everyone in the room cheered, all of us exchanging fist bumps on the bench.

Of course, Lila's gaze snagged on me for a second, and her expression instantly soured.

So did my mood.

I broke eye contact, but not before letting her see me roll my eyes and laugh. Then I bumped shoulders with Val, who laughed, and we carried on with putting on our gear and getting psyched for the game.

Yeah, I see you, I hoped Lila heard. *And you are* not *getting under my skin.*

Moments later, we were heading out onto the ice for warmups.

A lot of people had told me before I came here that Pittsburgh loved sports. As Coach Reilly had said, this was a sports town, through and through, just like Seattle.

As we hit the ice, the fans did not disappoint. People were still coming in, but there was a dense crowd along the glass all the way around our end of the arena. People held up signs, banged on the glass, waved, cheered—I could play hockey until I was ninety and this would never get old. Especially the part where there were dozens and dozens of little girls smiling so big their faces must've hurt.

One redhead who couldn't have been more than seven or eight held up a sign with Anya's number and the words, *I'M A GOALIE TOO!*

Beside her, a Black girl of about ten watched us in awe as

she gripped a sign reading, *I'M GOING TO BE A BEARCAT SOMEDAY!*

I tossed pucks over the glass to both of them, loving the way their eyes lit up. They dropped their signs and clutched the pucks, turning around and waving them at their parents as if they couldn't believe it.

I tapped my stick against the glass, gave them each a fist bump, and continued my warmup routine.

It really didn't get any better than this.

I was a little in awe myself. This was my second season in the League, but that awestruck feeling was still here. Still nearly as intense as it had been when I'd taken the ice in Seattle a year ago. It hadn't been all that many years since a pro women's league had been a fantasy. A league that was this big and this popular? Pure fiction.

And for me personally, the chance—the *freedom*—to join that league? To be a professional hockey player at this level? A pipe dream.

But here I was. Here we were. Somehow, we'd all made it to this. Somehow, I'd made it out from under everything that had tried to keep me away from the sport I loved.

People still asked me why I'd teared up during warmups at my first game in Seattle. They were going to be asking the same thing about tonight, that was for sure. What could I say? It was hard not to get emotional when I was finally living the dream I'd had to fight so hard for.

After warmups, my teammates and I trooped back to the locker room. Since this was opening night, we'd all be introduced before puck drop, so after the Zambonis had finished resurfacing the ice, we lined up in the tunnel for our intros.

As captain, I'd go out last, so I took my place at the back of the line.

Lila clomped past me, and our eyes locked for a second—just long enough for her sneer to make my hackles go up.

As she continued toward her own place in line, I rolled my eyes and dug my nails into the insides of my gloves.

She wasn't going to get to me. She wasn't going to ruin this night, this season, this team—nothing. Whatever her problem was, she could get the hell over it.

The announcements started. In numerical order (aside from me and the two alternate captains, who would be introduced last), the announcer called out each player by their hometown, number and name.

"From Boston, Massachusetts, number fifty-three— Simone Yates!"

"From Kazan, Russia, number sixty-one— Anastasia Ilyasov!"

The names went on, each player skating out to the cheers of the crowd before taking her place around the circle at center ice.

"From Bethesda, Maryland, number seventy-two—Lila Hamilton!"

My stomach knotted at the sound of her name. I refused to shift my gaze away as she skated out, and I made sure to keep my expression pleasant. The last thing I needed was a camera catching me scowling over Lila. I could only imagine the fur that would fly if some reporter wrote an article like *"Rivalry Brewing Between Sabrina McAvoy and Lila Hamilton?"*

Yeah, right. More like, 'Rivalry Brewing between Doran McAvoy's Daughter and Lila Hamilton.'

That thought almost had me letting my distaste into my expression, but I schooled my face.

The alternate captains were announced. And then...

"From Buffalo, New York, your captain, number five—Sabrina McAvoy!"

The roar from the crowd intensified so hard, I swore it almost knocked me off my skates. Dazed, I skated to my place in the circle. I sensed Lila's icy stare as I skated past her, but I ignored her. This wasn't her night. This was *our* night. If she wanted to be miserable, that was on her.

The announcer's voice boomed over the crowd, "Please welcome—for their inaugural Women's Hockey Professional League season—the Pittsburgh Bearcats!"

The crowd kept cheering. Loud. Long. On their feet.

Listen to them, Dad, and tell me this sport doesn't matter.

After the introductions, we saluted the crowd.

The starting lineup was announced, and then there were the national anthems, and then it was *finally* time for what everyone came for—*hockey.*

I skated up to center ice for the faceoff. On the other side of the dot was Bea Olsson, and we exchanged brief grins. We'd been teammates more than once over the years, and we'd roomed together at the Olympics.

Roomed together. Yeah. *That's* what the kids were calling it these days.

And it took me until I was in my late twenties to figure out I was a lesbian?

I shook that train of thought away as the ref held the puck between us. I could reminisce later.

Right now? Hockey.

The puck dropped. Bea was lightning fast on faceoffs, but I was faster. I snatched the puck away and immediately passed it to Laws, and we were barreling toward Montreal's zone.

Laws passed it to me, and I forced my way between a pair of defenders, keeping the puck securely against my blade even as they tried to steal it. A sharp *smack-smack* of stick on ice told me one of my teammates was calling for the puck, and I glanced her way a second before I passed to her. A Montreal forward zipped in between us and grabbed it, but Sims shoulder-checked her out of the way before snapping the puck back to me.

I almost lost the puck to an aggressive defender, but I managed to get away from her, and that was when I realized Laws was at the goal, standing just outside the crease. Our eyes locked for a split second, and I sent her the puck.

The goalie reacted, but she went low.

Laws chipped the puck up and over the netminder's shoulder.

The red light came on, and the goal horn was almost drowned out by the roar of the crowd as they shot to their feet.

We all crushed Laws in hugs, then skated toward the bench for fist bumps.

Barely a minute into the first period of our first game, the Pittsburgh Bearcats were on the board with our first ever goal.

And I couldn't wait for our next one.

Everyone in the locker room was exuberant after the game was over. We'd won our first game, and the way we were celebrating, we might as well have just clinched the Cup.

"The Pittsburgh Bearcats are undefeated!" Laws shouted. "The only team in the League that's never been beaten!"

We all laughed at that. It was technically true, especially since the only other expansion team to play tonight had lost, and the other four didn't play until tomorrow. So... yeah, we were *technically* undefeated as a franchise. Might as well celebrate that while it lasted.

Much like our undefeated streak undoubtedly would be, though, my good spirits were short-lived. The locker room was packed with people. Not just staff, and media along with players and their spouses and kids, which was normal. Most of my teammates' parents, siblings, and even a few grandparents had come to the home opener. There were so many people, staff had to leave some out in the hallway and carefully manage how many went into and out of the locker room. As players finished showering and dressing, they joined their families in the hall, and the whole ice level of the arena probably echoed with the sounds of excitement and celebration.

It reminded me of the locker room after we'd medaled at World Junior Women's and at the Olympics. Or after our major junior playoff games. Or my youth team's championship games. So many supportive family members. So much love.

I had that love and support, too. Zoe and my mom were here. My brother had texted me before and after the game; he was playing in Los Angeles tomorrow night, so he couldn't make it to mine. I understood that, and I had always appreciated his support.

But just like every major game since my U8 days, I was painfully aware of who *wasn't* here. Who *refused* to be here.

I wasn't surprised—he'd needed his arm twisted to watch me play at the Olympics, after all, and even then he'd only given in for the sake of his own reputation. It still hurt just as much as it had the first time, though.

I tried to ignore that rock in the pit of my stomach. Tried to focus on being happy we'd won, and on celebrating with my mom, sister, and teammates. I loved that Mom and Zoe were always here for me. That they'd supported me all this time, even when they'd had to do it in secret. And I appreciated Mark's love and support even when he couldn't be in the same place as me.

I couldn't lie, though—nights like this were hard.

Especially because there were *so many* dads here.

Anya's husband and kids were crowded around her locker stall along with both her parents *and* her in-laws. Her father-in-law looked as proud as if his own daughter had been out there tonight. Sims's stepfather, who'd been her dad since she was six, was on crutches after a recent ankle surgery, and he'd still almost knocked her over with a hug.

And then there were Lila's parents. Not just their presence and their obvious love and support for their daughter but for as long as I'd played alongside her, I'd always envied the way she lit up whenever they were there. They always beamed with pride whether we'd won or lost, and Lila never smiled like that except when they were around.

Every damn time, her dad would come into the locker room, wrap her in a huge bear hug no matter how much she stunk after a game, and tell her he was proud of her. If we'd lost, he'd reassure her that she'd played her best, and that the next game would be better. And if we'd won... Well, he was the reason I understood when people described someone as being so happy they could burst.

It made me so jealous I could barely see straight.

Just like I had so many times from U8 on up to the Olympics, I couldn't help asking myself that same awful question:

Why can't my dad love me like that?

I took a deep swig of water to push back the lump trying to rise in my throat, and I turned to my mom and sister. "We should go eat. Before they run out of the good stuff."

Mom laughed. "They make plenty, don't they?"

"Well, yeah, for the team and staff." I gestured around. "Not *this* many people."

"Mmhmm. I'm pretty sure the cooking crew knows to anticipate..." She mimicked my gesture.

"Okay, fine. How about we go eat before I start chewing off my arm?"

"Uh-oh." Zoe grimaced theatrically. "Don't want Beans getting hangry."

At least that got us out of the locker room. The lounge wasn't much better, but eating and talking with my mom and sister kept me distracted from everything else.

Well, mostly.

The celebratory vibe had followed us in here. The whole

room thrummed with excitement and elation, which just made my food sit in my stomach like a rock.

It didn't help when one of the reporters swung by our table. She was getting interviews and clips of players with their families, and she promptly lost interest in me after she realized my dad wasn't here.

As she walked away, I sat back and picked at my food. "Never fails, does it?"

Mom frowned and shook her head. "I wish I could tell you that'll go away, but..."

Zoe made a face. "So nice of them to want to celebrate a man in an article about women's hockey."

That got humorless laughs out of both Mom and me.

Right then, Lila and her parents strode in. She was laughing at something her dad was saying, and I almost fumbled with my fork.

There was that bolt of jealousy of course, but also something much more pleasant. Yeah, I envied how happy she was —how loved she was by *both* of her parents—but that relaxed, perfect smile was just...

Oh my God.

Her eyes flicked toward me, and her mood dampened ever so slightly. She quickly jerked her gaze away.

I dropped mine to my plate.

My dad wasn't here and he never would be.

The most beautiful woman on my team couldn't look at me without scowling.

Well, at least the game had been fun, because the rest of this evening was depressing as hell.

CHAPTER 9

LILA

For an entirely new team playing against other teams who had a few seasons under their belts, we were holding our own. We'd crushed the opposing teams in our home opener and the game after that, only to get utterly blown out in Charlotte. That loss was probably good for us; Charlotte was one of the Original Ten, and they were well-established and solid, but they weren't one of the top tier teams like New York or Calgary. Having them make mincemeat of us—destroying us 8-2—was more than enough to bring us out of the clouds after going 2-0-0 for our first two games.

"Oh, right," we all realized. *"We have to actually work at this if we want to win."*

Yeah, that was common sense, but sometimes it only took a couple of easy wins for a team to get lazy. That thoroughly humbling game in Charlotte definitely reminded us to keep our foot on the gas.

After that, we held our own, even if we didn't win every

game. By the end of our first month as a team, we had a respectable 7-3-0 record, which was enough to give us a firm hold on the third place spot in our division. Detroit was only a point behind us, though, so we needed to stay on our game.

We'd come in late last night from a game in Denver, and today was a day off. No practice. No game. No morning skate. We didn't even have a team meeting. Days like this were rare during the regular season, and everyone was taking full advantage. My teammates posted on social media about outings with their families, sleeping in, or spending the day at the spa.

I took advantage in my own way—I hit the gym at the training center, seizing the opportunity for a quiet workout on my own. Maybe one of these days I'd be able to afford a place with my own private home gym, but Faith and I didn't have the space or budget for that.

Fortunately, the training center had state-of-the-art everything. Great strength trainers, too, but I wasn't working with anyone today. I loved being able to have a gym to myself and just lift some weights and hit the bike without needing to drown anything out with my Air Pods. I hated wearing those things anyway, and right now was great—lifting happily while a local radio station played on the gym's stereo system.

My knee was sore today thanks to an awkward collision a couple of nights ago. It wasn't reinjured, just achy after I'd checked another player and our skates had tangled a little. Collette and my orthopedist weren't worried about it, but I did take it easy today, focusing on my arms instead of my legs. Even my back and shoulder workouts could put some strain on my knee, but arm workouts weren't too bad on the lower body.

I was halfway through my third set of hammer curls when the door opened from the hall. Damn. So much for having the place to myself. It was hardly *my* gym, though, so I couldn't really be upset.

Oh, but I could be annoyed as hell when the mirror showed me *who* had just walked in.

Seriously?

Yeah, seriously.

Unaware of my mood taking a nosedive, Sabrina put her water bottle into the cup holder on one of the bikes.

Eh. Whatever. The gym was open to all of us. I could be an adult and get over her being here even if I wasn't nearly as focused or relaxed anymore.

I *tried* to focus. I *tried* to relax. I was more or less successful with that, too, while she was on the bike. I was still aware of her presence, and I was still irritated because I had no desire to be around her—well, aside from that one really intense desire to be *very* close to her, which could shut right up—but she was over there and I was over here.

Fine.

Until she got up from the bike and, out of all the possible directions she could've gone in this enormous gym, she came to where I was working out. She put her towel and water bottle down two benches over from mine. Because of course she did.

Didn't she have a fancy, swanky-ass home gym she could use? Did she have to come here? I understood using it during off-ice team workouts, but on her own? On our day off?

Just give me some breathing room. Jesus.

That was ridiculous and I knew it. She had as much right to be here as I did. I just didn't want her here.

I couldn't control what anyone else did, but I could sure control what I did, so… fuck it. I was done working out.

I was so fixated on cleaning the bench and getting out of here, it only vaguely registered that she'd said something to me. Asked me a question, maybe? Damn, could've used some Air Pods right about then; great excuse to pretend I didn't hear someone.

I wasn't in the mood to engage, so I just grabbed my water bottle and towel, and started for the locker room without so much as a, "See you tomorrow."

I only made it two steps before Sabrina dropped the dumbbell she'd been holding, nearly hitting her foot, though she barely seemed to notice that *or* the loud *clank.* "Okay. What is your problem?"

I straightened, still startled from her throwing the weight and now caught off-guard by her question. "What?"

"Don't play stupid. You've had it out for me since day one." She crossed her arms across her sweaty tank top. "You're either taking swipes at me, or you're ignoring me like we're a couple of girls in high school who aren't speaking. What's—"

"I don't come to the gym to socialize," I said flatly. "If you do, then—"

"Oh don't even try that." She rolled her eyes. "I literally just asked if you were done with a set of weights. That's not socializing. And ignoring me, racking those weights, and storming off is obnoxious." She worked her jaw. "We're stuck playing together for the foreseeable future, so whatever your problem is..." She flailed a hand before letting it smack onto her other forearm. "Out with it."

The temptation to blow her off and stalk out of the gym was strong. I liked to think I was reasonably mature and not prone to catty bullshit, but what could I say? When I was around her, that side of me surfaced. All the resentment. All the frustration. Spend a few years constantly being in someone's shadow and see how charitable *you* are about them.

"Fine." I wiped the towel over my face, then dropped it onto a bench and faced her. "Maybe it's just frustrating as hell to work so hard to get here"—I gestured all around us —"only to be overshadowed by someone who gets a red carpet rolled out in front of her everywhere she does."

"Oh for fuck's sake," she snapped. "Are you still hung up on that?"

"Why shouldn't I be? You're still benefitting from everything that was handed to you, so why shouldn't—"

"Don't you *dare* tell me I've had anything handed to me." Sabrina stepped closer, dark eyes narrowing. "Don't you fucking dare."

Mirroring her, I crossed my arms and inclined my head. "You skated in here with a household name. This league isn't stupid, and neither is this team. They want you so people outside of women's hockey will actually—"

"And you think that could carry me this far?" She motioned in the general direction of the rink. "You think I could just go out there and do cardio while the rest of you do the work, because my name gets attention? My jersey didn't rack up those points, Lila." She tapped her chest. "*I* did."

"Uh-huh." I glared right back at her. "And it must've been so hard to learn when you had access to all the equipment and coaches and—"

"You have *no idea* what I've been up against my entire life," she snarled.

I was about to throw back that she could cry me a river. It must've been so hard, being the privileged daughter of a hockey legend, never having to worry about money or fight for a spot on a team. Yeah, must've been awful.

But the words caught in my throat when the overhead lights caught the tears welling up in her eyes.

And I froze.

Sabrina's jaw worked, and her voice was quieter now, with a ragged edge I hadn't expected. "You have no idea," she repeated. "You can make all the same assumptions everyone does. You can tell yourself and anyone who will listen that I was just handed a hockey career because I'm Doran McAvoy's daughter." She swiped at her eyes and swore, and that rawness in her voice was even more pronounced as she ground out for a third time, "You have *no idea.*"

Before I could make sense of anything, never mind respond, she brushed past me, leaving her water bottle by the bench along with the weights she hadn't racked.

It was a pet peeve of mine when people didn't rack their weights or wipe down their bench, but this time...

This time, I was hard-pressed to expect her to stay a second longer.

And my catty mean streak was fully MIA, too. I just felt like a jerk now. All this time, I'd thought of her like a spoiled rich girl who always had everything on easy mode, but clearly

I'd miscalculated somewhere. Clearly I'd messed up. Now things were going to be unbearable with my teammate, and that fell squarely on me.

"Shit," I muttered into the mostly silent gym.

I put away her weights, wiped down the bench, and collected her water bottle. By now, she was probably in the shower, so I could just leave it by her locker. In theory, I could do that and then slip out before we crossed paths again. Shower at home or something.

But I wasn't going to be a coward. I'd already been an asshole.

So, with my heart pounding, I sat on the bench and waited.

She emerged from the showers a few minutes later, now wearing a dry T-shirt and shorts with her hair up in a white towel. A few dark, wet strands framed her face, which was fixed with fury as she gathered her things. She didn't look at me even once.

After she'd dressed, I said, "Listen, can we—"

She snatched her shoes, gym bag, and keys up off the bench and stormed out of the locker room.

I stared at the doorway she'd gone through, my mouth still open with the words I hadn't finished saying.

What the hell? She wasn't even going to give me a chance to apologize?

Maybe she needed time to cool off. Or maybe she was just going to cold-shoulder me until the end of time.

Sighing, I gathered my own things into my bag and headed out to the parking lot. As I walked, I hoped I'd find her out there, waiting to catch me off-guard and confront me.

I didn't really relish the idea, but I hoped it played out that way; she deserved to say her piece, and I also wanted her to hear my apology.

But when I stepped outside, the day was still and silent. The parking lot was deserted except for my car.

Sabrina was gone.

CHAPTER 10

SABRINA

"What the actual fuck?" I huffed as I shoved my water bottle under the faucet to fill it up. "I'm just working out, minding my own damn business, and she has to..." I flailed my other hand. "*Ugh.*"

I mean, yes, I *had* asked her what the hell her problem was, but still. What the hell.

Zoe watched me over the island, her arms folded loosely across her Bearcats T-shirt. "That's really weird. She's been kind of a bitch to you ever since you both came to Pittsburgh, though, hasn't she?"

"She has." I shut off the faucet and capped my water bottle. "And she's taken little swipes about nepotism and whatever, but I figured that was just low-hanging fruit for her to be catty over. Kind of wondered what her actual problem was. I guess now I know." I rolled my eyes. "Same old story, isn't it? Every goddamned time a teammate is prickly toward me..." I just sighed and headed into the living room.

"Same shit, different team," Zoe muttered as she followed me.

"Seriously." I flopped onto the couch and pulled my legs up under me. "I know people think that about me. I'm not stupid, you know? I know what people say. But is it too much to ask for my *teammates* to take me at face value? Like, even if I *did* come up the way they all think, I can still play hockey, you know?"

"You can," my sister acknowledged, easing onto the other end of the couch. "And at least from where I'm sitting, the rest of your team gets that. It's just Hamilton who can't seem to get it through her head that even one of Dad's kids wouldn't be playing at this level without some actual skill."

"I know, right?" Sighing, I sat back and ran a hand through my hair. "I'm just so damn tired of it. All I want is to play hockey."

"And to be *respected* for playing hockey," Zoe supplied.

The words thumped against my chest. "Is that really too much to ask?"

"It shouldn't be. You're one of the best out there. Even if it was true that Dad had you working under the best coaches in the world from the time you could walk, you still had to put in the work." She twisted toward me, resting her elbow on the back of the couch and her head against her loose fist. "How many other generational talents out there have kids who aren't that great at hockey?"

"A lot," I grumbled before taking a swig of water.

"Right. I mean, look at Cary Olson's boys."

I hated that the reason I could instantly recall how "badly" those three had taken to hockey was that our father never shut up about it. Cary had been Dad's linemate for ten years, and he'd retired about six years before Dad did. They'd been magic together—two of the best two-hundred foot players in the men's league—but most people had no idea that they couldn't stand each other off the ice. Dad's ego pissed off Cary, and Dad never forgave Cary for defending our mom one night after Dad made a comment about her. No one but them and their teammates knew what exactly the comment had been, only that it had been in Mom's defense and Dad had blackened Cary's eye for it. Cary and his boys had also helped Mom and us kids move out of the house when she'd finally divorced Dad.

Dad couldn't bitch about Cary supporting Mom without looking like an asshole, and he knew it, but he happily grabbed every opportunity to rip on his linemate's sons' failure to become hockey stars. They hadn't even been "failures," really. Anton had been drafted in the second round by Los Angeles, traded two seasons later, and was now having a respectable career in Seattle. Greg had been undrafted, but signed with Boston, and though he only played about half a dozen games at the major league level, he'd led Boston's minor league affiliate to three championships in a row. Evan made it into major juniors and did all right, but ultimately decided not to pursue a pro career.

By any hockey parent's standards, all three of Cary's sons had done just fine. To hear my father tell it, though, they were abject failures. Even Anton was a disappointment despite being firmly situated in the men's league. Compared to my father and brother, they were mediocre and forgettable.

With a sigh, I pressed my water bottle against my throbbing forehead. "Guess it's a good thing Cary didn't have any daughters who decided to play hockey."

"Oh my God," Zoe groaned. "Dad would be *insufferable* about that."

"He would." Lowering the bottle, I looked at my sister. "I'm never going to change Dad's mind. I know I'm not. But I think... I mean, that's why it frustrates me so much when people act like he handed me a hockey career. It's the exact opposite."

"I get that. Everyone thinks you had it all handed to you from Dad, and no one will ever believe that you had to work twice as hard *because* of Dad."

I closed my eyes and pushed out a breath. "Exactly. And it's exhausting. Especially when someone comes along and reminds me. Like, for a little while, I *almost* forgot how everyone looks at me. I avoid reading articles or listening to commentators, and I just try not to think about it when reporters bring him up. So it kind of seemed like I was just playing hockey. As me. Not as Doran McAvoy's kid or Ty Caufield's ex-wife."

"Until your teammate threw it in your face," Zoe muttered.

I nodded and turned to her again. "The worst part is it makes me want to just walk away from it all."

My sister's eyes turned huge. "What? But you worked so hard to get to—"

"I know. I know." I gestured for her to calm down. "I'm not going to quit. I'm not giving this up. I just..." I let my shoulders drop as I slouched back against the couch. "It takes the fun right out of it, you know? Knowing I'm out there busting my ass, but people are absolutely sure the only reason I can skate that fast is because I've got a tailwind from Dad."

"Yeah, that makes sense." Zoe sighed. "I don't know how you play through it, honestly. I just really hope you don't give it up because one of your teammates is a bitch."

"If it was just one teammate, it probably wouldn't bother me as much. But all I can think is that she's the only one who's willing to say it out loud."

"Have any of your other teammates treated you badly?"

I considered it, then sheepishly shook my head. "No. And Lila's always hated me. I guess now I'm just worried who's being nice to my face while they secretly wish I'd leave so there'd be a spot for someone who's *earned* it."

"You did earn your spot," Zoe said.

"I know that. But do they?"

She looked like she wanted to argue, but then she deflated. "Ugh. Yeah, I guess it's hard to figure out who's buying into the rumors and who sees how you play right in front of their damn faces."

"Exactly," I whispered, and I felt even worse now. They had to recognize that my dad's name and influence could only carry me so far, right? I still had to be able to skate, protect the puck, score goals—that came from my head, hands, and legs, not the name across my back.

But Lila had to see those things too, and still, after all these years of seeing me play and playing together, she thought I'd had it all handed to me. Which meant that my other teammates—the ones who were less confrontational and could be sweet to my face—might very well think the same thing, too.

To my sister, I said, "I don't know what to do going forward. I don't know how to play through that." I laughed bitterly and added, "Not that I don't have years of practice."

Zoe scowled. "Honestly? If I were you?" She shrugged. "I'd probably just go out there and play for myself. Fuck the haters. Fuck the reporters. Fuck your teammates who don't think you deserve to be there."

"Kind of hard to do on a team," I said dryly.

"Maybe? But at some point, when you're racking up points and playing like everyone knows you can, they're going to have to admit it's you, not Dad."

"That hasn't worked yet."

"No, but at least then you don't have to care what anyone thinks."

I pursed my lips. On the surface, she had a point. And the ability to stop caring what other people thought *would* definitely make my life easier. If I could just ignore the comments and criticism, focus on the game, and play the level of hockey I knew I could, then I'd feel a hell of a lot better.

But given how much I still held out hope that my *dad* would change *his* tune about me and my hockey...

I wasn't optimistic about shutting off how much I cared what anyone else thought.

CHAPTER 11

LILA

I knew I'd messed up with Sabrina, but I didn't grasp just how badly I'd messed up until she showed up for our morning skate the next day.

I fully expected her to cold-shoulder me. Between now and when I could pull her aside and apologize, the air between us was going to be colder than the ice we skated on. Totally predictable and understandable.

What caught me by surprise was how she cold-shouldered *everyone*. When Laws said, "Good morning," to her, Sabrina's response was monosyllabic, her expression flat. While we all put on our gear and everyone chattered about whatever, she didn't say a word to anyone. And as soon as we hit the ice, she was off in her own world, skating like this was the middle of a playoff game and firing pucks into the boards so hard they echoed into the arena's high rafters.

Ooh, boy. There was no way this was a coincidence. That

she just happened to be in an uncharacteristically foul mood the day after I'd shot off my mouth.

This was bad, and I needed to fix it. I owed it to her *and* to our team.

Shit, I thought as I went about my own warmup routine. If I hadn't already felt like the world's biggest asshole, I sure did now.

The other problem? There wasn't a lot of opportunity to take care of the situation, especially today. This was a Sunday game, so puck drop was at 1:00 instead of 7:00. That meant our window of time for pre-game routines was a lot shorter than usual, and I knew better than to interrupt another player's routine under the best of circumstances.

After the game, then.

Except...

Jesus Christ. Twenty-three minutes into tonight's game, I knew waiting had been a mistake. This game was not going well, and even though it wasn't because of how I was playing, it was absolutely my fault.

"Pittsburgh number five," the ref said three minutes into the second period. "Two minute minor for roughing."

Sabrina shook her head as she took her seat in the penalty box, anger written all over her face. The call was a fair one; Nashville's blue liner had been trying to goad her, and Sabrina—usually so damned disciplined—had taken the bait. The other woman had wisely not punched back, so only Sabrina was penalized.

Jesus. This wasn't like Sabrina at all. Throughout our major junior days and whenever we'd played in international competition, she'd always been one of the most well-disciplined players on the ice. By the end of a season, she usually had a fraction of the penalty minutes as everyone else, and half of the ones she did get weren't really a lack of discipline. Accidentally tripping someone or high-sticking them; those were just part of the game.

Roughing? In the same game where she'd already taken a double minor for high-sticking?

This seriously wasn't like her.

And I couldn't avoid the fact that the way she was playing —angry, undisciplined, too aggressive—had all started after we'd had words in the gym. Every puck she'd hit this morning had practically screamed for mercy, and her checks this afternoon were harder than usual.

Now she was in the box because someone had successfully provoked her into roughing.

Oh my God, I thought as I watched her fuming behind the Plexiglas door. *This really is my fault.*

There was nothing I could do to fix it—not while the game was still going—but I could do my level best to minimize the damage. If Nashville scored a power play goal on us, they'd take the lead. If that ended up being their game-winning goal, Sabrina would feel even worse than she must have already.

No power play goal, then, I told myself as I set up with the penalty kill. *Not this game.*

Nashville wasn't going to make it easy, though. Their center won the faceoff in our zone, and they immediately started cycling the puck. We practiced for that, but there was only so much we could do. The point of it was to wear down the defenders, and it worked because we had to follow the puck if we didn't want to leave our goalie vulnerable.

The one saving grace? They weren't as good at this as they thought they were. As they cycled, I watched how they worked, same as I had during their last two power plays, and they were way too predictable. When a player at the point got the puck, she sent it to the other, who then passed it to the forward closest to her, who in turn passed it to the one closest to herself, and on to the next one, then back to the point. No changing things up.

Which meant when that second defender had the puck, I knew exactly where it was going.

It was a risk, but I left my own defensive position. Worth it—the puck landed right on my stick. I was about to clear it to the other end of the ice, but then I realized there was nothing but wide-open space between me and Nashville's goal. While the power play had cycled the puck, they'd been moving around, and they'd misjudged their spacing.

Instead of clearing the puck, I took it on my stick and bolted for the neutral zone. I sensed one of their players on my heels, but I skated like hell across the neutral zone and into the offensive zone, the crowd roaring with approval and anticipation.

With mere feet to go to the goal, I faked, then shot on the backhand.

The goalie was fast. She made the save, but the rebound got away from her.

There was a flash of black and gold at the corner of my eye, and I turned just in time to see Anastasia—who'd apparently followed me into the zone—fire the puck right into the back of the net.

The fans absolutely lost their minds.

I was first to Anastasia and threw my arms around her. "Nice shorty!"

"Nice setup!" She slapped my back. "That was amazing!"

A second later, our other two teammates were there, congratulating both of us. We had the lead now, and the jail-break goal had Sabrina out of the penalty box.

Hopefully that meant a big relief for her and a small redemption for me.

As Sabrina skated across the ice to the bench, she smiled at Anastasia. When her gaze landed on me, though, the smile vanished, and she just continued toward the bench.

My heart sank. I deserved that. I knew I did. I hoped the effort to keep Nashville from converting would earn me a little bit of grace, but I wasn't surprised that it didn't. She didn't owe me a damn thing after what I'd said. Getting her out of the box and helping our team to a lead wasn't—and shouldn't have been—enough.

After the game, I promised myself as I went to the bench.

I needed to make things right with her anyway. Pride be damned, I couldn't just let this fester. And now that it was affecting the team, there was no way around it. I'd set this in motion, and I needed to be the one to put a stop to it, ideally before it cost us a game or something.

One of the downsides with this sport, though, was how fast things moved, and not just on the ice. When the game ended, we were encouraged to take off our gear and shower quickly so the media could come in. Before the reporters had even left the locker room, we were being ushered into the lounge to eat, reminded multiple times that we were leaving for the airport soon.

Then it was onto the bus, into the airport, onto the plane, and into the air. Before we'd even leveled out, Sabrina was asleep. Not long after, so was I. Then we were landing and being ushered off the plane and onto another bus, which took us to the hotel.

Room keys in hand, we all dispersed to our rooms.

Several of our teammates were going to hit the bar for a nightcap. It was still reasonably early, and anyway, the nap on the plane gave some people a second wind. They needed to wind down a bit before they called it a night. I was dead on my feet, ready pass out even though it was only 9:00 (Pittsburgh time, anyway; God only knew what time it was in... wherever we were). Still, I joined them, hoping Sabrina would too. Then I could find a chance to discreetly pull her aside and clear the air. Ideally before Tuesday night's game.

But she didn't come down to the bar.

CHAPTER 12

SABRINA

We're going to the bar. You joining us?

The text from Laws made my chest tight. I wanted to hang out with my teammates. I really did.

But I was just not feeling it tonight.

Going to call it an early night. See you at breakfast.

Then I lay back on the hotel bed, still fully dressed, and just stared at the ceiling. I needed to get out of this funk. Ever since that confrontation with Lila in the locker room, I'd been off my game. Quite literally off it today—I hadn't taken that many penalty minutes in one game since my youth days. Here I was thinking I needed to play my butt off so everyone could see that I deserved to be there, and what did I do? Give Nashville *three* power play opportunities.

My team had managed to jailbreak me from one of them, but the other two—well, I'd just been lucky that Nashville's power play was mediocre at best. If we'd been playing against

Calgary or Seattle, it would've been a massacre even with our top-notch penalty kill.

Our top-notch penalty kill, which included Lila Hamilton, who'd gotten a well-deserved primary assist on that jailbreak goal.

I closed my eyes and sighed. Was it too soon to request a trade out of Pittsburgh? I liked the city and I liked most of my team, but I wasn't so sure I could keep playing on a roster with someone who openly thought I shouldn't be there. I was so worried that the rest of the team might think the same thing, and it was driving me up a wall.

This morning, when I'd arrived for our morning skate, I'd caught myself looking from one teammate to the next, wondering who was smiling to my face while sneering at my back. By the time I'd hit the ice, I'd been angry. So, so angry. By the time the puck had dropped for this afternoon's game, I'd been too angry to play well. Too unfocused. Too undisciplined. And it had nearly cost my team. At least I'd managed a goal in the first period; a violent slapshot of a goal that had left me feeling raw and angry instead of victorious because that was all I felt today—raw and angry.

So which is worse? Playing well and letting them all think I'm just here because of my dad? Or falling apart and giving them a reason to say I never belonged here in the first place?

I covered my face with both hands and groaned into the stillness. How much of this was in my head and how much of it was real? Couldn't I just, like, play hockey and enjoy the sport I loved? Did it have to be so fraught and full of suspicious people who thought I'd been handed a spot at the level they'd had to bust their asses to reach?

How much longer was my love of hockey going to keep me going before I gave up and did something else? Because right now, I wasn't loving hockey. If I was honest with myself, the only things that were really keeping me going were spite and stubbornness. I couldn't give up because I couldn't let my detractors—least of all my own father—be right. I needed to stay here—visible, playing professional hockey with that C on my chest—because fuck everyone who said I didn't belong here.

That had carried me through a lot of funks from my youth days all the way up through major juniors, and it was doing a lot of heavy lifting right now. But how long was it going to be enough? How long before it was okay to say I was done fighting and—

My phone screamed to life in my pocket, and I swore loud enough that whoever was next door probably heard me. Again when the iPhone's screen confirmed what the ringtone had already told me:

Dad.

Ugh. Really? I did not have it in me to deal with him tonight. I just didn't.

But I also didn't have it in me to have passive-aggressive voicemails festering on my phone, so... fine.

I put the phone to my ear and rested my free hand over my eyes. "Hi, Dad."

"Oh good, you're still awake."

"It's only..." What time was it? "It's not that late."

"Yes, well," he said, sounding just *slightly* patronizing, "I know what it's like, playing a game and traveling on the same day."

I rolled my eyes beneath my hand. "Just part of the sport."

"Mmhmm. It's probably not nearly as demanding for you, though, which is why I figured you'd still be up."

It took all I had not to push out a frustrated breath. I'd walked right into that, hadn't I? Should've seen it coming from a mile away. Sort of like I should've known Cady Williams had been trying to draw a penalty from me earlier, and that I shouldn't have taken her goddamned bait, and—

"Well, I'm up." I kept my voice as neutral as I could. "How are things?"

"Things are fine." He sounded dismissive, which meant he hadn't called to talk about "things." He didn't keep me hanging about why he *had* called, either: "Sabrina, how long are you going to embarrass yourself out there?"

"Embarrass myself?" I dropped my arm to the bed and stared up at the ceiling. "What do you mean? It was *one* bad night." The words, *"You had them, too"* stuck in my throat.

Dad scoffed. "Any night spent playing in this joke of a league is a bad night."

I rolled my eyes again, then rubbed them with my thumb and forefinger. "I'm committed for at least two years. So, even if I wanted to quit, which I don't..."

I didn't hear what Dad said next. I was vaguely aware of the disapproval and irritation coming down the line, but I was mostly focused on my own words.

"Even if I wanted to quit, which I don't..."

I *didn't* want to quit.

Did I?

No, I was pretty sure I didn't. But I couldn't lie—right now, just the thought of putting on my gear and hitting the ice again made me want to bury my head under the pillows and sleep for a month. I hated myself for the way I'd played today. I hated how I'd felt around my teammates. I hated how one conversation with one teammate—one who'd always thought I was shit on her shoe—had thrown off my concentration, my love of the game, my—

"Sabrina!" my dad snapped. "Are you listening to me?"

I jumped. "Hmm? What?" I paused. "I think my phone cut out for a second. The reception here isn't that great."

He laughed haughtily. "That league is putting you girls up in *luxury* hotels, aren't they?"

I pinched the bridge of my nose. This was the same hotel the men's league used, but I wasn't in the mood to argue with him about that. Or about anything, but whatever. "What were you saying before my phone went wonky?"

Dad gave an impatient huff. "There are a million other things you could be doing with your time and your family's good name. Why don't you start an organization like your sister-in-law? She's doing a ton of good things for people."

I literally bit my tongue. He was forever telling me to follow in my sister-in-law's footsteps, since she—unlike my mother and me—was the epitome of the flawless hockey wife. Imani was the model-perfect face beside my brother, and she ran a non-profit that helped underprivileged children. I adored her, and she did amazing things for a lot of people, but —as Dad was forever reminding me—I *wasn't* her.

"This is what I want to do, Dad," I said flatly, and my stomach curdled because I didn't know how honest I was being in that moment. "I want to play hockey, and I'm good at it."

The harsh laugh on the other end made my heart sink deeper. I was struggling hard enough to hold on to my love of the sport and my desire to play. It was a temporary funk, I hoped—I wasn't one to let people like Lila Hamilton get under my skin—but it still sucked. Listening to my dad shit all over what I was doing really, really didn't help.

Before he could say anything, I said, "Oh, I just got a text from the coaches. Team meeting. I need to go."

He chuckled again, but at least he didn't try to stop me from going to the "meeting." He might crap on my dreams and degrade my league at every possible opportunity, but even he wouldn't cause me to get disciplined. Good to know the man had *some* consideration where my sport was concerned. Probably because of how it would reflect on him if his daughter was not only playing women's hockey, she was irresponsible and unreliable. Not acceptable for a McAvoy.

"All right, kiddo. But think about what I told you, will you? This whole league—it's a waste of your time and my good name."

I hated how little energy I could muster to argue with him. I hated the lump in my throat that I couldn't quite force down.

"I'll talk to you later, Dad."

"Love you, Sabrina."

"Love you, too."

Then I ended the call and let the phone fall onto the mattress beside me. Tears stung, and I tried to hold them back, but I didn't succeed.

Spite and stubbornness had carried me through a lot, but they were MIA right now. I was just tired. I was hurt. My own father wanted me to stop playing because it embarrassed him to have his name associated with women's hockey. At least one of my teammates—one whose dad loved and supported her to the moon and back—thought I was here through nepotism and couldn't stand the sight of me. Nights like this, it was hard to stay stubborn. It was hard to feel that spite that had pulled me through so many times before.

Nights like this, I wanted to ask the team to release me from my contract so I could go live a private life somewhere. Maybe play on a beer league now and then just to scratch that itch. Do something where I could be Sabrina McAvoy instead of Doran McAvoy's daughter. Maybe even do something Doran McAvoy thought was worth doing.

Most of the time, I didn't care what he thought of me playing hockey. I was going to do it because fuck him.

But nights like this...

God, was it too much to ask for my dad to be happy that I was doing what I loved? That I was doing something I was good at it?

I can't believe everyone thinks you're the reason I have this career.

How much better would I be if you hadn't tried to keep me down?

CHAPTER 13

LILA

My chance to get Sabrina alone finally presented itself, and the location wasn't much different than the place I'd pissed her off—in the workout center at the arena in Charlotte.

We'd had a team meeting this morning, followed by a morning skate, and then everyone was heading out for their pre-game naps and routines, but I'd overheard her tell Anastasia she wanted to spend some time in the gym before she left.

I'd done a light off-ice workout myself before practice, so there was no point in going into the gym again. Plus I didn't want to distract her from her own routine, especially on game day.

But we did need to have this talk, and we needed to do it before the festering bullshit messed her up for another game.

As I expected, she went from the workout center to the showers, then came into the locker room, one towel around her hair and the other around her body. She probably only expected to find a few staff members wandering around; the equipment managers were always hard at work, and some of the coaching staff were usually nearby.

From the look on her face when she saw me, she definitely hadn't expected to find me here. Or at least, I was the last person she *hoped* she'd see.

She shot me a withering glare, then went to her locker stall and started pulling out another set of shorts and a team shirt. With those on the bench, she continued drying off from her shower.

I didn't watch her get dressed; we were all used to seeing each other naked, but staring at her while we were the only ones in here would be seriously disrespectful. And anyway, with everything hanging in the air between us, getting caught ogling her would not help our situation.

Once she had on her shorts and T-shirt, I turned her way. As she toweled her hair, I cleared my throat. "Look, I'm..." I swallowed hard. "What I said about you having everything handed to you—I'm sorry. You're right—I *don't* know what your life has been like." I paused, studying her. "Something tells me no one does."

She eyed me warily, her guard still firmly in place.

But before I could try again to get past those defenses, her shoulders dropped, and she pushed out a breath. She sat down on the bench, watching herself play with the towel between her long fingers. Her voice was soft, almost apologetic as she murmured, "No one does, no."

She sounded tired. As if she were absolutely wrung out, and not by her gym routine.

I chewed my lip as I studied her. Then, cautiously, I

moved closer, sitting down on the bench but leaving some breathing room between us. "You don't have to tell me. But... I'm curious."

Sabrina turned to me, strands of wet hair falling in front of her eyes. Why was it so hard to resist brushing them out of her face and tucking them behind her ear? She drew the tip of her tongue along the inside of her lip. "Why do you want to know?"

I half-shrugged. "All I've ever had to go by is what people have said. I, um... I thought it was the whole story." I had to almost literally swallow my pride before I added, "Apparently I was wrong."

She lowered her gaze again. "Is that why you don't like me? Because you think my dad handed me a hockey career?"

When she put it like that, I sounded like an even bigger asshole. Sighing, I nodded. "I've seen so many girls struggle to get to even major juniors. I thought..." I exhaled. "I'm sorry."

She studied me through her lashes, and I fully expected her to tell me I was full of shit before she stormed out.

Instead, something in her seemed to... collapse. She slumped a little, all the remaining anger melting out of her expression, replaced by what looked like pure fatigue. "*No one* knows the truth about my dad's influence on my career."

I swallowed. "What is the truth?"

She searched my eyes as if to ask, *"Do you really want to know, or are you just going to shoot down whatever I say?"*

Before I could insist I was coming from a genuine place, though, Sabrina took a deep breath and started talking, the words tumbling out as if she'd been holding them back forever and just couldn't anymore.

"Everyone's convinced my dad's name has been my golden ticket to everything hockey. And maybe it has been. I..." She sighed heavily and lifted a shoulder in a minute half-shrug. "I can't control the decisions or assumptions people make. The part people don't know is that the only thing my name might have gotten me is some more open doors. And yes, I know, that's a privilege. I know a lot of people don't have that. It isn't fair." She turned to me again, her eyes filled with fatigue and sadness. "But once those doors are open, I still have to earn the right to stay. I still have to play hockey. And the part people don't realize is that I had to fight hard to even learn to play in the first place."

I tilted my head. "What do you mean?"

"I mean my brother had everything he could ever need at his fingertips. He was skating before he was out of diapers. He had private coaches. My dad coached him. He took Mark to practices with him so he could learn from professional coaches and teammates." Sabrina swallowed like it took some work, and she shook her head. "I didn't have any of that. I learned to skate young because my mom wanted me and my sister to learn. But hockey?" She swiped at her eyes, which had started to well up again. "I wasn't allowed to play hockey. Not even in the driveway."

My lips parted. "What? Why not?"

"Because my dad thinks women's hockey is a joke. And he didn't want his name being used to legitimize the sport." She leaned back, letting her head rest against the divider between locker stalls. She closed her eyes, and when she spoke again, she sounded even more exhausted. "He hated that I was involved in getting the League off the ground. Even after I got married and changed my name, he didn't want me doing anything related to hockey—especially playing—because everyone still knew I was his daughter. So his name was still getting dragged into it." She rolled her eyes. "He was pissed that I changed my name, and then he was pissed that I was dragging his name near women's hockey. I can't win, I swear."

"Wow," I whispered. I considered everything she'd said, then I moistened my lips. "Can I ask something else? Again, you don't have to answer."

She met my gaze, eyes wet but curious.

"With all the shit everyone said about you riding your dad's name..." I hesitated, not sure how to continue.

In a resigned voice, she asked, "Why did I change it back after I got divorced?"

I nodded.

Sabrina stared at the floor again and gave a wet, miserable laugh. "Everyone's convinced I did that so I could land a contract in the League. Because Dad's name definitely carries more weight than Ty's."

"Right," I said quietly. "I, um... That's what I heard."

Her laughter, such as it was, faded, and she watched herself tracing the logo on her water bottle with her thumb. "I knew that's what people would think. And I dreaded it, because..." She sighed and shook her head. "At the end of the day, I'd rather let people say I'm using my dad's name for nepotism than keep Ty's name."

That caught me off-guard, and I stared at her. "Why's that?"

Sabrina brushed some wet hair out of her face. "The

thing is, no matter what the rumors say, I didn't retire from competition because of Ty's money." She turned to me. "I retired because Ty didn't want to be married to a hockey player. And he did everything he could to keep me from playing."

"What? Why? And how?"

"Why?" She huffed a near silent laugh. "Who knows? In hindsight, he married me for exactly the reason everyone thinks the League signed me—because of my dad. He loved the idea of being Doran McAvoy's son-in-law. When I wanted to declare myself for the draft the first year of the League, he had a million reasons why I shouldn't." She started ticking off the points on her fingers. "It would make my physique too hard and unattractive. The women's teams usually play on the road while the men's teams are at home and vice versa, so we'd barely see each other. It..." She dropped her hand onto her thigh with a heavy smack. "I don't know what the real reason was. Just that I got tired of fighting about it, especially because I'd spent my whole life fighting so hard against my dad over the same thing, so I just... gave in."

"That sounds..."

"Miserable?" She laughed bitterly. "You could say that. And I mean, Ty wasn't physically abusive or anything. I wasn't afraid of him. He just knew how to wear me down mentally and emotionally until he got whatever he wanted. By the time I realized I needed to leave, I couldn't. He had control of all the money. Everything was in his name. I couldn't afford to get my own place, never mind a lawyer." She sat up a little and rolled her shoulders. Then she turned to look right in my eyes, and though hers were still wet, there was a fierceness I hadn't seen before. "That was when I reached out to Laura Davies—Seattle's GM."

I straightened. "You did?"

Sabrina nodded. "She coached me in major juniors, so I knew her. I reached out and told her the God's honest truth—that I wanted to leave my husband, but I didn't have the means, and that I wanted to come back to hockey. I knew I wasn't ready to play again—not yet—but if I could get out from under my husband's thumb..."

"Oh my God," I whispered.

"Yeah, it was..." She laughed dryly and ran a hand through her wet hair. "So she fronted me enough money to get out and get a lawyer. She promised me it was no strings attached, but I busted my butt for ten months to get back in condition. Once I was, she offered me a PTO, and after I proved at training camp that I was still a solid player, she gave me a one-year deal."

Jesus. I felt like the worst human being on the planet after hearing Sabrina's side of the story. There'd been so many rumors and assumptions about her—every one of which I'd swallowed whole—and no one had come to her defense. "Did your family help you get away from your ex?"

Sabrina shook her head again, staring at the lockers with unfocused eyes. "My mom and sister supported me a lot emotionally, and they encouraged me to leave, but they were both struggling financially."

"Really?" I stared at her. "Your dad is richer than God, but they're...?"

She nodded. "He and Mom had a prenup, and Dad's lawyer threatened to turn it into an ugly custody battle if she didn't back down on splitting assets. She was scared to death of losing custody of us, especially my sister and me, so she took a small settlement and walked. The money she does have now is from working a regular job all these years."

"Holy shit. Your dad doesn't sound like, um..."

"Like the super nice family man who adored his kids and was devastated when his bitch of a wife took them and left? Yeah, I know. Amazing what does and doesn't make it into the press." She rubbed her eyes and sighed. "Sort of like how everyone still thinks I left Ty because I decided to become a lesbian."

That rumor had definitely made the rounds. As had the photos of her with the woman she'd dated—or at least hooked up with—after her divorce. "So you're bi, then?"

"No, no, I'm a lesbian." She reached up to knead the back of her neck with both hands. "Just a little slow on the uptake, I guess. And then before I had a chance to really come to terms with it and come out to my family, someone outed me." She stared up at the ceiling, still rubbing her neck, and I thought her eyes welled up again. "God, I would absolutely *kill* for some goddamned privacy."

"I bet."

"Everyone thinks being a McAvoy must be the greatest and most privileged thing ever." She lowered her hands and turned to me, and yep, there were fresh tears clinging to her lashes. "But all it's ever brought me is public humiliation."

If I'd felt like an asshole before... Jesus.

"I'm sorry," I said softly. "For all of that, and for..." I chewed my lip as heat rose in my face. "I'm sorry."

"I know." She stared down at her wringing hands again.

"You didn't know. Most people don't. And there's a ton of rumors and bullshit backfilling what everyone doesn't know, so they *think* they do, and..." She waved a hand in a heavy, tired gesture.

"Still. I'm sorry. It's... I obviously didn't have the whole story. None of us did." I grimaced. "I should've known what we all heard was..." I trailed off, not sure what to say.

"It's all been repeated so many times and so many ways..." She shrugged. "I can't blame anyone for believing it. And it isn't like I've ever done much to change the narrative."

"Why not?"

Another shrug, this one heavier than before. "The handful of times I've tried, I just get painted as a spoiled brat. The only thing I've ever been able to do to prove my dad wrong about anything is to play hockey like it's what I was born to do."

I nodded as she spoke. "I'm surprised your dad hasn't changed his tune about you playing. Even if he's got a stick up his ass about women's hockey, you're..." Why was I blushing? Because I felt like I was blushing. "You're really good."

A faint smile curled her full lips, but it faded fast. "I'd love to think he'll come around one of these days. But if the World Junior Women's and Olympic medals haven't convinced him..." She trailed off into a sigh.

"Ugh. Yeah. That sounds like someone who's seriously committed to his narrative."

"You have no idea," she muttered. "Plus, even if he could get past me having the audacity to be a woman playing hockey, he hates my playing style. That's literally the only thing he's ever acknowledged about my involvement with the sport—that I shouldn't do it, and that my playing style is wrong."

I blinked. "What? Why? What the hell is wrong with the way you play?"

She gave another ghost of a laugh. "Because I'm a playmaker. If I'm that happy racking up assists, I should just play defense and be done with it."

"For fuck's sake," I said, rolling my eyes. "The points benefit the team exactly the same way whether you get the goal or the assist. And you get a ton of goals, too!"

"I know, but he was always out for glory. And apparently if I absolutely *must* sully his name by playing women's hockey, I should at least be a goal scorer more than anything else. That would be almost respectable in his eyes."

"But he'd still shit on it."

"Absolutely." Sabrina's shoulders sagged again, and she wiped a hand over her face. "All I've ever wanted to do was play hockey, and I've done that. I'm doing it. It just doesn't seem like too much to ask for my dad to be proud of me too."

My heart dropped into my feet and the guilt over what I'd said the other day burrowed even deeper. "No, it's not too much to ask." I slid a little closer on the bench. "I'm sorry, Sabrina. I really am. For what I said, and… God, that you have to play with that albatross around your neck. It's…" I chewed my lip as I searched for the words. "Honestly, knowing what you've been up against all this time—it's even more impressive that you're as good as you are."

Sabrina stared at me as if she hadn't heard me right.

"I've always envied you as a player," I admitted. "Yeah, I thought you had it easy getting to that level, but I always wished I could play as well as you. But realizing now that you had someone holding you back all this time?" I whistled, shaking my head. "That's *incredible*."

Some color bloomed in her cheeks, and she managed a small smile. "Thanks. I just wish other people could see it." She dropped her gaze to her wringing hands. "I wish my dad could see it."

"Fuck him."

Her head snapped up.

I shrugged. "He's done everything he can to stop you. The best revenge is to play like hell and show the world that you're an even bigger generational talent than he ever was."

Sabrina's lips parted.

"I get that you want his approval," I went on. "I would too. But since he's going to be a dick about it, I say make sure that whenever he talks trash about women's hockey—especially you playing it—people are like, 'bruh, have you *seen* what your daughter is doing out there?'"

She stared at me, then laughed. "So, play so well that he looks like an ass whenever he talks shit?"

"Exactly!"

Her laughter had some more feeling this time. "I've always said most of my success has come from spite and stubbornness. Might as well stay on that track."

"That's the spirit." I held up my fist, and she bumped it. Sobering a little, I said, "And I mean it—I'm sorry."

"I know." To my surprise, Sabrina gathered me into a hug. As her damp hair cooled the side of my face, she said, "Maybe it wasn't so bad, because I think this conversation is exactly what I needed."

My heart fluttered with relief. "Still. I'm glad this helped, but I'm sorry about what I said."

"I know you are." Drawing back, she smiled at me, oblivious to how utterly gorgeous she was, even under the harsh locker room lights. "We're good."

"Okay. Okay, great." I laughed just to get my breath moving. "What do you say we go find something to eat? We've got warmups in a few hours."

"Sounds good." She gestured over her shoulder. "Let me put on my shoes."

As she did that, I basked in the broken tension and the settling dust. Maybe she was right and this conversation was something she needed. Maybe the end did justify the means.

But I still felt awful for what I'd said and for what a bitch I'd been to her.

And I was more grateful than she could imagine for her forgiveness.

CHAPTER 14

SABRINA

I probably shouldn't have been surprised that settling things with Lila made playing alongside her a million times easier. It was never good for a team when two players were at odds; it was something people could work around to a certain extent, but having teammates who disliked each other was far from ideal.

I was a little worried I'd been too quick to forgive her, but honestly, I was just so damn relieved that we'd put this thing to bed, I embraced our new dynamic. She seemed to be genuinely contrite, and it wasn't her fault she'd heard all the same poison about me that everyone else did. Could I really fault anyone for believing it?

Or maybe I just couldn't cope with conflict on my team because I got so damn much of it at home. Did I let things with her go too fast? Yeah, I might've. But I couldn't justify dragging it out because that was miserable for *me*.

For the rest of our teammates, too. Now that Lila and I

could be in the same room and on the same ice without wanting to gnash our teeth, I felt even guiltier for the tension we'd brought into the locker room. Though none of our team-mates had said anything about it—at least not to me—they weren't stupid, and it was clear from the new general air of relaxation that they'd picked up on the bad vibes. Definitely not good for anyone—least of all the goddamned team captain —to be causing that much stress for her teammates.

Way to go, Lila and Sabrina!

But we were good now.

Practices were easier. Games were easier. Even traveling for away games or sharing a meal with teammates was easier now that no one had to make sure Lila and I didn't end up near each other. Now that we sometimes sat together, I real-ized how much our teammates had been subtly keeping us apart. The lack of tension now made everyone's previous discomfort painfully obvious.

Hopefully we could make it up to them going forward.

There was one small fly in the ointment about this newfound understanding, though. While it improved things for us and our team, it also made those things more difficult in a way I didn't expect, but probably should have.

When we hadn't liked each other, I'd just catch a glimpse of her and feel irritated. With that out of the way, every glance in her direction sparked an entirely different kind of distraction. One that did not bode well for things like, you know, playing hockey.

Lila was lean in that way hockey players were—toned and tight from head to toe. Her hips and thighs were all power, and her shoulders made my mouth water, especially when she was wearing a T-back tank top like she almost always did while lifting weights. Lila was the complete package—that gorgeous build along with a wicked smile and disarming blue eyes.

God. Maybe we should've gone back to disliking each other. At least then I could stay on my skates and handle my stick without faceplanting on the ice.

Get a grip, Sabrina. Jesus.

Honestly, it was still a little weird to be driven to distraction by a woman like this at all. Or, well, to *admit* that I was. Looking back, I'd always had crushes on women, and there were multiple instances in my life where I'd barely been able to think while in the orbit of a particularly stunning woman. In hindsight, my sexuality could not have been more obvious.

I'd had a few flings and hookups with women over the years. Each time, I'd snapped right back to dating guys because, damn it, I was *not* a lesbian. I'd spent so long being defensive about that, I shoved myself back into the closet because... hell, I didn't even know why. It had made sense in the moment. Now it just felt like an exhausting waste of too many years.

It had taken three years of marriage to Ty to drive home the point that, yeah... I was a lesbian. Not even bisexual. After my divorce, I'd had a brief thing with a woman—one that had unfortunately made it into the media—and suddenly I was out before I actually wanted to be. That had tarnished the whole process of accepting myself; I'd finally figured out who the hell I was, only to have the press turn it into a circus because Kendra and I got careless and let a camera catch us.

But at least now I knew who I was... and why I was having a hell of a time concentrating around Lila Hamilton.

I just wish I knew what to do about that, because it was—

"Hey. Mac." Sims tapped my shinpad with her skate. "You coming?"

I shook myself and looked around. Oh, fuck me. While I'd been lost in thought—while I should've been getting into the right headspace for the game—my teammates had geared up and were starting to head out for warmups.

Face burning, I pushed myself up and grabbed my helmet. "Yeah. Yeah, I'm coming."

She gave me an odd look but let it go and followed our teammates out. Good thing the captain was always the last onto the ice, so I still had time to put on my gloves and helmet before catching up. With any luck, Sims was the only one who'd noticed me spacing out.

Hopefully no cameras had.

And *hopefully* I hadn't been stupidly staring at Lila the whole time. That would be hard to dismiss as nothing.

By some miracle, I pulled my head together enough that I didn't fall on my face as soon as I hit the ice. I found my place in the team's warmup routine, and I focused on skating, stretching, and (finally) getting my stupid head in the game. We were up against Boston tonight, and there was a reason they were situated *very* firmly in second place in their division. The only way to beat them was to stay on our game for the full sixty minutes plus any overtime that came along. Every team in the League had quickly learned that Boston would take full advantage if a team took their foot off the gas even briefly.

We had to bring our A-game tonight, and halfway through warmups, I was in the zone I needed to be in. Physically, I was ready. There was a little twinge in my hip, but it was just one of those old injuries that came back to haunt me sometimes. Our athletic trainers had checked me out earlier today and were confident there was nothing to worry about.

"Let us know if it gets worse," Connie had told me. "If anything moves in a way it shouldn't, or it doesn't feel right, say so. Otherwise, you're good to go."

So... normal. Nobody got to this level of hockey without a few lingering problems, and we all learned quickly how to tell the difference between pain that meant something was wrong and pain that just meant something was cranky.

I skated a few extra circles toward the end of warmups, followed by a couple of relaxed backward circles, just to work the twinge out a little. It helped, even if it didn't completely resolve the problem.

My body was as ready as it was going to be tonight. I could work with that.

My head was in a good spot now, too. All through my warmup, I'd mentally replayed the film we'd reviewed as a team yesterday and this morning. I worked through strategies to keep Boston from breaking away, and noted again and again that their second defensive pair frequently fell apart during odd man rushes. If we could take advantage of that, we'd be good. Exploit their weaknesses. Don't let them get breakaways. Oh, and don't try to five-hole this goalie—our offensive coach had been emphatic during film review that this netminder was okay at stopping top shelf shots, but nothing down low would get past her. Biggest weak point? Up high, blocker side. So just aim for—

Someone skated past me, same as all my teammates did a million times during warmups, but the blonde hair beneath her helmet told me a second before I saw her number that it was Lila.

She crossed over, effortlessly carrying a puck on her stick as she wound between other players before passing it to Sims.

Something about the way she moved...

I looked down at the puck I'd been carrying on my own stick, and hell if I could remember what I'd been planning to do with it. And what was I thinking about the other team's goalie? Something, something, top shelf?

I shook myself and fired my puck at the goal, then continued skating if only to keep anyone from noticing my brain had short-circuited.

Get a grip, Sabrina. Holy shit.

At least the buzzer sounding the end of warmups snapped my mind back into gear. I'd been playing hockey for so long, that it was almost an automatic shift—once warmups ended, everything else was shut off except for the game.

Except, apparently, my inability to look away from Lila as I walked up the chute behind her. Even with her pads and gear on, she was just—

Sabrina.

Come on.

What the hell?

I shook myself, and in the locker room, I called upon the same habit I had while she and I had been at odds—don't fucking look at her. Look anywhere *but* at her. Pretend she wasn't there. Don't think about her, don't look at her—no, seriously, don't think about her. Or those eyes. Or that body. Or that smile. Or—

"All right, ladies!" Coach Reilly said. "Let's go do this!"

Oh, crap. She was done with her pre-game speech and everyone was once again heading for the ice.

Well, I'd made it through games before where I was even more distracted by much worse things than my hot teammate. Breakups, fights with my dad, my grandma in the hospital—if I could play through those, I could play through this.

Granted in those situations, I didn't have the object of my distraction right there the whole time, but whatever. I'd make it work. I had to.

When the puck dropped, my scattered mind snapped into focus. Time to win a hockey game.

I lost the faceoff, but Laws managed to pick the other player's pocket just before they crossed into our defensive zone.

It was a grind. Every inch of the ice we gained against this team was an absolute battle. They managed to score on us twice in the first period, but we rallied and squeaked one in just before the buzzer sounded. The vibe in the locker room was frustrated but optimistic—this was a tough, tough team to beat, but they weren't unstoppable. We could do this. Next period, we'd carry the momentum from Anastasia's goal and tie things up. Then we'd focus on obtaining, holding, and extending a lead.

The second period started with the same back-and-forth energy, but determination radiated off all my teammates. When the third line got out there, they managed to get

Boston into their own end and keep them there, hemming them in so they couldn't risk a line change. With their skaters starting to get fatigued, ours started to peel away one at a time so my line could go out.

By the time Anastasia, Laws, and I were out on the ice with Sims at the blue line and Lila in the fray with us, Boston's skaters were absolutely gassed. Perfect.

We cycled the puck to wear them down a little more while we found a shooting lane. I realized I wasn't in a good position, so I carried the puck around behind the goal, and when I came out the other side, I searched for someone to pass to or a scoring chance of my own.

I'd barely made it out of the trapezoid before a Boston defender checked me. Fortunately, I'd seen her coming, and I stayed on my skates *and* held on to the puck.

She was coming back for more, though, and there was another player closing in.

"Hams!" I called out, and when Lila turned her head, the puck was already halfway to her.

It landed right on her tape. I thought she'd pass to Laws, but instead she fired a beautiful one-timer from the point.

The puck sailed right through a dense screen of players and over the goaltender's left shoulder.

Lila pumped her stick in the air and shouted, though her voice and the goal horn were both swallowed up by the roar of the crowd.

She had her first goal of the season, and the Pittsburgh Bearcats had the lead.

We celebrated with her, almost toppling her with hugs, and as I embraced her against the glass—

Oh. Hell.

The crowd disappeared. The goal song faded to nothing. There was just...

Do you have any idea how beautiful you are?

Thank God, Sims picked that moment to smack my back, and the spell was broken. Lila and I broke eye contact, and hopefully no one thought the extra color in both our faces was anything other than exertion. Then we were skating toward the bench for fist bumps, Lila leading the pack since she'd been the one to score.

After our brief celebration with the team, the five of us took our seats while the second line and second pair went out. As we cooled down, I stole a glance at Lila, who was at the other end of the bench with the defenders.

She picked that same moment to steal a glance at me.

Our eyes locked for a second.

Then she smiled. So did I.

Facing the game again, I blamed my racing heart on the intense shift I'd just played and the thrill of a goal. That had to be it. That was all it was.

There was a lot of pressure right now. We'd tied up a game against a team favored to go deep in the postseason. We had to keep our foot on the gas if we wanted to win this one. Yeah, that was all it was—pressure. Hockey. Normal stress during a game.

I was more subtle about glancing Lila's way this time.

She didn't meet my gaze, but my pulse spiked again. She had her helmet off, wet strands of blond hair tumbling down either side of her face as she had an animated conversation with the defensive coach.

I gulped, facing the ice again as my heart slammed against my ribs.

Aww, fuck.

I am so screwed.

In the end, despite fighting hard from start to finish, we lost that game in overtime. It was a struggle all night long, and there were a few times I thought we would lose in regulation. A buzzer beater from Val kept us alive, and we held our own in OT for almost the full five minutes. With twenty-two seconds left on the clock, Boston broke away, and though Anya tried like hell, she couldn't stop that shot from their star center.

None of us were thrilled about the loss, but it was a hard-fought game and we did still get a point, so it wasn't a disaster.

Three nights later, we brought down the house in Orlando, breaking their four-game winning streak with a 5-3 win. A lot of Pittsburgh fans were in the crowd, and it was as loud and raucous as a home game. I loved it, and I especially loved getting us back into the win column.

While my teammates went to the bar to celebrate afterward, though, I was ready for some quiet. I said goodnight to everyone, then headed up to my room.

And wouldn't you know it—I'd barely taken off my jacket before that all too familiar ringtone went off.

I sat on the edge of the bed and glared at the screen.

Dad.

God, I didn't need his bullshit tonight. Not on the heels

of an exhilarating win. The calls after those games were the worst.

I tossed my phone aside, buried my face in my hands, and groaned. I was in a good mood, damn it. I didn't want to talk to him. I didn't want to hear whatever he had to say about the way I'd played tonight.

Because he *would* have an issue with something.

I needed to stop being a hero and playing long shifts, because when I got tired, I got sloppy. Didn't matter that I hadn't had the opportunity to go to the bench—we'd been hemmed into our own end, Val had been without a stick, and the other team had been making drive after drive for our goal. I'd been gassed, but so were my linemates, and we couldn't just take off and leave Anya vulnerable.

Or he'd be pissy because I had, yet again, racked up multiple assists without a single goal. Or maybe it was that penalty I took in the third period? No, I hadn't intended to trip the other player, but accidental tripping was still tripping. I didn't make the rules.

My ringtone stopped. A solid minute later came the chirp to indicate a voicemail.

For a long moment, I lay there, listening to my heart thumping against my ribs. There was a second chirp to remind me Dad had left a message. I ignored that, too, though my pulse ratcheted up again. This wasn't nearly as pleasant as the feeling whenever I looked at Lila. When my heart would start going wild just because she smiled or brushed her hair out of her face or... who was I kidding? Because she existed.

That stressed me out for different reasons, but it was way more fun than this bullshit.

So why am I up here trying to talk myself into listening to Dad's message when I could be downstairs with my team?

With Lila?

Without a second thought, I pushed myself up. I left my phone in the room, grabbed my keycard, and went downstairs to the bar.

I tried not to read too much into the way Lila's eyes lit up when I came into the bar. "Oh, hey!" She smiled. "You decided to join us after all?"

I shrugged, keeping my own smile in place to hide my soured mood. "Wasn't as tired as I thought I was."

Her expression faltered slightly, and she tilted her head. "You good?"

Crap. She saw right through me. But I just waved the concern away as I slid onto a barstool. "I'm good. Tired, but not tired enough to go to sleep yet, apparently."

"Well, this is as good a place as any to hang out, right?" She winked, unaware of what that did to my nerve endings, and then flagged down a server so I could order a drink.

Truthfully, I did feel better hanging out with my team-mates than I did sitting up in my room and wondering about my dad, but I still felt like crap. I didn't contribute much to the conversation, instead just sipping on my cocktail while I listened to my far more energized teammates talking. They were speculating about some trade rumors, and also discussing some of the prospects who were likely going to be in-demand during the upcoming draft. Pittsburgh had quite a few first and second round picks for this year, and if our GM was savvy, she could snag us some incredible talent.

"If the teams ahead of us don't pick Stella Persson," Sims said, "Chloe should snatch her up. She's one of the best goalies in any of the major junior leagues right now."

"She is," Lila acknowledged, "but both Montreal and Omaha are picking ahead of us, and their biggest weaknesses are goaltending. I can't imagine them passing her over."

"I don't know," Val said. "They need goaltending solutions right now, not three or four years down the road when Persson is ready to play at this level."

"Hey, stranger things have happened." Sims shrugged. "The men's league has goalies who've gone straight from being drafted onto the roster."

"True," Val said. "And she's good, don't get me wrong. But is she good enough to pick that early in the draft? Because there are some *incredible* defenders up for grabs this season."

As much as I didn't have the energy to contribute, it was fun listening to my teammates debate the merits of various players. They all had some interesting insights, especially about prospects who played in their positions. Like when Laws thought Danielle Curtiss was a promising defender, but both Lila and Sims shook their heads.

"She's good," Lila said, "but she's going to need *years* of development before she's ready at this level."

Sims nodded in agreement. "She's a hundred percent defense. She's not going to make it here if she isn't solid offensively, too."

"Unless she's paired with a solid offensive defender,"

Laws pointed out. "I mean, the two of you have a good arrangement." She gestured at Sims and Lila. "Not that Sims can't play offense, but your strength is in being a really strong defender. So then Hams can go on ahead and help the offense."

Sims gave another nod. "The problem with Curtiss is that in those moments when she *needs* to be on the offense, she falls apart. It's nothing that can't be fixed with more development, and obviously she's great defensively if she's made it as far as she has, but that development is going to take time."

"I hope we do draft her," Lila said. "Even if she ends up in the minors for a few years, she'll get opportunities to train with us." She half-shrugged. "That can do wonders for a player's development."

At that, Sims smiled fondly. "Putting in some hours on the ice with you would do any young defender a *lot* of good."

Lila actually blushed, and suddenly my drink wasn't nearly cold enough.

"Well," she said with a quiet laugh, "maybe I'll get a chance to work with her. Guess we'll see who Chloe picks in the draft."

The conversation continued like that for a while, and eventually, people started peeling away to call it a night. When I got up to leave, I was surprised that Lila did, too. We paid our tabs, then headed for the elevator. We exchanged smiles as we waited, and neither of us said anything on the way up.

When we stepped out, though, Lila stopped. "Hey, before you go..."

I halted too, turning to her. "Hmm?"

She studied me. "You sure you're okay tonight?"

No. "I'm good." *Not even close.*

Her skepticism should've made me angry. Should've had me lashing out defensively because what right did she have to grill me?

But the truth was... I was tired. Not just from the game and the flight and everything else.

So, what the hell. I took a deep breath and admitted, "My dad called earlier."

Lila grimaced. "What did he say?"

"That's the thing—I don't know." I rubbed the back of my neck as all this fatigue settled in hard on my shoulders. "I didn't answer. And I haven't listened to his voicemail."

"From what you've told me, I don't blame you."

I appreciated that, but I didn't feel much better. "I'm going to regret it. I know I am."

She watched me for a moment. "But wouldn't you also regret listening to his message and calling him back?"

That brought me up short. "I... I hadn't thought of that, honestly."

She offered a sympathetic grimace. "Kind of sounds like you can't win for losing with him."

"No, I really can't." I pressed my back against the wall. "It's exhausting."

"I bet it is. But maybe tonight, you just picked the regret you can live with. Next time..." Lila half-shrugged. "You'll talk to him because that's the regret you can live with then."

"That's what I usually do."

"Do you feel worse now than you do on those nights?"

I thought about it. "I don't know. I feel like crap, but it's different." I looked at her through my lashes. "Talking to him always leaves me feeling like I just played a really bad game. Like I scored an own goal or something. I just... I feel like shit. But this?" I chewed my lip as I tried to find the words. "I don't know. It sucks, it's just... different."

"Yikes. I don't know how you do it."

The laugh that escaped my lips was dry as dust. "What choice do I have?"

Her eyes met mine, and I could see the answers she wasn't saying out loud. The same ones other people had given over time.

You could put your foot down.

You could tell him you're not going to tolerate that behavior.

You could go no-contact with him.

Yeah. I could. But it wasn't that simple. I had no idea how to explain why—I'd never been able to spell it out to anyone else, and I couldn't spell it out to Lila. I wasn't even sure I could explain to myself.

Because I'm sure it'll blow up in my face somehow just like cutting him off blows up in everyone else's face?

Because I'm holding out hope that someday he'll see the light?

Because I don't want to admit I'll never have the dad I know I'll never have?

I finally sighed and pushed myself off the wall. "I'll figure something out. For now, we should probably get some sleep."

"Yeah. We should." Lila smiled sadly. "Will you be okay tonight?"

"I'll be fine." I returned the smile, hoping it was convincing.

Maybe it was, maybe it wasn't. Whatever the case, Lila stepped closer and hugged me gently. "We've all got your back," she told me softly. "The whole team."

I almost wanted to laugh at that. It was true and I knew it, but it still seemed so wildly unreal that, of all people, Lila Hamilton had my back.

And yet, it also felt completely right and sincere. As if that rivalry had just been a dream or something between immature teenagers in major juniors.

Either way...

"Thanks," I whispered, and let her go. "I really appreciate..."

Our eyes met.

There was no crowd this time. No teammates. No cameras. Just the two of us in a deserted hotel hallway, standing way too close together and holding each other's gazes for one, two, six beats too long.

I opened my mouth to speak, not even sure what I intended to say, but Lila spoke first.

"We should get some sleep." She cleared her throat as she subtly put some space between us. "I'll see you at breakfast?"

"Yeah. Yeah, good idea." I took another step back myself, pretending I didn't feel an almost magnetic force drawing me back in. "I'll, uh... See you at breakfast."

Fuck me, that smile.

Thank God, she turned to go, and I managed to do the same. In my room, I deadbolted the door and then leaned against it, closing my eyes.

Yeah, I'd see her at breakfast tomorrow. And on the bus. And on the plane. And at the next hotel. And at practice. And...

I wiped a hand over my face and pushed out a breath.

I am so screwed.

CHAPTER 15

LILA

As we geared up for our next home game, Sabrina was edgy and nervous in ways I hadn't seen her before a game. Not even a critical one at the Olympics.

The way she kept chewing her lip? How twitchy she was, especially when the press came in? It made the hair on my neck stand up. Something was off.

I finished putting on my gear, then clomped over to her stall. "Hey. You okay?"

For a second, she looked like she was going to insist she was fine. Only for a second, though.

Deflating a little, she said, "Marci caught wind that my dad bought out an entire section in the lower bowl. Aside from the seats held by season ticket holders, anyway, so... *most* of the section."

I arched an eyebrow. "And that's a... bad thing?" Given that her dad was the one involved—yeah, that checked out. Even if I couldn't put the pieces together about *how* it was bad, something must've been sending up a red flag for Sabrina.

"On paper, it doesn't sound like a bad thing." She turned to me, her eyes full of worry. "But I know my dad. Somehow..." She shook her head.

"Shit," I whispered. "What do you think he's going to do?"

"No idea. I just hope it's something I can ignore while I'm playing."

"I hope so, too."

Unfortunately, it didn't look too promising as we skated out for warmups. One glace around the arena, and it didn't take a rocket scientist to figure out which section Doran McAvoy had bought out.

During warmups, the crowd was usually pretty thin anyway; a lot of people came to the glass, but others were still filtering in after getting beers and snacks. Most people would come to their seats in the ten or fifteen minutes ahead of the anthem.

But there were always people scattered throughout the arena. Always at *least* a few dozen trickling into each section throughout warmups.

Section 114, however, was almost deserted.

There were three couples in their seats, but the rest of the section was empty. Sections 113 and 115 both had twenty or thirty people so far with more wandering in, but 114 had... six.

And of course, that section was at the end of the arena where we warmed up. And the end we'd be attacking twice. Right in Sabrina's line of sight when she needed to concentrate the most.

I skated up to her. "It's 114, isn't it?"

She nodded grimly. "Yeah. And I have a feeling there isn't going to be anyone else in those seats."

Sure enough, when we returned for the anthems, only those six fans were in those seats. The arena was packed apart from that undeniably empty section.

Christ. What was his deal? What was he trying to do? Just mess with her head? Start rumors? Give people a reason to snap a photo and spread it all over the internet saying "Look at this abysmal crowd at a WHPL game"? Because that last thing—people had definitely done that. They'd take photos between periods when a lot of fans left to get beer or use the restroom, or when the gates had just opened and people had barely started coming into the arena. Then they'd create this narrative that no one came to our games, so it was a waste of time.

Of course, the arenas would just post the ticket sales and crowd size for each game, and fans posted their own photos of the dense crowds, but it was still enough for haters to talk shit.

As for all of us on the ice, we were conditioned to pay as little attention as possible to the crowd. They could be distracting, so we had to ignore them as much as we could. That was hard sometimes; it was why the Wave was so damned annoying, because that much movement beyond that glass was bound to catch our eyes.

For the most part, aside from the Wave, we could ignore just about anything beyond the glass. The big gap was as conspicuous as a defender's missing tooth, but it wasn't moving unlike the damned Wave, and it wasn't like anyone else knew who'd bought out that section.

Only Sabrina knew.

I wondered if that was the point. From the way Sabrina was clearly trying to not to look anywhere near section 114... it was working.

God, please don't let it mess with her concentration.

At least we couldn't hear the sports commentators, because they were guaranteed to be speculating about it. Fans probably wondered what the deal was. Our teammates undoubtedly noticed the gap in the crowd.

But Sabrina knew exactly why it was empty.

For her, it wasn't just an unusual visual or something to catch her eye at an inopportune moment. It was the most blatant way Doran McAvoy could tell her how little he cared about what she did. He might buy out an entire section of seats, but could he bother to show up? Or have anyone else show up and use those tickets? Absolutely the fuck not.

I skated by her as we set up for a faceoff. "You good?"

Her jaw was tight, but she nodded sharply. "I'm good. Let's do this."

I flashed her a smile, and the corners of her mouth twitched ever so slightly upward.

Sabrina won the faceoff. Like, decisively. I didn't think the other center's stick had even touched the ice before Sabrina was off and running with the puck. She passed it to Laws, who bullied her way past a defender into the offensive zone.

Sims hung back near the blue line, so I went in to join the

fray, and I was almost immediately in a puck battle against the wall with two of their players and one of our forwards.

Then a stick appeared out of nowhere, darting between my skate and another player's. An instant later, both the stick and puck were gone.

I'd barely turned around before Sabrina fired the puck to Anastasia at the edge of the crease, and Anastasia tipped it in behind the goalie's back.

The roar of the hometown crowd after a goal was always intoxicating, but it had nothing on the sheer triumph on Sabrina's face. As she nearly bowled over Anastasia with a hug, she was beaming as if everything in her world was absolutely perfect.

I joined my teammates for celebratory hugs.

Sabrina clapped my back with her glove. "Pretty sure you're getting the secondary assist on that one."

I blinked. "I am?"

"I think so. The puck was on your stick when I grabbed it."

I scowled playfully. "So you robbed me!"

Her smile turned to an innocent grin. "I figured you wouldn't mind. And I mean..." She gestured up at the Jumbotron, which still showed GOAL in flashing red letters.

I gave her a fake punch to the shoulder. "Whatever."

She cackled all the way back to the bench for fist bumps.

As we took our seats on the bench and let the next shift hit the ice, I threw back some water, then leaned forward and stole a look at Sabrina. Her attention was fixed on the players even as she and Anastasia had an animated discussion about something. Strategizing, probably. Maybe deciding on a set play for their next shift.

She didn't look once toward section 114. Didn't look the least bit bothered by it, either.

Not until the buzzer sounded, signaling the end of the period. At that point, we were out on the ice again; Sims and I had just started our shift, and Sabrina had been out with her line for over a minute and a half. As soon as the period ended, her façade slipped a little. Her gaze flicked toward 114, which was the only section that didn't have people filing out to refill beers and hit the restroom.

I skated up to her and clapped her shoulder with my glove. "Hey. You good?"

Pressing her lips together, she nodded. "Yeah." We started toward the bench. "Just still can't believe he..." She trailed off, shaking her head.

"Well, it's his loss."

She turned to me, eyebrows up.

I shrugged. "He's the one missing out on an awesome game." I paused. "I'd say don't let him get to you, but a dick move like that..." I rolled my eyes.

She laughed humorlessly. "Yeah. I wish he didn't get to me."

"He's your dad," I said as we clomped off the ice and into the chute. On the way down the hall to the locker room, I added, "I think it would get to anyone."

Sabrina nodded.

At the locker room door, she stopped, so I did too. Gazing back toward the ice, she let her shoulders sag beneath her pads. "It's exhausting, you know? Just trying to live my damn life and enjoy my career, and he never misses an opportunity to take a dig." She gestured at the ice with her stick. "This is probably because I was stupid enough to ignore his call the other night and not listen to his voicemail."

I stiffened. "Oh. Shit. You think that's what this is about?"

"Maybe? Because, I mean, I know better. I know it'll always come back and bite me in the ass. But I just... I was so done with his bullshit, you know? So now... this." She scowled, leaning against the wall. "Probably why he made it seem like he was coming to a game. So he can rub it in my face that I didn't bother returning his call, so why should he bother coming to my game?"

"Those... don't sound like they're on equal footing."

She snorted derisively. "They do if you know my dad." Exhaling heavily, she picked at a thread on her glove. "Honestly, I knew he wasn't going to come, and that this was just him being an ass. That part doesn't bother me. It just..." She chewed her lip.

I nudged her gently. "What?"

Sabrina pushed out a ragged breath and met my gaze. "I don't know if he's doing it on purpose, or if he's too oblivious to even know it. But the reason this bothers me so much is because all I've ever wanted since I was a little kid was for my dad to come to one of my games." She swallowed hard, like it took some actual work. "Having him cheer for me was probably too much to ask, but I would've given anything for him to *just show up*."

Just listening to the raw hurt in her voice made my chest ache. I'd gotten the impression for a while that Doran McAvoy was an ass, but holy crap.

She laughed again, the sound bitter and resigned. "God, I sound like I'm still that little kid. I'm living my dream, but what do I want?" She flailed a hand toward the ice. "For my dad to show up and act like it matters."

I took off my glove and squeezed her forearm. "You're not a little kid, but you *are* his daughter. I think anyone wants their parents to support them. And the fact that he'll do something like *that*"—I nodded in the direction she'd gestured —"says a lot about what kind of person he is."

"I know, right?" She let her head fall back against the wall. "But like, I know who he is. I've always known who he is." She sighed, gazing at the locker room door with unfocused eyes. "I wish I could learn how to stop caring that he doesn't care."

My heart ached for her. For the millionth time, I felt guilty for ever thinking she had an easy ride to the top. I couldn't imagine fighting against that strong of a current and still landing here.

I wish I knew what to tell her to make her feel better. But really, what could make someone feel better after a lifetime of bullshit from a person who should've been one of the loudest members of her cheering squad?

"I have to admit," she said softly, meeting my gaze, "I've always envied you in that department."

"You have?"

She gave a near soundless laugh. "Your parents are *always* there. They always seem so happy and supportive, and I mean, they've been to *how* many games this season?"

I wasn't sure why some heat rushed into my face. "They...

Yeah, they've always been amazing about that. And now that they're only a few hours away..."

"I'm glad they can come to your games. My mom does, too, and my sister. Just..." She rolled her eyes and scowled. "Not my dad."

My heart ached beneath my chest protecter. It was both empathy and guilt; I'd been so sure she'd had everything handed to her, but I couldn't imagine playing hockey—hell, just living my life—without my family's enthusiastic support. There'd been times as a teenager when I'd resented having to work part-time jobs to pay for hockey, but I understood now that my parents had just been stretched too thin. They'd tried so, so hard, sacrificed so, so much, and sometimes they couldn't quite cover everything.

Even during those petulant moments of hating that I had to work between school and hockey, I'd never—not *once*—doubted my parents' support, both of my hockey and of me in general. I'd never—not even during the most hormone-soaked teenage fits of anger—questioned how much they loved me.

Sabrina... God, how did someone deal with that? And on top of it all, play at the level she did?

"That really sucks," I whispered. "Your dad—he should've supported you. And he should support you now."

"I know." She blew out a breath and managed a faint smile. "But I'm glad I'm in the minority. Most people I've played with—their experiences are better. And yours... Like I said, I've always envied you for your parents."

I had to swallow hard to push back the sudden lump in my throat. "You should've had that too."

The answer to that was a heavy shrug.

"You going to be okay for the rest of the game?" I asked.

Sabrina seemed to consider it. Then she rolled her shoulders and met my gaze as she nodded. "Yeah. I've played through worse."

I wasn't sure I wanted to know what was worse than her dad buying out an empty section.

Now definitely wasn't the time to ask for a tour of her Memory Lane, though, especially since she really did seem to be pulling herself together. She had her game face on, and anyway, we only had so much time left on this intermission.

So I gave her arm another reassuring squeeze, and we continued into the locker room to go about our intermission rituals.

A few minutes later, everyone started back to the ice. Sabrina put on her gloves and helmet, and as she headed out, she looked like she had it together. God, no wonder she was such dynamite on the ice—she was so used to playing under the weight of unimaginable bullshit from her dad *on top of* all the assumptions that she didn't deserve to be here at all.

Sabrina had to be one of the strongest women I'd ever met. We were lucky to have her as a teammate and captain, and I was damn lucky she was forgiving enough to treat me like a friend.

I followed my teammates out, Sabrina and the alternate captains bringing up the rear as always. After I'd skated a small circle, I looked her way, making sure she still had that game face on.

But right when I looked her direction, she did a double take and almost stumbled. I followed her gaze, and hell, I nearly lost my edge, too.

Section 114 wasn't empty anymore. The first few rows were full, and the ushers were guiding a long line of kids down the steps to fill the rest.

What the hell?

At our bench, Sabrina asked Tanya if she knew what was going on.

Our team reporter smiled. "They're kids who were sitting in the charity suites or whose teams had been invited to the VIP suites. I guess they all saw the big empty section and asked if they could sit closer." She half-shrugged. "Since the ticket holders for those seats hadn't shown up during the second period..."

I stared at the stream of kids coming down to take those seats. Then I turned to Sabrina, who was smiling as she too watched the kids.

Shifting my weight on my skates, I quietly asked, "Won't your dad just try to grab all the credit he can for buying seats for them?"

Sabrina shook her head. "Then he'll have to explain why the seats were empty for most of the game." She laughed with some actual feeling. "He's probably watching this on TV and losing his mind right now."

"You think he's actually watching?"

She pursed her lips. "Maybe? If nothing else, to see how I react to the big empty section that we both know he bought." She grinned. "I hope he's enjoying the show."

I laughed. "Think he's thrown a beer can at the TV yet?"

Sabrina cackled. "Probably. I'll bet he's apoplectic." Her eyes danced with mischief. "Let's piss him off even more by winning."

"Ooh, good idea. Especially since if we win, we'll leapfrog Detroit in the conference standings."

The way her face lit up made my heart skip. "Let's do it."

We bumped fists, and when the game started up again, we played our hearts out to do exactly that.

I hated that her dad was such a dick to her, but his come-uppance—even if only he and Sabrina knew about it—was thoroughly satisfying. All the kids in section 114 screamed their heads off and had an amazing time. Sabrina even tossed them some signed pucks during a stoppage, which clearly made their night.

I hoped Doran saw the whole thing. All the smiling kids. All of them cheering for Sabrina. Her enormous smile while she signed pucks and threw them over the glass. I could imagine him fuming and snarling over it, and I loved it.

And I especially hoped a commentator mentioned that the section was sold out but empty, so the arena staff made the decision to move the charity group kids into those seats. That way Doran couldn't pretend he'd done it on purpose to give those kids a chance to sit closer. Maybe we'd even get lucky and a reporter would have the spine to ask him why he bought that many seats and left them unoccupied. I couldn't wait to see how he'd try to back pedal from *that*.

They probably wouldn't ask—no one dared put Doran McAvoy on the spot—but I could dream. Either way, if he wanted to be miserable and spiteful instead of celebrating his talented, hard-working daughter, then fine.

Sabrina was, despite his best efforts, enjoying the game and having a great night. She was playing like the superstar he'd tried so hard to stop her from being.

I'd always been impressed by her hockey. Even during those times when I'd wanted to hate her and would try to tell myself she wasn't that good, I knew she *was* that good. Realizing now how much she'd had to overcome to be this star— how everything that we all believed gave her a boost had actually held her back—I was awestruck by her.

That she'd come out of it as a strong, kind person. That she'd soared to this level on her own power, not through nepotism.

And as I watched her taking a selfie with a kid through the glass, that huge smile on her face and her dark eyes sparkling...

I kind of wondered how I was going to be able to play next to her after all.

Do you have any idea how beautiful you really are?

CHAPTER 16

SABRINA

The buzzer sounding the end of that game may as well have been singing angels. I was so relieved, I almost collapsed right there on the ice.

Finally. It was over. In overtime, too—Anastasia scored with twelve seconds left on the clock, earning us an OT win and saving us from going to a shootout. I was good at shootouts, and they were kind of fun, but I wasn't in the right headspace for it tonight.

Not after that stunt my dad had pulled.

I didn't know what message he was trying to send, or if it was just his way of thumbing his nose at me and my sport, but I'd spent the entire game trying not to let it get under my skin. To some extent, it had, but at least I'd managed to play as if it hadn't. If Dad had been watching—to see his trolling take effect, not to see his daughter playing hockey—then I wasn't about to give him the satisfaction of hurting my performance.

So I'd played my heart out. Two goals. Two assists. I'd drawn the penalty that had given us the power play that led to our game-tying goal in the final minute of the third period. For a few panicked minutes, I'd been afraid we'd take the L in overtime, but a highlight-reel steal by Anastasia followed by a dagger of a goal had ended the game in our favor.

I'd given my father nothing to criticize. Of course, he'd find something. That turnover in the second period that led to a scoring chance. Losing an edge at just the right time to allow an odd-man rush. The fact that I was suited up for a women's hockey game in the first place.

But everybody made mistakes every single game. Even the most legendary players lost edges and turned over pucks and did just bone-headed stupid shit sometimes. It was part of hockey. I'd played a solid, respectable game. He'd have to work at it to find a reason to shit on me tonight.

And he wasn't going to keep me in suspense about it, either—I'd finished getting dressed and was heading into the lounge to eat when his ringtone chirped in my pocket.

"For fuck's sake," I muttered, and I stayed out in the hall for some relative privacy while I answered. "Hi, Dad."

"Hey, kiddo. You home?"

"Still at the arena. The game just ended."

"*Oh*, that's right," he said, letting the sarcasm drip. "You had a game tonight, didn't you?"

"Mmhmm. I did."

There was silence on the line for a solid thirty seconds. It was a type of staring contest I was used to with him. There was an elephant in the room, and we were each waiting for the other to break eye contact and look at it.

I was way too irritated tonight—and too stubborn in general—to let him win this one.

Eventually, he spoke, his tone light and casual but with a taunting edge: "You know, ticket sales for girls' hockey must be through the roof if almost an entire section was available."

I rolled my eyes, grateful he couldn't see me. "Lower bowl tickets are expensive. Sometimes people can't—"

"Sure they are."

I pinched the bridge of my nose, fighting back the temptation to push out an exhausted sigh. If I had to guess, Dad had bought all those tickets back when they'd first gone on sale. Back when enormous swathes of the arena were available. He was probably gleeful as all hell that the night I ignored his call was just before this game. Was that why he'd been calling so much lately? Because he knew I'd eventually ignore him and he'd be able to throw that in my face?

"He is such a goddamned *child* sometimes," I remembered my mom telling her sister one night when she didn't think any of us kids could hear her. "How does a grown man think this is the right way to act?"

I'd never forgotten my aunt's caustic retort of, "Do you honestly think Doran counts as a grown man?"

There'd been a time when Mom would chastise her sister for making fun of Dad or his perpetual immaturity, but that night, she'd just laughed, shaken her head, and taken a *big* gulp of wine.

In the present, Dad gave a quiet chuckle. "Well, you did tell me that the ticket sellers don't care who's buying the tickets or filling the seats."

I gritted my teeth. For fuck's sake. That was an angle I

hadn't considered. "So you bought a whole section and left it empty—why? Just to prove a point? *What* point?"

"You wanted me to support you," he said in that patronizing way that drove me up a wall. "So I bought tickets to your game. A lot of them."

"But you left all the seats empty."

"I'm in Buffalo, Sabrina."

I pinched the bridge of my nose and fought to keep my frustration out of my voice. He was baiting me. Trying to set me off and make me emotional, because then he could tell me how I needed to be rational and logical rather than being led around by my emotions. It was how he'd manipulated my mother, too—whenever she'd approach him with something that bothered her or that they disagreed on, he'd push her until she got angry. He'd keep pushing until she finally lashed out like any human would sooner or later, and then he'd lecture her about how she needed to calm down and be logical.

I wasn't falling for it. My ex-husband had done the exact same thing, and I'd learned with him that my best weapon against this kind of bullshit was to keep my cool until he either lost his own or lost interest.

Or, if I was in the mood to provoke him and let *him* get "emotional," change the subject and let him know how utterly unimportant his opinion was.

Lowering my hand, I said, "Well, it was good talking to you, Dad. But I've got media availability, and they're bringing in some of the kids who were sitting in your section. So I need to let you go."

"The kids? What?"

"Oh, you didn't know?" I couldn't keep the smile out of my voice. "The arena staff moved a bunch of kids down from the charity suites. Since no one had taken your seats by the second intermission, they decided it was a shame to just leave them empty." As much as I wanted to listen to him lose his mind over it, which he inevitably would, I also wanted to make sure he knew who was calling the shots. "Anyway. I have media availability. I have to run. Talk to you later."

"I... You're..." he stammered. Then he sighed, the defeat more delicious than it should've been. "All right. Love you, kiddo."

Sure you do.

"Love you too, Dad."

I ended the call and breathed a heavy sigh of relief. I'd had my media availability right after the game ended, so I didn't actually need to go anywhere. I just wanted to be off the phone.

Mission accomplished. I'd won—I'd turned his bullshit back on him, and I'd ended the conversation on my terms.

But I couldn't say I felt any better.

The one upshot to Dad's constant trolling and messing with my head was that I was so used to it, I could shake it off pretty quickly. Sure, I was pissed off in the moment, and I'd gone to bed in a foul mood that night, but by the next morning, my attention had shifted to more important things. Things like coffee. Packing for the next away game. Getting to the rink for practice.

Yeah, on some level, I was still vaguely irritated when I thought about his stunt with section 114, but I was more annoyed with that old, persistent low grade throb in my hip and with some jackass on the freeway who wouldn't let me change lanes.

By the time I was on the ice for practice, my hip was starting to loosen up and the rude guy on the freeway was a distant memory. The stands here in the rink were crowded for a weekday—no conspicuous void sticking out like a middle finger—and I tossed pucks to a couple of smiling little kids before shifting my attention to practice.

After that, it was the usual routine—showers, media availability, food. We were in Seattle for the next game, so we boarded the bus instead of driving home, and by about 3:00, we were in the air. Between the long flight, the bus ride to the hotel, and the time it took to settle in, it was almost 8:00 local time—so 11:00 Pittsburgh time—before I came down from my room to join my teammates in the bar. Everyone had eaten on the plane, and we were tired and jetlagged, but there were always a few people who came down for a nightcap.

I wasn't usually one of them, hence the surprised, "Oh, hey, Mac!" from Sims as I joined them in the bar.

"Hey." I smiled. "Room for one more?"

"Of course!" Our teammates shuffled around a bit, and I sat down at the table.

No one drank heavily—that was for after a game, not the night before one—but I got a glass of wine and some of my other teammates had beers or cocktails. Most of the conversation was about Pittsburgh. We were all fairly new to the city, aside from Val, who'd grown up here, and Nora, who'd played for RMU in college.

We all compared notes on places to eat and neighborhoods we were thinking of buying or renting houses. All of us who'd spent part of our careers in Canada—growing up there or playing in major juniors, plus a few who'd been on WHPL teams up there—agreed that we had zero complaints about Pittsburgh in the winter. That, of course, got us going down the familiar track of comparing winters in various cities we'd played in; since most of us had played in Canada or the coldest U.S. states, we all had strong opinions about this time of year.

Sims was from Vancouver, which didn't exactly have the monstrous winters that were pretty notorious throughout the rest of Canada, but like me, she'd spent her major juniors seasons in Calgary. "Those winters can go straight to hell."

I nodded. "I loved it there, don't get me wrong, but two winters in Calgary was *more* than enough."

"Ugh, same." Nora, who'd also been in major juniors with us, bumped fists with me over the table. "The city is amazing, but the winter?" She tsked and shook her head. "That is just... barbaric."

Laws made a "world's smallest violin" gesture. "Come talk to me when you spend four winters in *Winnipeg*."

That had everyone shaking our heads and murmuring, "Nope. No. No, thanks." I'd played there plenty of times in my career, often in the dead of winter, and that kind of cold was no joke.

The conversation continued like that, and after a while, a

few people started to peel away. They'd say their goodnights and pay their tabs, and the small crowd around our table thinned.

Which was how I wound up sitting across from Lila.

She glanced at our other remaining teammates, who were currently discussing their kids, and then faced me and lowered her voice. "I meant to ask—how are you doing after last night?"

After last night? What was—

Oh. Right.

That.

I picked up my glass—just water now—and took a sip. "I'm good, honestly."

Her brow pinched. "Did your dad say anything to you?"

Rolling my eyes, I nodded. "Yeah. He called after the game, but..." I waved a hand. "To tell you the truth, I'm so used to his bullshit, I was pretty much over it by this morning."

"Yeah?"

"Mmhmm." Not entirely true, but my anger had cooled to a simmer of annoyance, so... close enough.

"Wow." She absently swirled what remained of her cocktail. "You're tougher than me. I'd be a mess if my dad pulled something like that."

I half-shrugged. "I think I'm just used to it."

Lila wrinkled her nose. "That's a shitty thing to have to get used to."

"So are old injuries, but..."

That made her laugh softly. "Isn't that the truth?"

"Right? But I mean, I think years of putting up with his bullshit has—okay, it hasn't quite given me the ability to let things roll off like water on a duck's back. It's more like..." I thought about it. "I guess it's more like when a dog wallows in the mud, but then the mud dries and falls off, and before you know it, you forget he was ever in the mud at all." I paused, then laughed. "Okay, that's probably not the best analogy."

"Well, given what your dad does, I'd have said it's more like a dog rolling in shit, but..."

I snorted. "I was trying to be polite."

"Why?" She gestured at herself. "I'm not."

I just laughed, and the little grin told me that was the desired effect. It also scrambled my brain just like always. God, I was such a wreck over her.

It didn't help that she looked smoking hot tonight. She was dressed casually since we weren't subject to the League's dress code right now, and the blue tank top she was wearing screwed with my concentration. It showed off her ink and her toned arms, not to mention the slightest peek at her cleavage.

And I was staring.

Shit!

I went for my drink again, and after I'd swallowed it, I cleared my throat. Time to change the subject.

"So." I folded my arms on the edge of the table and met her gaze. "How did you get into hockey in the first place?"

Lila played with the straw in her cocktail. "All the kids in my neighborhood played street hockey. I used to watch them when I was really little, and when I was like five, I finally convinced them to let me play."

"Aww, so does that mean there's pictures somewhere of tiny Lila playing street hockey?"

Her shy laugh and that blush were mesmerizing. "My parents have videos, too. Tons of them."

"Okay, that all sounds super adorable."

She rolled her eyes, blushing even brighter. "There's actually one my parents tried to send to one of those funny home video TV shows. One of the older boys kept getting pissy that the other kids would let me play, and he was ranting about it while my dad was trying to get a video of us playing. He was all about how I was too small and weak to even move the ball, never mind get it into the goal, and I could barely skate, and..." She rolled her hand. "Just bullshit, you know?"

I nodded. "One at every rink, isn't there?"

"God, right?" She huffed. "Anyway, so right when Mom was about to tell the kid to go home," Lila went on, "I hit the ball toward the net, but missed and hit him right in the butt." She laughed quietly. "And like, he's on roller blades, ranting and raving, and suddenly something clocks him from behind."

"Oh my God!" I giggled. "So, windmill followed by a faceplant?"

"Mmhmm. It was hilarious. I've seen that video at least ten thousand times, and it still cracks me up."

"It sounds funny as hell! Was he mad?"

"Oh, yeah. He grabbed his stick and left. He still played with us after that, but he stopped being such an ass to me."

"Good." I gestured with my drink. "Valuable life lesson for him."

"Exactly! And actually, a few months after that, he

stopped coming around. I thought he was mad about me playing, but then I found out it was because he had joined an ice
hockey team. Which was how I learned ice hockey was a
thing. So I talked my parents into getting me lessons, and here
I am."

"Wow. Does that kid know you're at this level now?"

She laughed. "Well, considering he's married to my sister
now, he can't really avoid it."

I let out a laugh of disbelief. "Oh, yeah? What does he
think?"

"He's super supportive, just like the rest of my family. As
I was getting older and he realized I was getting serious about
hockey, he started helping me. Like we'd do little drills and
scrimmages on the street, and if we were at the rink at the
same time, he'd give me pointers."

"Oh. Damn. So he really turned it around."

"Maturity." She shrugged. "It's a beautiful thing."

"There is that. Does he still play?"

Lila nodded. "Not pro or anything. He's in a beer league,
and he still plays in the street with my nieces and nephews
and some of the neighbor kids. I sometimes join him, too. But
he kind of saw how much hockey had to take over someone's
life if they wanted to pursue it as a career." Her expression
turned a little sad. "I knew I wanted to go to the Olympics the
first year I saw women's hockey at the Games, so I was on a
serious trajectory from the time I was like eleven. I think Ian
saw how much I had to pour myself into the sport, how
expensive it was for my parents—all of that. And he just
decided that wasn't for him."

I studied her, wondering how far to pursue this. I was

curious about her history, but especially with as much as she'd resented the version of me she'd thought was real, it might've been a minefield of sorts. Treading carefully, I asked, "It was tough coming up, then? Playing hockey as a kid?"

She stared at the table, her expression distant. "It was hard. Like... really hard."

"Yeah?"

Without looking up, she nodded. "My parents were amazing about supporting me, but hockey is stupid expensive. Especially when a kid grows out of their gear faster than they can wear it out."

"I remember," I said quietly. "After the divorce, my mom had a hard time paying for a lot of it."

"My parents did too. I wore a lot of very, very used gear."

I gave a cautious laugh. "Hey, some of that stuff wasn't bad, though. It was already broken in."

"I know, right?" She laughed too, and with some actual feeling. "The first time I got a new chest protector, I was like, what's up with this bullshit?"

"Seriously. It was skates for me."

"You didn't use new skates?"

"Not until I was almost sixteen. My brother always gave me his old skates, so they were totally broken in."

Lila groaned, absently stabbing at one of the remaining ice cubes in her glass. "Ugh, I wish I could go back and tell younger me to appreciate the used skates. Breaking in a new pair is just..." She made a hilariously disgusted face.

"Right?" I chuckled. "I'd wear my skates until they fell apart if the equipment managers would let me."

"No kidding." She stabbed at the ice cube again, then

nudged the drink aside. She picked up her phone, but instead of looking at the screen, she just turned the device over and over with her long fingers as if she needed something to keep her hands occupied. "Anyway, so yeah, the equipment was expensive, plus all the fees and travel. That was tough on my parents, but they did the best they could."

"That's great," I said. "That you had their support."

"It is. And the other tough thing was... I'm a girl. When I was playing in U8 and U10, nobody really cared that I was a girl playing alongside the boys. Some of the boys could be a little weird, but... I mean, they were eight-year-old boys." She shrugged. "We were all weird at that age."

I laughed softly. "No kidding. Throw a bunch of eight-year-olds on skates and into the rink, and things are bound to get weird."

"Right?" Her eyes flicked up to meet mine for a second, the faintest smile curling her lips. Then she dropped her gaze again, and the smile went with it. "Anyway, as I was getting old enough for the AA league, most of the boys were fine with it. They knew I could hold my own, and they just cared about winning, you know?" Sighing, she sat back. "The parents, though..."

I grimaced. "Yeah, I remember those days."

"You do?"

"Are you kidding?" I stabbed at some ice cubes with my straw. "I think it's a rite of passage for girls who play hockey if they don't live in a place with a AA all-girls team."

"Yeah, you're probably right." Lila shook her head. "It's so stupid. And they tried to make it sound like they were just worried I'd get beat up or something. They even tried to campaign for me to be a forward instead of playing defense because it would be"—she made air quotes—"*safer.*"

I rolled my eyes. "Oh, that's bullshit."

"Seriously. But my coaches called them out. I didn't make the connection until they said something, but they pointed out that the only reason the parents wanted me to play offense was because they knew I'd be cut."

"Because you had the chops to play defense," I said, "so they wanted you in a position where you were weaker so you playing on the team would be a moot point."

Lila's chuckle was low and caustic. "Sounds like you've seen that movie."

"Mmhmm." I huffed sharply. "When I was U16, someone tried to make a case for making me play goalie."

"*Goalie?*" Lila barked a laugh. "You? I mean, no offense, but…"

"None taken. The thing is, I was one of the tallest on the team at that point. The skaters' parents all said it gave me an unfair advantage, and they should use my height in the net." I tsked. "Everyone knew I'd be cut the second I tried to play goalie."

Lila studied me, then slowly exhaled. "I wonder how often that kind of thing happened to other girls."

"I'm sure there were leagues where it didn't," I said. "But I swear every girl I played with in major juniors had some story about butthurt parents of boys. If it wasn't the parents of their own teammates, it was opposing players."

She groaned. "Oh, God, they were the *worst.*" She picked up her drink. "You know one of them actually got caught telling her son to try to take me out of the game?"

My jaw went slack. "No shit? You mean she wasn't even smart enough to say it in the car or something where no one would hear?"

"Apparently not." She paused, lips quirked. "Honestly, looking back, her son might've ratted her out. I never heard the full story, but I played against him a few times and with him for one season, and he was a good kid. So it wouldn't surprise me if he told the refs or his coach."

"Well, good on him."

"No kidding." Lila smirked. "Though after that, every time he checked me, he'd just shrug and say his mom told him to."

A laugh burst out of me. "What a little shit!"

"I know, right?" The smirk turned to a cocky grin that had no business being that sexy. "He blocked one of my shots one time. Caught right in the inner thigh."

I grimaced and rubbed a spot on my own inner thigh where a blocked shot had left a nasty bruise a few years ago.

"He went down," Lila went on, "because, I mean, that shit hurts, right? So as he's getting helped back to the bench, I skated by and said, 'tell your mom that one was from me.'"

"Oh my God! And you didn't get an unsportsmanlike for that?"

"Nah." She shook her head. "Even he thought it was funny. The ref tried to give me a dirty look over it, but he couldn't help laughing."

"Everybody knew about the incident with his mom, didn't they?"

"Yep. And I don't think anybody ever let him forget it." She tapped her thumb on the edge of her phone case. "So most people were good, you know? And especially after they saw me play, they usually didn't bitch about me being on teams. It was really just a struggle to pay for it all, you know? Like I said, my parents got me as much equipment as they could, but hockey gear isn't cheap." She laughed softly. "From the time I was about twelve or thirteen, I worked a *lot* of hours at the rink's concession stand just so I could keep my skates sharp and replace broken sticks."

"They let you do that? The rinks, I mean?"

"Oh, yeah." She shrugged. "They were hard up for staff, and my parents didn't object, so they let me work and paid me under the table. I doubt they could get away with it now, but I'm glad they did then."

"No kidding." I paused. "I'm glad you had that support. Especially from your family."

"Me too. I went through some periods where I wanted to give it up, and they kept me going."

The pang of envy over that support was almost physically painful. "You wanted to quit?"

She shrugged. "Not seriously. But you know how it is—when you're a teenager and everything is a bigger crisis than it actually is, so an embarrassingly bad game just feels like the end of the world."

"Oh, man. Yeah. I know exactly what you mean."

She raised her eyebrows. "Did you ever have those moments?"

"Absolutely. I don't think I ever wanted to quit hockey, but there were days when I wondered if I was cut out for it. Like after a really bad loss, or if I'd taken some awful penalty that had cost us the game. That stuff is tough to shake off now. Back then?" I whistled, shaking my head.

"Ugh, no kidding. I think also I saw how much my family was struggling so hard to make it work for me, and I'd just... I'd feel like I was letting them down. One season, my U16 team came in dead last in our division, and I thought, what the hell am I doing? My parents are killing themselves to make this happen for me, and my team just went 12-26-12."

I winced. "Ouch."

"It was bad." Lila shuddered. "I do not miss that season. So I was all ready to give it up and be done with it, but my parents sat me down and said I wasn't a failure. The whole team had been a mess, and there were already rumors that the entire coaching staff was getting replaced—which they were. They reminded me that they knew I had talent, and that I'd worked so hard to get where I was. I shouldn't give it up because of bad season. Then Dad told me about Cleveland in the men's league, and how they had these two godawful seasons during their rebuild. Then five years later, they won the Cup. So... I shouldn't let a funk drive me away from the sport I love, you know?"

The story, especially that last part, had a lump rising in my throat. My mom had been that supportive. My brother and sister, too. But had my dad ever sat me down and reminded me that even teams at his level could have catastrophically terrible seasons followed by glory years? No. Not once.

I'd have worked every shift available at my childhood practice rink's concession stand in exchange for just one pep talk like that from my father.

I swallowed the last of my drink, and as I pushed the glass away, I said, "I'm really glad you had that kind of support."

"Me too." She smiled. "I wouldn't be here without it."

"I don't know." I returned the smile. "Somehow I think you're exactly the kind of tenacious and stubborn player who'd have clawed her way to this level no matter what."

She laughed, making the bar a few degrees warmer. "Well, I'm just glad I didn't have to do that. Not without help, anyway."

"Yeah. Me too."

We exchanged smiles.

Then Lila looked around, and her spine slowly straightened. "Are we... Are we the only ones left?"

"Are we?" I glanced at the other side of our table, which was empty. When I scanned the room, sure enough, there wasn't a single familiar face in sight. A handful of people were still here, but no one from the Bearcats. Which meant... I grabbed my phone, then laughed when I saw the screen. "Oh crap! It's almost 1:00!"

"It is?" Lila flipped her phone over so she could see the screen, and the way she laughed did things to my heart that I was too tired to think too much about. "Oh shit. We should get some sleep!"

"Yeah, we should." I pushed my chair back. "We're going to be dead on our skates tomorrow morning."

She groaned as she got up too. "Ugh. Can't we have maintenance days tomorrow?"

"I wish."

We paid our tabs, then headed for the elevator. On the way up to our floor, I stole a glance at her in the mirror, drinking in the sculpted, tattooed arms, and how that tank top sat just right. God, this woman was gorgeous.

And without all the animosity between us, I was lucky I could think around her. After tonight's conversation? Getting a more intimate look at her past—at *her*—than I'd ever had?

Jesus. I was never going to concentrate on the ice again.

CHAPTER 17

LILA

"Okay, you've been on another planet lately." Faith dropped onto the couch and eyed me. "What's going on?"

"What?" I laughed. "I'm good. I blew that shot at practice, but I was—"

"No, no, no, no, no." She shook her head emphatically. "I don't mean when you're playing hockey. I mean just... you. In general. Whenever you're not on the ice or working out, you're..." She gestured like something flying away. Shooting me a pointed look, she added, "I'd tell you to be straight with me, but..."

I tossed a throw pillow at her.

She laughed, caught it, and wrapped her arms around it. "Okay, seriously. I need you to *level* with me—what's going on? Because you've kind of been a mess since you found out you were coming to Pittsburgh, and you're a different kind of mess now."

"I feel like a better mess," I tried.

"Uh-huh. But still a mess. What's going on and why do I think it has to do with McAvoy?"

The heat that rushed into my face meant there was no pretending she hadn't found her mark. I had to be as red as the goal light, and her cackle made me groan.

"I knew it! I knew it!" She nudged me with her bare foot. "I totally knew it."

"Shut up," I muttered.

She giggled, but then studied me. "What happened, anyway?" She lowered her chin a little and eyed me. "One minute, you couldn't stand her and wanted her launched into the sun. Now you're suddenly..." She flailed a hand at me. "Very much *not* wanting her launched into the sun."

I avoided her gaze and chewed the inside of my cheek.

"If you've got a crush on her," Faith mused, "you can tell me."

Groaning, I buried my face in my hands. It wasn't like I could hide anything from her, and I had no idea why I bothered trying.

"I figured as much," Faith said, but she sounded sympathetic. "I'm just surprised. You know, because of the whole wanting her launched into the sun thing. What changed?"

I ran a hand through my hair and exhaled. "She's attractive as hell, okay? I mean, have you *looked* at her?"

"Enough to know she's a hundred percent your type, yes."

Renewed heat rose in my face. "Do I have a type?"

"Um, yes?" My friend eyed me like I'd lost my mind. "Tall and femme with a butt that doesn't quit? Hair that spends more time in a messy ponytail than not? And like, you've got a serious competency kink, and you spend every day seeing exactly how competent she is at hockey." Faith cocked a brow. "Did I miss anything?"

I let my face fall into my hands and groaned. "Oh my God, I am so fucked."

"Or, well... not fucked. Which seems to be the issue."

I gave her the finger, prompting a giggle. Raising my head, I said, "But she's a teammate. Getting involved with a teammate is—"

"Oh, stop it." Faith gestured dismissively. "There are two married couples on your team and another that's this close to getting engaged. Literally no one cares if you get involved with a teammate."

I pressed my lips together. Okay. Fine. She did have a point. Even as I'd said it, I'd known it was a weak argument. Hell, the forward who'd assisted on our gold medal game-winning goal at the Olympics married the goalie she'd scored on like two months later. The men's league still got the vapors if they found out a player was gay, but in ours, lesbian and bisexual women were not exactly a rarity.

"All right, so no one cares if I get involved with a teammate." I grimaced. "But let's not kid ourselves—she's not going to be interested in me. I was an unholy bitch to her when we got here."

"You were, and I don't think I'm the only one who's noticed that that's changed. Like, *dramatically* changed." Faith laughed. "In fact, it was such a dramatic change, I'd bet money that the only person on the planet who doesn't know you're into Sabrina McAvoy is Sabrina McAvoy."

I chewed the inside of my cheek. "You don't think she

knows?" I didn't think she did, but it sure would make things easier.

"Of course she doesn't." Faith waved her hand and reached for her drink. "Have you ever met a woman who can tell when another woman is into her?"

I managed a laugh. "Fair point."

"Which is probably how *you* haven't caught on that she is absolutely into *you*."

I choked on nothing. "She—what? What are you talking about?"

Faith rolled her eyes. "See what I mean? Everyone on the planet can see it, but neither of you are going to catch on until one holds up a sign that says '*Hey, stupid, I'm into you.*'"

I laughed, but it came out kind of high. I was still a little off-guard by her suggestion that Sabrina was into me. Yeah, yeah, I was always slow on the uptake when it came to figuring out if a woman wanted me, but... *Sabrina?* No way.

"Okay, so no one on the team will care if we're together," I said. "But... the last time I dated a teammate, it was a disaster. And it was distracting on the ice."

"Do you think it'll be any more distracting than all this sexual tension you idiots keep ignoring?"

"Maybe? With Leann, it was *bad*. I'm lucky I didn't get thrown off the team."

Faith rolled her eyes. "You were sixteen. Everything is ten times more dramatic and distracting when you're sixteen."

Ugh. Fine. Once again, she was right. Attraction and breakups were still enough to short circuit my brain now, but not like they had been when I was a teenager. I was an adult now. As much as I was and always would be a hothead on the ice, I was a professional, and I'd played through all kinds of things that would've had teenage Lila crying in the showers.

"But what about the whole thing where we didn't get along at first?" I groaned. "God, I was such a jerk to her."

"I'm glad you recognize that," Faith said. "What changed?"

"Besides me not being a jerk to her anymore?"

"Well, I'm assuming there was a reason for that. Aside from, you know, you realizing it was uncalled for."

Trust her to be blunt and to the point.

"Okay, okay." I waved a hand. "I realized it was uncalled for." There was a lot more to it—a lot of things I hadn't known and still felt like an asshole for assuming—but that wasn't my story to tell someone else. "The way things are now... I mean, what should I do? I've never been good at approaching women."

"And? She's into you. Flirt back a little. Ask her to get drinks or dinner. And, you know, maybe tell her it's a date because if she's anything like me, it'll be your twelfth date before she realizes what's going on."

I laughed, because yeah, I'd done the same thing. "Okay, okay. I'll try. Maybe. But like, if I flub this, I'll still have to see her every day."

"So what if you do?" Faith shrugged. "Haven't we all made asses of ourselves with a woman, and then laughed about it with her in bed later?"

I didn't know why that made me blush, but it did. "It's not just me?"

She barked a laugh and shook her head. "Oh Lord, no. I

was so ridiculously awkward with Elena when we met, and look at us now."

"Eh, good point."

"Hey. You're not supposed to agree with me."

I shrugged unrepentantly, earning me an eyeroll.

"Anyway. Speaking of my lovely wife…" Faith pushed herself to her feet. "I need to go FaceTime her and the kids."

I nodded. "Tell them all I said hi."

"Will do. And you'll figure this thing out with Sabrina." She squeezed my shoulder as she walked behind the couch. "Talk to her. Ask her out. If you'll check her into the boards during practice just because you don't like her, you have to be able to ask her to get drinks because you *do*."

"You know it's not really that easy," I called after her.

She just cackled, and I laughed as I rolled my eyes. She made a good point. A lot of them, actually. I still didn't quite buy that Sabrina was into me, but hey, nothing ventured, nothing gained. And honestly, I didn't see how asking her out could make things any more excruciatingly awkward than they'd been during training camp. I cringed just thinking about that.

I'd talk to her, then. Maybe. Eventually. I could work up the nerve, couldn't I? I'd done it before.

Not with someone as hot as Sabrina.

Not with someone I'd already screwed up this badly with.

Yikes. This won't be easy.

Worth a try, though.

In the next room, I heard Faith's kids squeal in delight over the phone, their voices distant and tinny, and I smiled to myself. I envied the marriage and family she had.

On the other hand, I had no idea how they did it. Elena was playing for Seattle while Faith worked for Pittsburgh, so they spent the season living apart. The kids stayed with Elena because her parents lived locally and could take them whenever she was on the road. Neither of them had any family in Pittsburgh, so they wouldn't have that support network here. Keeping the kids in Seattle was a no-brainer.

They seemed to do all right with that arrangement, but it had to be hard as hell. I'd never done a long-distance relationship, and I wasn't so sure I was wired for it. Then again, if I was in a relationship with someone and our circumstances changed... Well, I'd either have to rewire myself for the long-distance thing or let her go. I couldn't imagine Faith letting go of Elena, and their separation wouldn't be forever. So maybe LDRs were one of those things you didn't necessarily sign up for—you just dealt with it if the circumstances arose, kind of like how I dealt with my knee problems now that I had them.

It occurred to me that if I pursued Sabrina, and if I somehow managed to pull a miracle out of my ass and charm her into hooking up with me or dating me, we might have to do the long-distance thing at some point. Hockey was a fickle thing, and there was no guarantee either of us would stay in Pittsburgh. Trades. Free agency. Anything could happen. There wasn't even any guarantee we'd both see the end of the season with this team; there'd been an absolute storm of trades last year right before the trade deadline, and that could happen this year, too.

There was also another expansion coming in the next couple of years, and the team would only be able to protect so many players. They'd probably put Sabrina on the protected list, but me? I kind of cynically wanted to think no one would snatch up me and my knee for their expansion team. I was still amazed Pittsburgh had signed me at all, so I wasn't banking on that lightning striking twice, either as a UFA or during the expansion draft. But if it did... where would that leave me and Sabrina?

It was so much easier to not like her, but now I did like her. I liked her a lot. I'd misunderstood things about her, and I'd unfairly disliked her, and now... God, my tune had changed about her, that was for sure.

It didn't help that I was *painfully* attracted to her. And, I mean, okay, Faith was right about Sabrina being my type, but there was more to it than that. Sabrina didn't just check all my boxes—she was like the gold standard of all of them. Now that I wasn't determined to despise her, I was lucky I could think around her, never mind speak or skate. When I'd still hated her, I'd been annoyed by how much the camera loved her smile. Now, I completely understood why the camera was so infatuated with it. Who wouldn't be?

The competency kink Faith had mentioned—I couldn't deny that either. Both that I definitely had one, even if I hadn't realized that was what it was, and that Sabrina person-ified the kind of competency that made my pulse race. Now that I wasn't watching her through resentment-colored glasses, and now that I knew the truth about her rise to hockey stardom, it was impossible not to see how incredible she really was.

Even if her father *had* connected her to the best hockey coaches on planet earth, genes and mentors could only take someone so far. The way Sabrina saw the ice? The way her mind worked? You couldn't teach that. I'd been so angry that her name had given her an express ticket to the top of this sport, I'd never stopped to realize that Sabrina truly *was* a generational talent. Not a dynastic one—her gift had nothing to do with her father and everything to do with her hockey IQ and her work ethic.

That level of competency? Oh, yeah. That did it for me.

And now that I knew just how much of an uphill battle it had been for her to get here? How little had been handed to her and how much she'd been held back? How intensely stubborn and fiercely determined she had to be to fight through all of that to earn her place as a hockey star?

Oh, hell. There was no pretending I didn't admire that... or that I wasn't ridiculously attracted to it.

I swore into the silence of the living room and rubbed my eyes with the heels of my hands. Hating her for what had turned out to be nothing had been easy. Being this stupid for her? How the hell was I supposed to function like this?

And what was I supposed to do with it? Approach her? Have... Well, have faith in Faith that she knew what she saw and that this attraction was mutual?

The thought made my heart race. I wanted to do that. I wanted to know what Sabrina looked like when she was flirty. When she was flattered. When she was so turned on she didn't know which way was up. I wanted all of that.

But... was I setting myself up for heartbreak? Either because she wasn't as into me as Faith somehow thought she was, or because we'd wind up on different teams and wouldn't be able to weather the distance? What if we got together and then—

Yo. Lila. Get a grip.

I took and released a deep breath. I was getting ahead of myself. Way, *way* ahead of myself.

Instead of thinking about all the reasons Sabrina and I would inevitably break up, I needed to think about being *teammates* with her. Being *friends* with her. Making up for the incredibly bumpy start we'd had because of my stupidity. See if she actually liked me after the novelty wore off that I wasn't being a complete asshole to her.

Then, and only then, maybe I could see if I was imagining this spark.

CHAPTER 18

SABRINA

WHPL EXPANSION TEAMS PROVING TO BE SOLID CONTENDERS

Pittsburgh, Alburquerque dominate their divisions while Nashville and Denver make strong cases for wild card finishes

DENVER – Four of the six expansion teams added to the Women's Hockey Professional League this season are proving their mettle right out of the gate. Five weeks into the season, the Albuquerque Ice Crystals (12-4-2) are just two points behind the Las Vegas Saints (13-2-3) in the Southwestern division.

In the east, the Pittsburgh Bearcats (14-3-2) are solidly number two in the Great Lakes division, and a mere two points behind the Toronto Ice Queens (14-1-4) in the Eastern Conference. If Toronto continues their current skid (four losses in a row) and Pittsburgh extends their five-game winning streak, we could see the new team taking that number one spot.

The Anaheim Blizzard (4-9-5) and Cleveland Rebels (5-8-6) have struggled to find their game. Cleveland appears to be rallying, winning three of their last four after an abysmal start. Anaheim seemed to do the same in late October, but after blowing three multiple-goal leads in recent games, it's clear something needs to change for this team.

Both the Denver Stampeders (10-3-5) and the Nashville Outlaws (9-6-3) have established themselves as strong contenders for their respective wild card spots. Denver started their season weakly, recording three regulation and two overtime losses in their first six games. Since their disastrous 7-2 loss on October 15, the team has surged, boasting a record of 8-0-2 in their last ten, landing them firmly in the Western Conference's second wild card position.

Nashville lost their first five games in regulation. General Manager Toni Cochran swiftly demoted head coach Lena Talbot to assistant head coach and hired Kristen O'Connor to the team's helm. Under O'Connor's leadership, the Outlaws have played 9-1-0 in their last ten games.

Denver plays at Vancouver tonight, and Pittsburgh hosts the Seattle Winterhawks.

GENERATIONAL TALENTS MAKING THEIR MARK IN WOMEN'S LEAGUE
Ivy Tanneson on track for second 100-point

season; hockey legend Doran McAvoy's daughter leading spectacular power play in Pittsburgh

LOS ANGELES – On the eve of Thanksgiving—often a point at which the playoff picture begins to take shape—several WHPL players are standing out with exceptional performances.

First overall draft pick Ivy Tanneson has amassed 14 goals and 17 assists after just 25 games, putting the Los Angeles right winger on pace for her second 100-point season. Fans and analysts feared her disappointing rookie season—20 goals, 9 assists—had been portentous for her career, but after corrective surgery on her wrist following the playoffs, Tanneson is back on her superstar trajectory.

A surprise talent is emerging in Montreal's seventh round pick Noel Carter. Initially placed on the team's bottom six to provide some depth scoring, Carter has soared to the top line. After 27 games, she leads her team in points (31) and assists (18), and she ranks fourth in the League for power play goals.

Montreal general manager Naomi Ouellette says Carter "has come into her own and found her stride, and she will have her name in the sport's record books for sure."

And in Pittsburgh, the McAvoy hockey dynasty continues to reign supreme. The daughter of the legendary Doran McAvoy and sister of St. Louis star Mark McAvoy, Sabrina McAvoy is living up to her name and her genes. She's currently third in the Great Lakes division for goals and first in assists, and no one in the Eastern Conference has more points overall. Sabrina's playing style has always been that of a playmaker, notching an impressive number of assists on her teammates' goals. By contrast, her father was a record-setting goal scorer, but after just two seasons in the WHPL, Sabrina is on track to match or possibly surpass Doran's point totals.

Of his sister, Mark McAvoy says, "I'm not at all surprised. I was there when she was tearing up the ice on a team of boys who were all older than her." With a laugh, he adds, "If there's any woman who's going to make the jump from the women's league to our league? It's Sabrina. Guaranteed."

Doran McAvoy did not respond to requests for comments on his daughter's performance.

In the passenger seat, Zoe huffed sharply and put down her iPhone, where she'd been reading aloud the recent articles. "Are they ever going to be able to mention your name without bringing up Dad or Mark?"

I gave an irritated sniff and tapped my nails on the wheel. "They left Ty out this time, so I guess I can't complain too much."

"The hell you can't," she muttered. "Funny how they never call Mark the 'brother of women's hockey star Sabrina McAvoy.'"

"Yeah. *That'll* be the day."

"Right?" she grumbled. "Ugh. They don't even mention that you're the captain or that your team's power play is number one in the entire league. Don't they ever get tired of gargling Dad's balls?"

The laugh that burst out of me almost made me run off

the road, and Zoe giggled behind her hand. I playfully smacked her arm. "You're so gross!"

"I'm not wrong, though!" She gestured with her phone. "I mean, they can't even talk about your stats without comparing them to his. Like, why not just say you're probably going to set a points record in the League instead of saying... that?"

I pursed my lips as my humor died away. "Yeah. It's annoying. On the bright side, Dad probably won't see it and get pissed off about it since he doesn't read articles about women's hockey." Good thing, too—he'd bristle at the idea that his son might eclipse some of his records. He would *not* be pleased about anyone suggesting his *daughter* could do the same, especially since she was playing against women so it didn't really count anyway.

"You never know," my sister said. "He's just narcissistic enough to Google himself."

I groaned. "Ugh. True. Well, let's hope he doesn't read this one. That's a phone call I don't want to answer."

"I don't blame you. At least Mark has your back, though."

At that, I laughed with more feeling. "He better. He knows if he's a butthead, I'll get into his league just to play against him and beat him."

She giggled. "Those guys wouldn't know what hit them."

"Eh, some of them would. I'm pretty sure the guys I played with and against remember me."

"Think any of them are still bitter over you beating them?"

I grinned. "Probably."

We both laughed, and I continued driving. One guy from my U12 league had gone on to make the men's league, and two more were in the minors. One of the two in the minors had been on a team that had threatened to forfeit a game rather than play against a girl. When it became clear that my coach wasn't benching me, they'd grudgingly agreed to play. That kid had spent two minutes in the box for high-sticking me during the second period, and his coach had thrown such a tantrum over it—claiming it was impossible *not* to high stick a player as small as eight-year-old me—that he'd scored himself a bench penalty. In the resulting five-on-three power play, I'd scored, and the kid's team had been apoplectic.

I wondered sometimes if that had been in the back of his mind that time in major juniors when he'd tried to fight my brother over something stupid. Like if he saw the name MCAVOY across Mark's shoulders, and just sort of lost his mind. That, too, had cost his team a power play goal against. Scored by Mark, of course, since he hadn't taken the bait and thus hadn't taken a penalty.

The kid's stick had been in four pieces when he'd emerged red-faced from the box.

Temper, temper, I thought, suppressing a laugh.

The GPS piped up and told me to take an exit off the freeway. From there, it directed us into a neighborhood in Wexford where some of my teammates lived, and a few minutes later, we parked in front of Coach Reilly's house.

Usually a teammate—the captain or one of the alternates, typically—would host holidays, but since this was our first year as a team, Reilly had insisted on hosting Thanksgiving. Most of us were still settling into our places, and a lot of us had smallish rentals that might not accommodate the whole team. Next season, once everyone was more situated, it would probably be at one of our houses.

I wondered, not for the first time, if I should buy a place here. I liked my team so far, and I liked Pittsburgh, but this all felt tenuous. Maybe because I'd spent my whole life thinking hockey was a breath away from getting yanked out from under me. What if the team didn't stay in Pittsburgh? What if I was traded? What if I didn't get extended, or the fans lost interest in women's hockey and the whole league evaporated?

As I got out of the car and headed up the walk with Zoe, I wondered if anyone else on the team or in the League felt that way. If there was this constant certainty that we were a collective flash in the pan, and once the novelty wore off, this would all be gone.

Given the ticket sales and the enthusiastic demands for more teams in more cities... we probably weren't going anywhere.

Did that stop me from being absolutely sure we were hanging by a thread? Not even a little.

My train of thought derailed as soon as Reilly's husband let us into the house. Most of our teammates were already here, apart from those who'd gone home for the holiday, and the house was alive with chatter and activity. Kids were playing in the living room, and adults milled around there as well as the kitchen, the TV room, and the back deck.

And I wasn't even a little bit surprised when my gaze landed on Lila, and my heart did that familiar jump that I still didn't want to think too much about. She turned my way and offered a smile too, and I suddenly needed a beer. Not for the alcohol—just for something cold, damn it.

I really should've settled things with her in training camp, so I could've had camp and the preseason to get used to this part. Not that it would've helped; it had been almost a month now, and I was still mentally blue-screening in her presence.

At least I was better about skating and playing hockey, though. The rest of the time? When we were working out or socializing? God help me.

And today, when she was wearing that dark red pantsuit and a pair of simple diamond studs? When she had that silver chain resting just so across her collarbones? Fuuuck.

She just looked so damn *good*.

It was hard to believe Lila Hamilton was screwing with my brain like this. Not because of the bad blood we'd had for a little while, but because I'd known her since we were kids. Like so many of us, she had still been in the awkward teenager phase during major juniors. We were all gangly back then, and some of us had still been waiting on growth spurts to mercifully show up. Which they did. Eventually.

When we'd gone to Worlds and to the Olympics, we'd mostly settled into our adult bodies. I felt like I should've had a crush on her back then, just like I should've been attracted to some of my other teammates and opponents. I probably had the inklings of crushes at that time, but I was so focused on hockey, I didn't really give it any thought beyond telling people, "No, I am not a lesbian!" I'd been so deep in the closet that my passport was issued out of Narnia; I didn't *let* myself notice other girls.

I had no idea if I'd have been into Lila back then had I accepted who I was.

Years later, though, with those awkward teen days an

even more distant memory than my closet, Lila Hamilton definitely had my attention..

And eventually, sooner or later, I was going to figure out how to coexist with her without my mind going blank every time she smiled.

I wandered the party and socialized with teammates and their families until dinnertime. The meal was served buffet style. After we'd loaded our plates, we sat down at one of the two large tables that had been set up in the dining and living rooms.

I, of course, sat beside my sister.

The chair beside me was empty for a minute or so, but then someone sat down, and when I looked...

Oh God. How am I supposed to follow dinner conversation with you right next to me?

Lila gave me a smile, then focused on putting her napkin in her lap.

I took a deep swallow from my ice water. Not that it helped.

"Hey, Mac," Laws chirped from across the table as we started eating. "That was a nice write-up about you. That article about you and Ivy Tanneson? That's awesome."

"Oh. Right." I smiled thinly. "I'm glad to see Noel Carter getting some air time, too. She's really killing it out there."

"You are, too," Laws insisted.

"It's a shame they fall all over themselves to make everything you do about your dad and brother." Sims wrinkled her nose. "Does that bother you?"

I admittedly let the mask slip a little. "It's... I mean, it would be nice if they could talk about me as me rather than *his* daughter or *his* sister." I huffed a laugh. "At least this time they didn't mention that I'm *his* ex-wife."

That had a few other people scowling.

"The dad and brother part would be annoying." Val stabbed a piece of turkey on her plate. "But the ex-husband? *Eww.*"

Nods all around, and the support made me smile, if half-heartedly. "Yeah, it's, um... It's not fun. And like, this is *our* league. I'm sure my brother could do without always being compared to our dad, but at least they're both in the same league, you know? Can't we have our thing without constantly being compared to the guys?'

That prompted a chorus of "hear, hear," around the table.

Beside me, Lila made a face. "The press and commentators really just can't let you stand alone, can they?"

I sighed, bringing up my glass. "I guess it's to be expected."

"Maybe, but it's still grating."

I rolled my eyes. "You have no idea."

Our eyes met, and the subtlest wince in her expression made me regret my choice of words.

"But I'm glad no one here knows what it's like," I said quickly, "because it sucks. We earned the right to be here. All of us. The least they can do is say our names."

"Damn right," Laws said. "I'm glad they're talking you up —I'm glad they're talking up our league at all—but the click-bait is so transparent."

"Right?" I rolled my eyes.

My sister laughed quietly. "They might as well just make a headline, 'Hey Doran, Please Notice Me!'"

Everyone at the table laughed, and they were immediately calling out other ideas for headlines to kiss our father's butt.

In the midst of it all, I glanced at Lila.

And she smiled, her eyes dancing with mischief.

What were we all talking about again?

CHAPTER 19

LILA

The Pittsburgh Bearcats had only existed since the beginning of this season. That seemed way too early to have any clearcut rivals as far as I was concerned, but apparently I was wrong.

Tonight, we were playing in New York.

Maybe it was because the men's teams had a rivalry, and that had just carried over to us? I had no idea. Whatever the cause, both teams and both sets of fans were out for blood tonight. Halfway through the first period, there'd already been four two-minute minor penalties—one slashing, one hooking, and two for roughing. Those last two probably could've been given five for fighting, but by the time their gloves had come off, the refs were breaking them up, much to the crowd's disappointment.

Now we were seven minutes into the second period. Sims was in the box for slashing, but now it was four-on-four for twenty-one seconds because one of New York's forwards had taken a penalty for boarding.

If we hadn't already had a fire under our collective asses, we would've now, because Laws could've been seriously hurt by that player who boarded her. It was a genuine miracle no one had thrown gloves over that. That, or the refs got the offending player into the box before anyone had a chance to come at her. When she came out? All bets were off.

I stole a glance at her while we set up for a faceoff. Tonight was as good a night as any for my first fight in the WHPL.

Come and get it, bitch.

That would have to wait until she was out of the box, though. For the time being, we were focused on making the whole team pay by way of a goal. They were, of course, going to make us work for it, and I suspected they were going to try to jailbreak their player. As much as I wanted her out of the box so I could answer the bell for her nearly injuring my teammate, I didn't want it to be at the expense of a goal against.

New York got the puck at the faceoff, but they didn't have it for long before Val snatched it away. Both sides battled it out in the neutral zone, and then Sims was free.

Power play time.

Sims had barely hit the ice before a blur of white, black, and gold zipped past me.

I followed. Sims always stayed behind in the neutral zone in case the action turned back our way, so I shot across the blue line into New York's zone.

The player who'd whizzed past me came to a stop near the boards, and I got a look at her number.

Five.

Sabrina. I grinned behind my visor; should've known it was her by the superhuman speed.

By the time I made it across the blue line, Sabrina was engaged in a board battle with two of New York's skaters behind the goal. I itched to join in the fray, but Anastasia was closer. I'd be one body too many; I was better off staying somewhere they could pass the puck once they got it free. Or where I could snatch it away from a New York player if she won the fight and tried to break away.

That was exactly what happened, too—one of their skaters got the puck and flung it around the boards, probably to be intercepted by someone waiting at the blue line.

I don't think so.

I lunged for the puck and just managed to stop it with the tip of my blade. I bobbled it a little, but I got it under control.

Behind me, someone tapped her stick on the ice, and I whipped around to pass it to her.

It had barely hit Sabrina's stick before she wound back and slapped it toward the goal.

The netminder might've been ready, but Anastasia was screening her, and the puck sailed past both of them and right into the twine.

Sabrina pumped her fist in the air and shouted as the goal light came on. Along with our other teammates, I skated over to hug her and congratulate her. As I did, she had a huge smile on her face, and when she locked eyes with me—

Oh my God. Good thing I was hugging her into the glass, because had I been trying to support my own weight, I probably would've lost an edge.

And why was I suddenly overcome with this need to kiss her right there on the ice?

I let her go and followed her and our other teammates to the bench for fist bumps, all the while reeling from my own stupid thought.

What the hell? That wasn't who we were.

But maybe it's who I want us to be.

Okay. Sure. I had a crush on her, especially now that I knew everything I'd thought about her was wrong. But I knew it probably wasn't mutual—despite Faith's thoughts on the matter still ringing in my head. Either way, on the ice in the middle of a game wasn't exactly the time to do anything about this attraction.

I'm losing my damn mind.

Fortunately, I still had hockey to hold my focus. That was one of the great things about this sport—it *demanded* a person's full attention.

I could finish losing my mind later. For now? Hockey.

As we were setting up for a faceoff, the announcer spoke in that reluctant way they sometimes did when they called opposing goals. The booing crowd almost drowned her out, but I heard her anyway:

"Pittsburgh goal. Number five, Sabrina McAvoy. Assisted by number seventy-two, Lila Hamilton. McAvoy from Hamilton at three minutes, thirty-four seconds."

I grinned to myself. Another assist for me. Another goal for Sabrina. And now we had the lead. *And* the home team's fans were pissed off. Nice.

The chippiness continued into the third period. I loved

games like this—the competitiveness and the feistiness, what wasn't to love?

After an icing call, we set up again. Sabrina won the face-off, and we were off and running. There was a battle in the neutral zone, and New York almost got into our zone before I stole the puck away.

I quickly scanned the ice and realized two of my team-mates were wide open.

"Ana!" I called out, and as soon as Anastasia looked my way, I sent the puck to her. She passed it to Sims, who passed it back to me, and I sent it on to Val. She got into the zone, and we were once again setting up, cycling the puck and keeping the skaters' attention while we closed in on their goal.

I almost wanted to laugh because they were so focused on us and on the puck, and we were moving around so much, they hadn't noticed that only four of us were engaged in the puck-go-round.

From the corner of my eye, I tracked Sabrina, who'd quietly made her way from the faceoff dot around the back of the goal. I sensed when she was in the right position. The puck came to me. I wound back like I was going to send it to Sims, who was off to the goalie's right. When everyone—including the netminder—shifted toward Sims to anticipate the pass, I fired it to Sabrina.

Before the goalie or any of the skaters could course correct, Sabrina tipped it in just past the goalie's left skate.

The crowd made a collectively frustrated sound, and we all nearly toppled her as we went in for hugs.

"That's two!" I shouted over the noise. "Think you can get three tonight?"

Sabrina glanced up at the screen. Then she fixed a wicked grin on me that made me glad yet again that I was leaning some of my weight on her instead of balancing on my skates. "Hell, yeah. Let's do it."

Oh, yeah. We were doing it. We had seventeen minutes left in regulation. New York would be on her now that she was on hatty watch, but I had faith.

After fist bumps, Sims and I went to the bench along with Sabrina's line so some fresh bodies could come out. A couple of shifts later, Sabrina and her linemates were back out. About thirty seconds after that, Coach sent Sims and me to join them as the exhausted third D pair peeled off to come back to the bench.

We swung our legs over the boards and hurried toward the offensive zone, where the forwards were setting up.

Sims hung back by the point, and I skated closer to the action, watching the puck and my teammates. Anastasia passed it to me, and I sent it to Sims just to throw off New York's skaters. She sent it to Sabrina.

An opposing player managed to steal the puck mid-pass, and she darted toward the neutral zone. I followed, but something caught on my boot and I went flying, and the whistle blew before I'd even landed on my chest and forearms with a grunt. It wasn't a bad fall—not fun, but my gear did its job.

As I got up and dusted myself off, a player was arguing with a linesman. The crowd booed, and New York's coach was shouting something that looked like *"Embellishment!"*

Embellishment, my ass. You trip someone going as fast as I was, some airtime was a guarantee.

The ref made a gesture that I recognized as a warning to stop yapping unless the coach wanted a bench penalty.

Ooh, keep yapping. Let's make it a five-on-three. C'mon, Coach. I dare you.

She wisely shut her mouth, though. She clearly wasn't happy about it, and I was surprised smoke hadn't started curling out her ears, but she didn't continue arguing with the ref.

Fine. Five-on-*four*, then. We could handle that.

On the way into the offensive zone for the faceoff, Sabrina gave me two taps on the elbow. I nodded and skated over to pass the same gesture on to Sims. It was our sign for a set play from the faceoff. It was a risky one, but it could be deadly if it worked.

Sabrina won the faceoff and sent the puck to Sims. Sims headed for the blue line, ostensibly to set up at the point, but then—at least as it would appear to everyone watching—she lost control of the puck.

Predictably, the player who'd been skating after her doubled her efforts, lunging for the puck.

While that skater was slightly off balance, Sims seized the puck back and sent it past her, right onto my tape. I immediately passed it to Laws, who shot it between another skater's legs.

Sabrina was right at the edge of the crease. Both she and the goalie went for the puck, but Sabrina was faster. She snatched it away before it even reached the edge of the crease. The goalie had dived for the puck, and she couldn't get back up in time to stop Sabrina's shot.

For the third time tonight, the red light came on for

Sabrina. Our fans drowned out the booing New York fans. Usually, there were only a few hats if someone scored a hat trick at an away game. Tonight, though, the crowd was full of Pittsburgh fans, and hats rained down all around us.

Sabrina had the first hat trick in Pittsburgh Bearcats history. Her first as a professional.

There was a time not too long ago when I'd have been rolling my eyes and resenting the fact that she was the one to notch that record.

Tonight, though, I knew who she was and where she'd come from. I was glad she was the one to get our first hatty. She'd worked hard. She deserved it.

As the ice crew collected hats while a few more fluttered down, the goalie and one of the skaters tried to scream about goaltender interference, but two of the officials had had unobstructed views of the goal. Sabrina's skates and stick never crossed into the blue paint, and she never interfered with the goalie's ability to protect the goal. It was a good, clean goal, and the refs weren't about to review it.

When the Jumbotron showed the replay—yeah, no, there was no goaltender interference. The only reason Sabrina had hindered the netminder's ability to do her job was that the netminder herself had come out of the crease, and as she'd tried to make the save, her stick had tangled with Sabrina's legs. If anything, she was lucky she didn't get a penalty for tripping Sabrina; then again, if Sabrina had fallen like any other player would have in that scenario, the coaches would've lost their minds about embellishment all over again.

Ugh, teams like this were exhausting and so were their

fans. Not every goal against was a product of goaltender interference, and not every penalty was embellished. Get a grip.

But then the ref skated to the blue line, and the whole arena went silent.

"New York is challenging the goal for goaltender interference."

A mix of cheers and boos went up. Everyone on the Pittsburgh bench exchanged "is she for real?" looks.

The officials went to the penalty box and pulled on their headphones, and they reviewed the goal for an alarmingly long time.

"That's not good," I muttered to Sabrina.

She scowled and shook her head. "No, it isn't."

"They're probably just being thorough," Sims chimed in. "They said it was clean and wouldn't review it, so they're probably worried they missed something."

Sabrina and I both considered it, then shrugged. She might've been right.

As the replay appeared above our heads, dramatically slowed down, I had to assume the New York coach's heart was sinking. It was so obviously not goaltender interference. It had been obvious in the moment and in the initial replay, and in the super slow motion from above? Good God. The stick hadn't even interfered with Sabrina as much as I'd thought initially. At this speed, it was clear the only contact made between Sabrina and the netminder was the netminder bumping Sabrina's calf *after* she'd made the shot. And that was well outside the crease, too.

If that was goaltender interference, I'd eat my visor.

The referees broke from their huddle by the penalty box,

and one skated to the blue line. Instantly, the entire arena again fell silent.

"After review of the coach's challenge," the referee's voice echoed through the stadium, "there is no goaltender interference." She made a gesture like an umpire declaring a baserunner safe, and the mix of boos and cheers almost masked when she added, "We have a good goal." Then she motioned toward New York's bench. "New York has a two-minute penalty for delay of game. Pittsburgh will have a two-minute power play."

Beside me, Sabrina flashed a toothy grin. "Well, then." She tapped her stick against mine. "Let's see if we can put another in the net."

Sounded like a plan to me.

But about twelve seconds into my next shift, someone checked Sabrina hard from behind. Not a penalty, but I saw red.

Especially when I realized it was the same little shit who'd boarded Laws earlier.

Fuck it. We had a solid lead with only a handful of minutes to go.

I skated in front of her, locking eyes, and I dropped my gloves.

She flung off her gloves too, and as we squared off, her expression said, *"Bring it on."*

Game on, then.

I swung first, then grabbed a handful of her jersey. She did the same, but missed. The second time, her fist connected with my nose, which stunned me enough for her to throw me off-balance. As soon as I realized I was going down, I threw myself toward her, using her arm and her jersey for leverage.

She hit the ice first with me straddling her.

Then the refs were hauling us apart, blowing their whistles like their lives depended on it as our teammates banged their sticks on the ice and boards. The crowd was a mix of cheers and boos—typical.

I let the ref pull me up, and she barked, "Get in the box and clean yourself up."

Clean myself—

Oh. The telltale trickle above my upper lip told me I was bleeding, and when I touched my lip, my fingers indeed came away with a smear of blood.

Eh. I'd won the fight. I could live with a bloody nose.

I skated across the ice to the boos of the New York fans and the cheers of those from Pittsburgh. I sat down in the box and pressed a towel to my face. The bleeding wasn't too bad. My nose throbbed a little, and my jaw was sore. Had she hit me in the jaw, too? Maybe I'd caught an elbow on the way down. Everything had happened so fast, I'd lost track of every way we'd made contact.

She dropped into the other box and shouted something at me through the glass, but I ignored her. As heated as I was about her dirty checks—especially boarding Laws—I'd learned long ago that nothing pissed off a fired-up player more than ignoring them. She'd get even angrier, shouting and gesticulating at me, while I cooled down and caught my breath.

By the time our five-minute penalty was over, I'd be calm and collected. Hell, I already was—I'd defended my teammates and let her know that kind of bullshit wasn't okay. I wasn't fired up anymore. From the screaming and banging on the glass beside me? Well, that was the kind of pissed off that often led to sloppy play and costly penalties.

Keep it up, dear. Be my guest.

Oh, she did. When our penalties were over, only two minutes remained on the clock. A smart coach would've kept her fuming defender on the bench, but apparently she thought the better approach was to turn the angry player loose anyway. They'd pulled their goalie from the net so they could have a sixth skater on the ice, and they were valiantly trying to score the two goals they'd need to tie up the game.

Number thirty-six—the one I'd fought—decided that would be a good time to cross check Laws, which caused her to lose the puck.

The whistle blew.

New York's coach started losing her mind.

And once again, with less than two minutes on the clock, Pittsburgh was on the power play.

I wondered how number thirty-six felt as she sat in the box and watched Val and me assist Laws on a decisive power play goal.

In her skates, I'd have been super pissed. Mostly at myself.

In my own skates? With my team notching a decisive win against these rivals? I was thrilled.

The buzzer sounded not long after that. Third star went to New York's goaltender for making almost fifty saves.

Second star went to...

Me?

I blinked. "Wait, what?"

"Are you surprised?" Sims smacked my shoulder. "You got three assists tonight!"

My jaw fell open. I... holy crap. I had, hadn't I?

Well, shit. I might've ended up with a bloody nose and a bruised jaw, but three assists and the second star—couldn't complain about that.

First star was, of course, Sabrina.

Earlier in the season, I'd have fumed over that. Tonight, I knew better.

And tonight, I knew she'd earned that first star.

A couple of hours after the game, we were in an airport lounge waiting to board our charter. I'd eaten at the arena, but I couldn't resist a cup of coffee and a pastry.

I'd barely settled into one of the cushy leather chairs beside a little table when someone took the other. And somehow, I wasn't surprised—and yet was still startled as all hell—to see that it was Sabrina.

"Oh, hey." I couldn't help smiling, and I was irrationally sure she'd heard or felt my pulse jump. "Did you get one of the pastries?" I nodded toward the buffet.

"Of course." She gestured at her plate. "They're amazing."

"Always are." I took a bite of mine, mostly to avoid saying something stupid. I was sure I was going to say something stupid now that Sabrina was here. I'd had that feeling a lot lately, and it was... weird. I wasn't the smoothest in the world with attractive women, but I wasn't usually like this.

Mercifully oblivious to my mind spinning out over her, Sabrina held my gaze and grimaced. "How's your face? After that fight?"

I gingerly touched my jaw. "Sore in a few places, but I'll be okay." I grinned. "Totally worth it after what she did to you and Laws."

"No kidding." Sabrina scowled, shaking her head. "That was totally uncalled for. *Both* times."

"Right? But that seems to be how this team plays."

"It does. Can't wait to face them again."

I groaned. We were in the same division, so we'd be playing against each other three more times this season. Couldn't fucking wait.

A few minutes later, our boarding call was announced. As we got up, I caught myself feeling both relieved that I was no longer in danger of saying something stupid and... what could I say? I was disappointed that I was no longer sitting with her. That I'd squandered a chance to really talk to her, stupidity or awkwardness notwithstanding.

But to my surprise—and relief, and panic—as I took my seat on the plane, Sabrina gestured at the one beside me. "Can I join you?"

Oh fuck yes. Wait, no. How am I supposed to relax with you sitting here? God, yes, please sit here.

What the hell? Was I a teenager again?

Clearing my throat, I nodded. "Yeah. Of course."

She put her bag in the overhead bin, then settled beside me. We exchanged smiles, but didn't say much for a while.

Then she was checking something on her phone, and her expression suddenly darkened. "For fuck's sake," she muttered, and typed something with sharp, irritated taps on the screen.

After she'd apparently sent the message, I cautiously asked, "Bad news?"

"Not really." Sighing, she leaned back against the seat. "Just a reporter sniffing around, trying to get me to talk about Ty." Sabrina rolled her eyes. "They didn't ask me about him half as much while we were married as they do now."

"Wow, seriously?" I made a face. "What do they even want to know?"

She made a tired gesture before letting her hand drop onto the armrest. "I think they just want dirt. Like everyone is convinced there's something scandalous about it. Either I left him for Kendra, or he was cheating, or..." Closing her eyes, she sighed heavily. "I just tell them we weren't compatible. I wanted to play hockey, and he didn't want a wife who played hockey."

"Was that—was that actually the issue? Did he try to stop you from playing?"

She nodded slowly, gazing with unfocused eyes at the back of the seat in front of her. "That was what finally made me leave, yeah."

"And they don't think that's juicy enough?"

"Apparently not."

"Wow." I studied her. "Can I ask you about something personal?"

Sabrina let her head loll toward me as she raised her eyebrows. "Sure."

"When you were married—"

Her wince stopped me in my tracks.

I chewed my lip. "I'm sorry. We don't have to... If you don't..."

"It's fine." She picked up her glass. "It's wasn't a great time in my life, but I can talk about it."

I hesitated.

"It's fine," she said again. "What's on your mind?"

I proceeded cautiously. "Just... I saw some interviews with you during that time. And you were at a lot of his games —things like that." I paused, watching for signs that I really was treading where I didn't belong. "You never seemed happy."

She winced again and dropped her gaze. Before I could insist she didn't have to talk about it, she said, "I wasn't." She swallowed. "I never was."

I chewed my lip, not quite sure how to ask what I thought was the obvious question.

She watched her thumb running back and forth along the edge of the armrest. "To tell you the truth, I think Ty was more in love with my name than he was with me."

"But you changed your name when you were married to him."

"Yep." She laughed bitterly. "What better way for him to lay claim to me than to make me take his name? He wanted the clout of being Doran McAvoy's son-in-law and Mark McAvoy's brother-in-law, and he wanted the world to know that I was *his*."

My lips parted. "Seriously?"

Sabrina nodded, not looking at me. "It was, um... It was oppressive."

"That sounds miserable."

"It was. And looking back, I basically walked right into a marriage like my parents' marriage. In fact, my mom is a big part of why I got away from him when I did."

"Yeah?"

Sabrina nodded. "Ty and I came to visit during the off season. While he was golfing with my dad and brother, I went over to her place. She sat me down and said, 'You aren't going to want to hear this, but it's what I wish someone had told me while I was married to your father.'"

"Whoa."

"Yeah. And like, I knew she was miserable with him. I saw what she put up with and how he treated her. I just didn't think Ty was doing the same things, you know?" She huffed a caustic laugh, watching her fingers trace the condensation on her glass. "At first I was like, no, he's nothing like Dad. But she just calmly laid it all out. How he was just passive-aggressive enough to keep me in line. And how she could see him using me as a trophy wife so that everyone knew he was married to Doran McAvoy's daughter." Sabrina made a disgusted noise. "I went and watched a bunch of his interviews, and I realized he almost never missed an opportunity to mention my dad."

I wrinkled my nose. "What a brown-noser."

"Right?" She rolled her eyes. "Anyway, Mom didn't have that for my dad—a name or a family he could lord over people —but she *was* a model. He insisted she never left the house without a full face of makeup, her wedding rings, a Rolex—

the works. He wanted her at every home game, and he pushed her to be involved in—ideally in charge of—everything the team did for charity and whatever. Not because he cared about the causes, but because he wanted people to see his beautiful model wife doing things in his name."

I couldn't help making a disgusted face. "Oh my God. No shame whatsoever."

"None." Sabrina slumped back in her seat and rolled her shoulders a little. "So, yeah, Mom could see my marriage going the same way hers did, and she told me to get out. Especially since Ty wanted kids, and he'd been pushing me hard in that direction."

That caught me by surprise. "He was pressuring you? And you didn't want them?"

"I..." She chewed her lip, her eyes losing focus. "It wasn't that I didn't want them. I think deep down, even before my mom pointed everything out, I knew I didn't want kids *with him*. And once I realized I wanted out, I definitely didn't want to be chained to him. My mom was chained to my dad for eleven years after the divorce, until my sister turned eighteen, and Dad made it hell for her."

"Jesus Christ," I breathed.

"Right?" She laughed bitterly. "I feel so stupid. Getting manipulated right into the same situation I swore I'd never get into."

Frowning, I shook my head. "I don't think you were stupid. Manipulated, yes, but that's on him, not you."

"No, but I feel like I should've seen it coming." Sabrina rolled her eyes. "I guess I was just so used to Dad's bullshit, I didn't notice it coming from Ty. And it..." She hesitated. "It doesn't help that I was struggling with my sexuality, too." Her cheeks turned pink. "I'd known for a long time that I was attracted to women, but I spent years trying not to be. Or trying not to admit I was."

"Why's that?"

"Mostly because so many kids liked to tease me that I was a lesbian because I was into sports and I wasn't the girliest girl growing up." She rolled her eyes. "Of course a lot of that goes back to my dad, too. He said women's sports were just a place for dykes to pretend they were men."

"Oh, for fuck's sake."

"I know, right? And I think a part of me was afraid that if I admitted I was a lesbian—if I came out—then I'd just be proving him right." She scoffed and shook her head. "It's so stupid, and I hate that I—"

"No, it's not stupid," I said gently. "You've spent your whole life getting rejected and judged by your dad. If my dad acted like that, I wouldn't want to give him another reason to be a dick to me either."

"Still. I just wish he didn't have so much influence over me or my life anymore."

"Which makes it even *more* annoying is that no one can write about you or talk about you without mentioning him."

She scrunched up her face and nodded. "That part sucks, let me tell you."

I exhaled. "And here I was frustrated that they can't talk about me without rambling on about my knee and how it makes me a liability."

Sabrina shook her head. "It doesn't make you a liability. Half the League has had some kind of serious injury at some point in their career, and any one of us could have a career-ending injury at any time. You're not a liability. Hockey is."

I laughed because that was somehow the only way I could think of to express the relief that came from her comment. "Well, let's hope it doesn't mess up my knee again. Because I'm really enjoying this damn sport."

"Me too." Our eyes locked, and she finally smiled with some actual feeling.

Then, unexpectedly, she dropped her gaze and cleared her throat. "Listen, uh, one of the reasons I wanted to sit with you—" She glanced around as if to make sure none of our teammates were eavesdropping. Facing me again, she said, "It hasn't been announced officially yet, but Coach Reilly said I've been selected for the All-Stars."

I was shamefully aware of how much that would've irritated me before, but much like I was with her hat trick and first star, I was thrilled for her. "That's great! I don't think anyone will be surprised."

She laughed softly. "I don't know. We've got some pretty badass players on this team. But I was bringing it up because they said I can bring a plus one to the event." She lifted her eyebrows, and she actually sounded a little shy as she asked, "Would you want to come with me?"

I straightened. "You'd... want me to go with you?"

"Well, yeah." She shrugged as if it was no big deal, and maybe it wasn't. "Euli is bringing her wife and Val is bringing her daughter. I don't want to go alone, you know?"

My heart went into overdrive. Had Faith been right about her? That Sabrina was as into me as I was into her?

But... she could've just wanted me to come along as a

friend and teammate. Maybe no one else on the team could go. Maybe her sister was busy that weekend. It didn't... It didn't *have* to mean Sabrina was into me, and I really, really didn't want to make an ass of myself by assuming.

I did want to go, though, and we'd just have to see how things went between us.

"Sure, I'd love to go!" I smiled. "I've never been to the All-Stars. I mean, I went to our exhibition games at the men's All-Stars, but I've never been to ours, you know?"

"Neither have I. So, you're in?"

"Definitely!"

The way her face lit up should not have screwed with my pulse like that. But it absolutely did.

And so did the invitation to be her plus one for the All-Stars.

Holy fuck. Maybe Faith *was* right after all.

CHAPTER 20

SABRINA

I'd been to the men's league All-Stars plenty of times over the years. Early on, it was to cheer for my father. Later, my brother and—one season, by the absolute skin of his teeth—my ex-husband.

This was the first year I would be playing in the tournament myself. It was only the fifth year our league had even had our own All-Stars; it had taken a few years for us to graduate from having an exhibition game at the men's All-Stars to having an All-Star tournament of our own. It made sense now that the women's league was rolling on its own momentum. We had a huge and growing fanbase. We were selling enough tickets to actually get respectable salaries instead of—as was the case in the first couple of seasons—needing second jobs to make ends meet. We didn't *need* the endorsement of the men's league in order to be perceived as legitimate.

The men's league did still endorse us, though, and they always sent a few players for some of the fun stuff during the skills competition, as commentators, and even just to sign autographs. The fans loved it, and honestly, so did the male players. If there was one thing all fans of this sport could usually agree upon, it was "more hockey = good."

So I wasn't at all surprised to see an enormous crowd outside the arena this afternoon. Players were arriving for the skills competition, and fans were packed in along either side of the long red carpet leading up to the players' entrance. Lila and I got out of the car, and immediately we had both fans and journalists calling our names. Reporters held out microphones and pointed cameras at our faces. Fans waved phones, pucks, and photos at us.

"Did major junior you ever think this would be us?" Lila asked quietly as we gravitated toward the fans.

"I hoped." I flashed her a quick smile, which she returned. "Now here we are."

"About damn time," she said just loud enough for me to hear.

"Agreed."

Then we were right against the edge of the red carpet, signing pucks, photos, jerseys, and anything else people wanted. We posed for selfies—some together, some on our own—and steadily made our way down the line. Of course we did the obligatory posing for the reporters, but as much as we could, we stuck to the fans. They were the reason we were here, after all.

And what could I say? There was something amazing— something downright *addictive*—about all these young girls with wide, starstruck eyes telling us they played hockey too and they hoped they'd be here someday.

"How long have you been playing?" I asked a petite blonde girl as I signed a puck for her.

"Since I was four," she said, grinning broadly. "I want to play like you!"

I smiled back. "Keep working at it! You'll get there!"

The hope in her eyes melted my heart. But then she glanced over her shoulder, and her smile faltered just a little. "My dad says I might be too small."

Behind her, a man who might've been in his thirties met me with a sheepish shrug.

I frowned. "How tall are you?"

"She's about four-foot-three," her dad said.

"And how old?"

"Eleven," the girl said.

I smiled and shook my head. "Do you know who Joanna Lawson is?"

The girl's expression lit up once again. "She's so cool!"

"Uh-huh, and she's only about four-foot-ten." I glanced at the girl's father, then back at her. "Are you fast?"

"I'm the fastest!"

I laughed. "Well, being small and fast is good. Keep practicing—you're not too small."

She squealed with delight. At least her dad had the decency to look chagrined, and he mouthed, "Thank you," before I moved on to the next fans. I hoped he really did get the message. Considering he was here with her and she was playing hockey at all, she already had a leg up on me when it came to support from her father. If he could stop wringing his hands about her height, she'd probably do just fine.

As I started down the line again, I realized Lila had been

watching the whole exchange. When our eyes met, her soft smile did things I really didn't need to be thinking about right now. Just the fact that she'd accepted my invite for the weekend still had me off-balance.

Don't read to much into it, Sabrina. Friends travel together, too.

As we continued walking, Lila tilted her head slightly toward the girl and her dad. "Think she'll be on this side of the barrier someday?"

Grateful for something to focus on besides my suddenly spinning head, I shrugged. "Well, we got here. No reason she can't."

Lila's smile almost made me trip over my own feet, but I managed to keep my balance, and we continued down the line.

When we were nearly to the end, I glanced up ahead. There were some reporters waiting to interview us, and a few of the players from the men's league were milling around since they didn't really have anywhere to be for a while.

I caught a glimpse of my brother. Then another face caught my eye, and I stopped so abruptly, Lila almost ran into me.

"What's wrong?" she asked.

"I..." No amount of media training could pull the *"what the fuck?"* out of my expression.

I hadn't expected to see *him* here. My brother, yes; he'd always been a vocal supporter of the WHPL, much to our father's dismay, and he'd texted me saying he was super excited about this weekend. Not a surprise to see his big grin as I came up the red carpet.

Seeing my ex-husband?

Ugh. Seriously?

Lila's hand on the small of my back both startled me into the present and blanked my brain, and I turned to her. Eyes wide, she asked again, "What's wrong?"

You're touching me. Please don't stop.

"Ugh... I'm good. I'm good." I shook myself, finally managing to school my face so I didn't look like a deer in the headlights. "Ty's here."

"Oh for fuck's sake," she muttered, unaware of my brain again jerking to a stop when her hand disappeared from my back. "Why is *he* here?"

"No idea." I pushed my shoulders back. "But he's not ruining tonight."

"No, I think he's ruined enough nights for you."

I snickered. "You're not wrong."

She laughed and elbowed me, and when I met her mischievous gaze, some of my irritation melted away. Funny how quickly she'd gone from being the object of my aggravation to the salve I needed when someone else got on my nerves.

We continued up the red carpet toward my brother and ex, and I counted myself lucky that Ty had been talking to a reporter during my mental record scratch. He hadn't noticed me staring at him, so he wouldn't be able to rub it in my face. Someone probably had noticed and would tell him about it later, but at least right now, he'd been characteristically oblivious.

As we inched closer, I hoped someone important would

call him away and he'd be elsewhere when I reached the end of the carpet.

No such luck.

I was about ten feet away with Lila right beside me when Ty tilted his head and narrowed his eyes the way he always had when he was irritated with me. In an instant, my nerves about crossing paths with him gave way to pure annoyance.

"Well, look at that." His media smile had never looked so cold. "You made the All-Stars. Even if it's not the *real* All-Stars." He was clearly trying to make it sound like a joke to anyone who was listening, but I knew better.

"Mmhmm. I did." I forced myself to sound and look pleasant, if only because there were cameras and hot mics around. "So what brings you here? They have you as a guest commentator?"

The corners of his mouth twitched like he desperately wanted to scowl. It was admittedly a cheap shot—Ty's one attempt as a guest commentator had been an embarrassing disaster. He wasn't stupid by any means, but he was not comfortable in front of a camera like that.

After a second or two, Ty fixed his media smile into place. "Houston is campaigning to be included in the next expansion for a women's team. So some of my teammates and I are here to represent our team and the city." Though he had on that smile, his voice gave away how utterly displeased he was by this. Small wonder he couldn't hack it as a commentator.

Beside me, Lila gave a quiet laugh. "Is Houston actually in the running? Doesn't seem like there's much of a hockey culture there. Not anymore, anyway."

I had to literally bite my tongue to keep from laughing out

loud. Houston had been a thriving hockey town for almost twenty years, but in the last five—not so much. Fans were vocally frustrated with the team's poor performance and worse management. The club had the cheapest season tickets in the men's league and could barely sell them.

Ty rolled his eyes. To me, he said, "It was nice to see you, Sabrina. Good luck tonight and tomorrow." Again with that media smile to sell it to the cameras and microphones, but I knew him too well not to catch the sarcasm.

He turned to go, and I called to his back, "Good luck against New York next week."

Even his suit jacket couldn't hide the ripple of irritated tension that went through him, but he kept walking.

I watched him go, then shook myself and continued inside. I wasn't proud of the interaction. The whole mean girl thing wasn't my style. But damn if Ty didn't bring out the cattiness in me.

"New York?" Lila whispered as we walked. "Is that a nerve?"

I laughed. "Ooh, yeah. Houston is on a multi-year losing streak against New York. He *hates* playing against them." Humor fading, I glanced back in the direction he'd gone. Then I stood aside, out of the flow of traffic, and chewed my lip. "I... kind of feel bad for picking at him."

"Why?" Lila tilted her head. "Not to sound like a kid, but... he started it."

I managed to laugh but with a lot less feeling than before. "I know, but... I don't know. I just feel like..." I gnawed my lip again.

"Don't do that to yourself," she said softly. "He was an

asshole to you when you were married, and he was setting up to be an asshole to you just now. You had every right to shut him down before he had a chance to."

I glanced at her. "So why do I feel so bad for being catty?"

"Did he make you feel bad every time you stood up to him while you were married?"

"I..." I wavered on my feet a little. "Yeah. Yeah, he did."

"Right. So you're conditioned to just take his crap and then feel bad when you have the audacity to dish it back." She tugged me into the flow of traffic again, and with that hand on my back again, she gently propelled me forward. The contact made goose bumps spring up under my suit, and my brain record-scratched so hard I almost didn't hear her speak. "If you went out of your way to stomp on his raw nerves unprovoked, then yeah, I could see saying you're the problem." Shaking her head, she added, "You're just not putting up with his bullshit anymore."

I exhaled, letting her words—and let's be real, her hand on my back—soothe me and ease me down from the rafters. "You're right. Maybe eventually I'll learn not to feel like crap when I don't just take it."

"You will." She flashed me a wicked grin, her beautiful eyes sparkling with mischief. "And if I'm there, you'll have backup, which means he'll have two catty bitches to deal with." She winked. "If memory serves, he's not that great at defending against a two-man rush."

The laughter that poured out of me felt amazing, and we continued into the venue.

Bringing Lila as my plus one had been the best idea ever.

With her nearby, it would be a lot harder for me to even

notice Ty.

I managed to avoid Ty and his attitude for most of the day. And when we were in the same place, there were usually enough witnesses and recording devices present to keep us both from letting the cracks show. Plus I was pretty sure he wanted nothing to do with Lila, who was there most of the time.

Most of the time.

Just my luck, as I was leaving a photo shoot, I was alone. A reporter had asked Lila for an interview, and I was due to meet up with her after we were both finished.

I stepped out of the room where the shoots were being done, and I took out my phone. *The photographers are done with me. Where do you want to meet up?*

No response right away, so she was probably still in her interview. That, or she was somewhere she couldn't hear her phone. Either way, there was no hurry, so I leaned against the wall and thumbed through notifications and social media. I'd been warned that the All-Stars meant nonstop people and activity, and I was grateful for a moment to catch my breath.

Shame it didn't last.

There were people walking by in either direction. Someone in heels and in a hurry. Someone else in dress shoes walking at a more sedate pace while talking on his phone. A small group of people heading someplace on a mission.

But somehow, a set of footsteps hit my senses and made me look up from my phone. Maybe because it was a familiar gait. Maybe because I realized the person was coming toward me.

For a second I thought it might be Lila, even though I already knew it wasn't her. Wrong shoes. Wrong cadence.

No, it was...

Oh, for Christ's sake. Yeah, Ty was coming toward me, and he looked pissed.

I straightened against the wall as I pocketed my phone. I didn't say anything, though; I didn't want him to be able to blame me for igniting a confrontation, and I sure as hell didn't feel like giving him a polite hello.

He stopped a polite distance away, but he was still closer than I would've liked. "We need to talk."

"Do we?"

"Yes." His lips peeled back as he growled, "I'm tired of you talking shit about me to the media."

I blinked. "I don't talk about you at all."

"Bullshit you don't," he hissed just loud enough for me and no one else to hear. "You've told at least five reporters that you can play hockey now that we're divorced."

I stared at him, then huffed a humorless laugh. "Nice to see you're keeping up on articles about me. But also—that isn't exactly a *lie*."

He worked his jaw so hard I was surprised I couldn't hear his teeth grinding. "You could at least stop telling people I wouldn't *let* you play hockey."

I gave him a sarcastically innocent look I wouldn't have dared deploy during our marriage. "Why not? It's true, isn't it?"

He tsked and rolled his eyes. "It makes me look like an

asshole."

"Well, if the truth makes you look like an asshole..."

Ty huffed sharply. "Seriously, Sabrina?"

"Am I wrong?"

Another eyeroll. "For fuck's sake, you don't—"

"People ask me why I retired from hockey and why I decided to come back," I snapped. "It's a valid question. If you didn't want to be part of that narrative, you could've just—"

"So I'm the bad guy because I wanted a wife?" He sneered. "If I wanted to live with another hockey player, I'd move in with one of my teammates."

"Oh, stop it." My turn for a passive aggressive eyeroll. "I wanted a husband, too, but I wasn't at all threatened by you playing the same sport I did."

His laugh was sharp and caustic. "You wanted a husband, huh? That's not what I've been hearing." He narrowed his eyes. "That why you brought Hamilton with you? Because you want a"—he made air quotes—"husband?"

The response that came to the tip of my tongue was rude to say the least, and I bit it back.

But then I remembered the conversation I'd had with Lila. Why should I avoid his landmines when he danced all over mine?

So... fuck it.

"Well, when we got married," I said evenly, "I did want a husband. But three years with you finally broke through a lifetime of denial." I flashed him a brilliant smile. "Thanks for that! Should I tell reporters and fans that instead of the part where you wouldn't let me play hockey?"

The shock and anger in his face was almost too satisfying for words.

Then he swore, shook his head, called me something that didn't need to be repeated, and stalked away.

As he disappeared down the hall, I pushed out a breath, trying to ignore the jittery comedown from the adrenaline surge. I rubbed my forehead with the heel of my hand. How had I ever been married to that man?

Another set of footsteps broke away from the sparse traffic, but when I looked up this time, relief almost knocked my knees out from under me. Relief, and something I did *not* need to be thinking about when we'd be sharing a room tonight.

"Hey." Lila's brow was knitted with concern. "Everything okay?" She gestured down the hall. "I saw you guys talking, but..."

I swallowed as I rolled my shoulders. "It's fine. He was being an ass, but... I told him off."

"I saw that, and I'm glad you did." The concern lingered. "But the look on your face while you two were talking, it was..." She bit her lip.

"What?"

Lila glanced in the direction he'd gone again, then shifted her weight. "Okay, you can tell me if it's none of my business, but..." She studied me. "Was he ever, um... unsafe? Like...?"

I could read between those lines well enough, and I shook my head. "No. He never raised a hand to me, and I never thought he would." I exhaled, deflating as the memories pushed down on my shoulders. "He'd just get... loud. It scared me. Not like he'd actually touch me, but..."

"But like there's a man getting angry and loud right in your face," she said softly. "I think that would scare anyone."

The validation hit me in a soft spot, and I had to swallow hard as I nodded. "Living with that—it sucked."

"I can imagine." She searched my eyes. "Do you, um... Do you think he might've picked now to confront you as a way of messing with your head for tonight?"

I tensed. That hadn't even crossed my mind, but now that she mentioned it... "That *asshole*."

"Ugh." Lila took my elbow. "Come on. Let's go eat, and then we can do a little skating to get your mind back in the game."

I blinked. "You... want to help me practice for tonight?"

Her smile was cuter than it had any right to be. "I want to skate, because I'm a hockey player at a hockey event and I'm not playing hockey."

Rolling my eyes, I laughed. "Of course, it's all about you, rink rat."

"Absolutely. Now let's go."

Feeling lighter than I had just a moment earlier, I pushed myself off the wall, and we started toward the elevators. Yeah, Ty probably had intended to throw me off my game. He'd known while we were dating that picking a fight with me on game day would torpedo my performance, and it had taken me an embarrassingly long time to catch on to what he was doing.

Thank God Lila had picked up on it this time.

Nice try, Tyler. Your bullshit won't work when she's got my back.

CHAPTER 21

LILA

Lunch in an off-the-beaten-path restaurant seemed to help shake Sabrina out of her funk.

Some light practicing in the arena went a long way, too. There were a handful of other players on the ice, including one who'd brought her husband and kids out to hit some pucks back and forth. The rink was hardly crowded, though, and I was so focused on what we were doing, I mostly forgot there were other people here at all.

Focused on what *we* were doing?

Yeah, right.

As Sabrina and I played a low-key game of keep away, I was completely focused on *her*, and not just because I was trying to steal or hold on to the puck. I was mesmerized by the way she was laughing as we battled it out. The way she'd cackle when she stole the puck and fired it into the empty net? That way she'd try to look aggravated when I got the upper hand, but she couldn't quite hide her smile? Her happiness, especially after seeing her so rattled and frustrated with Ty, made me happy.

"Oh, come on!" she called after me as I swiped the puck off her stick. "That was a cheap shot!"

"What?" I skated around behind the net and flashed her a grin. "It was just a poke-check!"

"Uh-huh." She glided toward me. "So I just imagined the slew-footing?"

I half-shrugged. "Pretty much, yeah."

"Bitch," she muttered, but she was smiling.

The low rumble of an engine met my ears before I had a chance to snark back, and I turned to see the Zamboni pulling up to the gate. I glanced up at the clock and realized it was almost 3:30.

I nodded toward the Zamboni. "Guess we should get out of here."

We gathered up the pucks we'd been using and a few stray ones littering the ice. Once those were gone, we headed for the locker room to shower and change, and I was pleased that Sabrina was still smiling and chirping like normal. All traces of her encounter with her ex-husband were gone.

Mission accomplished.

Get wrecked, Ty, I thought as we stripped off our gear. *You have no power here.*

Her mood held as the day went on, so I was confident she'd shaken it off. We relaxed in our room for a while, then put on our suits and returned to the arena for the All-Star tournament.

This time, I could only go with her as far as the players' entrance. I'd be spending the game in the stands along with some of the spouses and families.

Outside the entrance, I turned to her. "You going to be okay? After earlier?" I'd been hesitant to bring it up and remind her of it, but I wanted to be sure.

Her smile deserved to be on magazine covers. "I'm good. Honestly, everything with him feels like it happened ages ago. So... thanks for that."

"Don't mention it." The impulse to draw her in and kiss her was almost irresistible.

I recovered, though, and I cleared my throat. "Well, good luck out there."

That smile. Fuck me.

"Thanks. Enjoy the show."

Oh, I would. As long as Sabrina was out there on skates, doing what she did best, I would definitely enjoy the show.

And maybe spend some of the time figuring out how to shut off the part of my brain that kept whispering *"Kiss her"* every time she looked my way.

A number of players from the men's league were out on the ice in their jerseys and skates with the All-Star competitors. Not all of them were here just to promote our league on behalf of theirs. Two of the guys beamed as they talked about how proud they were of their wives—one was married to Cleveland's goalie, the other to Vancouver's star center. A defenseman from Chicago cradled his infant son against his jersey while he raved about his fiancée and how she was definitely going to win the hardest shot competition. It was seriously cute.

Ty was down there, too, and like the others, he was interviewed, his face projected onto the Jumbotron for all to see. He plastered on his fake smile to talk about how excited he was at the prospect of Houston getting a WHPL team.

The whole time, he looked *deliciously* miserable. Every time the reporter started to speak, he seemed to brace a little as if he were expecting an uncomfortable question. Probably one about his ex-wife, her performance, and her selection to the All-Stars.

I was glad the reporter didn't ask about Sabrina. I didn't care at all if Ty was uncomfortable, but Sabrina didn't deserve to have her relationship picked apart as tabloid gossip. Especially since she was *right there*—she and another forward were warming up for fastest skater, which was the next event in the skills competition.

Eventually, the reporter moved on to someone else, and Ty became another face in the crowd around the edges of the ice. On the screen now was Alex McDaniels, who had retired a couple of years ago and was married to Nichole Manning, captain of Omaha. He was wearing the jersey of his old team, Kansas City, as part of the city's campaign for a WHPL team. As he was interviewed, he held his ten-month-old baby, and the whole arena was practically swooning over how cute they both were. Especially how cute he was as he gushed about his wife.

"I'm real proud of her," Alex said with a big smile as he

bounced the baby gently on his hip. "I mean, she had him, and like six months later, she's at training camp." He shook his head and laughed. "I'd have needed another *year*, and I definitely wouldn't have made the All-Stars my first season back."

Some of the guys behind him were nodding in agreement.

Everyone in the crowd chuckled at that. Alex had played through some pretty hardcore injuries in his career, so he wasn't a wimp by any means, but he was clearly awed by Nichole's recovery. We all were—here I was thinking I'd come a long way after my knee surgery, and here *she* was racking up points and dominating the ice a few months after pushing out a whole human.

The interviews ended, and everyone except a handful of skaters and officials moved to the side of the ice to make room for the fastest skater event. Sabrina was among the competitors, and she skated some lazy circles while she waited for the event to start.

My heart thumped as I watched. I'd done the backwards skating competition in the exhibition at the men's All-Star weekend a couple of years ago, and I'd been stressed as hell about that. Like any defender worth her salt, I could skate backwards all day long, but with a timer and that many people watching? It was seriously intimidating.

Come on, Sabrina. You can do this.

The first two skaters notched impressive times. 14.121 and 14.629. Not bad at all.

The third wiped out on a corner. I grimaced sympathetically as she got up and dusted herself off. She'd hit the boards when she went down, but she didn't seem any worse for wear; probably more frustrated than anything.

Sabrina was fourth. My pulse pounded even louder in my ears. The only thing worse than going right after someone with an incredible time was going after someone who'd fallen. The sight of someone going down could get stuck in a skater's head, make them second guess themselves or hesitate at the worst possible moment.

I pressed my hands together in front of my lips and held my breath as Sabrina glided up to the starting line.

Come on, come on, you can do this. You've got this.

The whistle blew, and she took off. She flew down the straightaway and whipped around the curve like a speed skater, her hand out and fingers nearly grazing the ice as she rounded the first corner, then the second. She powered down the longer straightaway, the crowd roaring as she raced the clock along the boards, then around the end of the ice, before giving everything she had in the final stretch to the finish.

In a blink, it was over, and her time flashed on the Jumbotron: 14.016.

I screamed along with the crowd. There were still two competitors left, but she'd bumped the leader into second place. It wasn't even that much of a surprise—Sabrina was one of the fastest skaters I'd ever seen—but it was a relief. She'd stayed on her skates, and she'd beaten at least three people.

As the crowd settled down, the next skater took her mark. Like Sabrina, she stayed up, but she was no match for Sabrina's time. She crossed the finish into fourth place with 15.001.

The final player was Eevi Heinonen, a Finnish forward who couldn't have been more than five feet tall. She was only nineteen, a rookie playing for Denver. An All-Star as a rookie? That was impressive.

She took her mark, and when she sped off the line, I was genuinely surprised flames didn't shoot out from her skates. Holy shit. She zipped around the first two corners like they were nothing, and her short legs didn't hold her back at all on the straightaway. The crowd was absolutely roaring when she sped over the finish.

Her time? 14.001.

Sabrina was the first to congratulate her, almost toppling the tiny rookie in a huge hug. Heinonen stared up at the screen, her jaw slack as her name lit up at the top of the leaderboard. Then she smiled, and the rest of the skaters came up to congratulate her.

Sabrina didn't look the least bit bothered that she'd been knocked into second place. I wouldn't have been either; her time was perfectly respectable—hell, it was insanely fast—and it was seriously cool to see a kid perform that well against veterans.

Then everyone cleared off for the next event. I dropped into my seat, dizzy and breathless from watching and cheering for Sabrina. Not too long ago, I'd have been so salty that she'd made the All-Stars. I'd probably be watching at home, rolling my eyes and telling Faith, "I'm so glad she lost to that rookie," while Faith rolled *her* eyes and told me I was an idiot.

Yeah. I was. But fortunately I wasn't anymore, and I was here with Sabrina, watching this play out in person and cheering for her like a friend and teammate should. I might've been slow on the uptake when it came to her, but I got my head out of my ass eventually.

Not a moment too soon.

As Sabrina skated past the bench where some of the guys were hanging out, she locked eyes with Ty. Even from this far away, it was obvious when they made eye contact. He said something to her, and her smile vanished.

One of the guys with him gave him a sort-of-playful punch to the shoulder, then spoke to Sabrina as he herded Ty in another direction.

I gritted my teeth.

For fuck's sake, dude. Can't you just let her enjoy the event?

Of course he couldn't. From everything Sabrina had told me, he was incapable of letting her enjoy something that didn't involve or prioritize him.

Fucking asshole.

At least she'd been able to shut him down a couple of times since we arrived, but this time... Ugh. There were too many cameras around, too many fans watching; she didn't dare make a scene, so she had to take whatever he said.

What a twat.

After that, the skills competition couldn't wrap up fast enough. There were still several events—hardest shot, backward skating, trick shots—and they took for-fucking-ever while I squirmed and waited to be able to see Sabrina.

The minute things started winding down, I took out my phone. Sabrina would be tied up for a while—showering, media availability, maybe eating—so I texted her, *Hey, are you good? I saw Mr. Douchewaffle talking to you.*

It was about fifteen minutes before she replied, *Yeah. He just made a snide comment about how our fastest skater wouldn't even place against the men's league.*

"Are you kidding me?" I muttered into the night. I wrote back, *What a jackass.*

I know, right? She's a rookie and she just won something she'll be talking about for years. Why shit on that?

I rolled my eyes. She didn't hear him, did she?

Fortunately, no. There was a pause, then, *I kind of wish she had, LOL. I was chatting with her in the locker room and she's spicy AF. She'd have made him wish he hadn't been born.*

At that, I laughed. *Oh man. That would've been funny.*

Right? Anyway, he's just trying to be a dick. On-brand for him. WTF was I thinking when I married him?

You said it, not me.

The response was a middle finger emoji, and I snorted.

Then she said, *Ok, gotta go talk to reporters. Should be done in about 30 min.*

Sounds good. I'll meet you outside.

I pocketed my phone and steadily made my way out of the stands with the rest of the crowd. I was glad Ty hadn't made it too far under her skin. At least he hadn't put a damper on her entire trip.

Maybe tonight, I could find a way to get him out of her mind entirely. Dinner out, maybe? Watch a game on TV or a movie? Hell, we could go to that ax-throwing bar down the road if she wanted to. I could probably even swing by the hotel's office center and print out some pictures of his face to pin to a target.

I'd feel her out when we got back to the hotel. Whatever she wanted to do, I was down.

Because over my dead body was that asshole ruining Sabrina's All-Star weekend.

CHAPTER 22

SABRINA

I was still irritated when we got back to the hotel. I was at the All-Stars, for God's sake. This was supposed to be fun, not a chance for my ex to mess with me.

But where he went, bullshit followed, and I shouldn't have even been surprised that he was here.

"You know what?" I looked at Lila as I unbuttoned my suit jacket in our room. "I'll bet you anything he begged to be here."

She raised her eyebrows. "You think so?"

"Oh, yeah." I sat on one of the beds. "He couldn't give a fuck about our league. In fact, he hates that it even exists."

"So why would he want to be here? If he doesn't—" She stopped. "You think he volunteered just so he'd have access to you?"

"I wouldn't put it past him," I muttered. "He was pissed that I left while he was at an away game and wouldn't talk to him except through my lawyer." I rolled my eyes. "He probably knew he'd stress me out just by being here."

"That's a lot of effort just to fuck with a woman who doesn't want you," she said dryly.

"I know, right?" I sighed. "But I don't think his ego has ever recovered from me leaving. Especially the part where I changed my name back."

"I take it he was angry about that then?"

"Oh my God." I rolled my eyes and wiped a hand over my face. "When he saw that I'd filed a petition to change my name, he blew up my phone for like a week."

"Was that something your lawyer would show him? Or something he dug up on his own?"

"I'm pretty sure he dug it up. Ugh. I wish he'd just... I don't know. Get over it. Get some therapy. Just move on and leave me the fuck alone."

She laughed humorlessly. "Why do I get the feeling he's not someone who would get therapy?"

"Oh. He's not. But hope springs eternal, right?"

"It really does." Lila watched me for a moment. Then she sat beside me and touched my forearm. "Listen. We've got the rest of the night to ourselves. Why don't we go out, eat some good food, and have a good time?" She grinned as her shoulder rose in a half-shrug. "Maybe he'll even see us and realize how much fun you're having without him."

My laugh felt better than anything had all damn week. And a night out with Lila? Perfect, regardless of what my ex thought. "That sounds like a great idea. Where do you want to go?"

"Um, well..." She pursed her lips and took out her phone.

"There are some nice places near the hotel. We might have to make a reservation, or we could just walk in and take our chances."

"Let's just take our chances." I shrugged. "Doesn't need to be anything fancy. I'm happy to eat in the hotel bar, honestly."

Lila met my gaze. "Are you sure? I'm sure we can find something nicer."

"Do *you* want do?"

"I'd *like* to," she said cautiously. "But if you're tired or..." Chewing her lip, she trailed off.

I thought about it, then rolled my shoulders. "You know what? Let's find something nice."

The way her face lit up made my breath hitch. Did she... Did she want to go somewhere upscale with me? Or did she just not want to settle for the hotel bar?

I mean, going to a nice restaurant together didn't necessarily mean going on a date.

But it also didn't necessarily *not* mean that, either.

As I freshened up to go out, a conversation drifted through my mind.

"It took her four dates to realize we were even dating," my teammate Carly Nelsson had laughed. "I swear, every woman I know who's dated women has the same story."

Okay. Maybe they did. But Lila wanting to go someplace nice for dinner didn't mean she was trying to take me out on a date. Neither did taking me to lunch to get my mind off my asshole ex. Or hitting the ice with me so I could think about something other than him.

She came to the All-Stars with you, doofus. This is what you want.

I studied her as she fixed her hair in the mirror beside the TV.

Was I reading too much into this? Was it wishful thinking?

Yeah, I'd asked her to come with me because I wanted her and hoped she reciprocated, but I was so bad at this. So new to dating women. Not that men had been any easier to read, but that didn't stop me from feeling utterly clueless or hoping Lila was taking the lead.

Maybe...

Maybe that was what she was doing? By suggesting dinner out?

"We were halfway through dinner," Sara James had said, rolling her eyes. "And she suddenly asks, 'wait, is this a date?'" She'd facepalmed. "Um, duh? How much clearer did I have to make it?"

"Ready to go?" Lila asked, snapping me out of my thoughts.

"I, um..." Oh my God, she looked amazing in that suit. And had she put on a touch of makeup, too? I shook myself. "Yeah. Yeah, I'm ready. Let's, uh..." I looked around for my phone and keycard, which I found on a nightstand. "Let's go."

I headed for the door, but those stupid, ridiculous questions kept beating on the inside of my skull alongside those stories my teammates had told. Were they going to keep pecking away at me all through dinner? Because *that* would help me relax and unwind.

I reached for the door but hesitated. "Uh. Before we go..."

"Hmm?"

"Is this, um..." I sensed her watching me, but I couldn't quite make myself look at her.

"Is this, what?" she prodded gently.

I swallowed hard as my cheeks burned. "I, uh..." Then I shook myself and laughed nervously. "Never mind. Never—we should get going."

Once again, I reached for the door. I still didn't get my hand on the handle, though, this time because Lila's gentle touch to my elbow halted the motion.

"We still have time." Her voice was softer than I'd ever heard it. "If something's bothering you, let's deal with it now instead of out there."

Okay, that made sense. And I wouldn't be any less awkward trying to ask in public. If anything, I'd be way more likely to just not ask, which was probably the best-case scenario, because if we—

"Sabrina?"

I closed my eyes and pushed out a breath. Then I turned to face her, and despite the fluttering in my stomach, I met her gaze.

Somehow, I found my voice, and I whispered, "When you suggested we go get dinner... just the two of us..."

Goddammit. So much for finding my voice.

Lila's eyebrows rose as she inclined her head. "Mmhmm?"

I swallowed. "Did you... Were you, like, just suggesting we go get something to eat? Or..."

The corner of her mouth twitched slightly, and I thought

some color rose in her face. "Or was I asking you out on a date?"

Hoping a mute response would be less embarrassing or awkward, I nodded.

Lila held my gaze, pressing her lips together as the pink in her cheeks deepened. "I... I mean, I kind of thought..." She gulped. "That's why we're here, isn't it?" She gestured around us.

"Um..." Oh. Fuck. This was what I'd wanted, yes, but now that it was happening—oh, God, I didn't know what I was doing. My heart was pounding harder than it had in the last minutes of our Olympic gold medal game. Lila was chewing her lip, studying me as if she were trying to figure out what to say to salvage the moment.

She took a breath and pushed her shoulders back. "Maybe I should phrase it like this—if I said I was hoping it *was* a date, and that that's what I kind of thought this whole *weekend* was—would you still want to go?"

I blinked, caught off guard by the bluntness. And by how oblivious I'd been to, well, everything. "I..."

"It's okay if you say no," she said quickly. "If you're not interested, and you don't want—"

"I'm not really interested in going out." I stepped closer and put a hand on her waist. "But I like the 'date' part of the equation."

And then I kissed her, stifling a startled yelp with my lips a second before she relaxed against me. Her fingers slid up into my hair, and the barely audible moan almost melted my spine.

Lila's lips had no business being that soft. Her touch had

no business being that perfect, her fingertips leaving goose bumps in their wake as she ran them through my hair. She was such a badass on the ice, but like this... wow. She was just so gentle and perfect. The few times in my life that I'd kissed a woman, it had felt right and magic in ways it never did with a man.

Kissing Lila Hamilton? Oh my God.

I ran my hands up her back, and her barely audible sigh turned my knees to liquid. Was this real? Oh, fuck. This was real. This gorgeous, amazing woman really was kissing me, and somehow... Somehow I wasn't fainting.

After an eternity, and still somehow too soon, she drew back. "So, um..." She sucked her lower lip into her mouth as she held my gaze with smoldering blue eyes. "Instead of going to dinner, you game to stay in and order room service?"

The shiver that ran through me had my toes curling in my shoes. "I like that idea." I drew her back in for another long, mind-blowing kiss. How was this woman so *hot*?

She broke the kiss again, and her eyes were absolutely on fire now. She was a little out of breath as she said, "As long as we're staying in, we don't need to be dressed up, do we?"

I licked my lips. "We don't need to be dressed at all."

Lila's eyebrows flicked up as if she hadn't expected that.

But then she grinned and started unbuttoning her blouse.

CHAPTER 23

LILA

Sinking naked onto this hotel bed with Sabrina was incredible and surreal. It wasn't the first time I'd seen her undressed —came with the territory in hockey—but I'd never had my hands on her before. I'd never run my fingers through her hair or slid my palms down her back and over her perfect butt.

And I had *definitely* never felt her hungry, *aggressive* touch. I didn't think I'd ever felt sexier in my life than I did in that moment—on my back with Sabrina McAvoy on top of me, her strong hands pinning my wrists to the pillow as she kissed down the side of my neck.

"Oh my God," I breathed. "I didn't... I didn't expect you to be a top."

Her laugh was a hot breath across my skin. "Surprise?"

I was halfway to delirium already, and laughing just made me higher. Then she was kissing me again, and when I parted my legs, her hips settled between my thighs.

She released my wrists and slid one hand up into my hair

while the other arm supported her weight. Now that my arms were no longer restrained, I wrapped them around her, tracing her perfect, powerful body and soft, warm skin. I hadn't been kissed or touched like this in ages. Had I *ever* been kissed or touched like this? Because I swore being with Sabrina was a whole new experience. My nerve endings lit up as if they'd never been touched this way before, and I couldn't help moaning into her kiss because oh my God, she was an incredible kisser.

Sabrina broke the kiss and pushed herself up. When she met my gaze, trembling and breathless, there was a hint of shyness in her eyes that caught me off-guard. She'd been so toppy from the moment we'd kissed, but now... this?

"Hey." I caressed her cheek. "You okay?"

"Yeah. Yeah, I'm good." She laughed self-consciously as a blush bloomed in her cheeks. "Just, um... Just fair warning—I haven't been with a lot of women."

"But you've been with some?"

She nodded, uncertainty still written across her beautiful face. "Just... not a lot." With an embarrassed laugh, she added, "What can I say? Denial isn't just a river in Egypt."

I smiled. "I get that. But you know what you like, right?"

Another nod.

I lifted my head and kissed her. "So... do that. If I like something different, I'll let you know."

A self-conscious look lingered, but then she smiled. "All right. Just, you know, keep your expectations—"

I cut her off with another kiss, gripping her hair tight as I explored her mouth all over again. When I was absolutely sure I'd kissed the uncertainty right out of her, I broke away just enough to breathlessly murmur, "You're doing just fine. Trust me."

Her lips curved against mine, and then we were off and kissing again. Just making out, and touching each other, and breathing each other in, and...

I could get lost in this woman. I *was* lost in this woman. She was more aggressive than I expected, but not overbearing in the least. And if this was her when she was uncertain, then once she found her confidence—ooh, that was going to be a ride.

She broke the kiss and started down my neck. I let her explore, just moaning and writhing under her as she touched and teased and tasted me all over. Given her cautions about her inexperience, I wasn't sure if she'd be game to go down on me.

Turned out she was *seriously* game for that.

As she pushed my thighs apart and went to town, I could barely find my breath. I didn't know what she was so worried about—her mouth was spectacular. Whether it was experience, instinct, or just some kind of divinely bestowed talent, Sabrina knew exactly how to lick and tease my pussy. Maybe out of tentativeness, maybe out of a desire to savor everything she did, she absolutely worshipped my clit with her tongue. Slow circles. Just the right amount of pressure in some places and lightness in all the others.

There were times in my past where this felt good, having a woman go down on me, but an orgasm wasn't going to happen. This... This was not going to be one of those times. Regardless of Sabrina's uncertainty or her lack of experience, I could already feel that telltale build; that electricity that meant she could absolutely send me over that edge.

God, yeah, baby. Take me there.

I reached back, searching for something to hold on to, but the hotel headboard didn't have anything I could grab. I couldn't find any purchase, so I clung to the pillow instead, trying not to levitate off the mattress.

Sabrina kept my hips still with her strong hands while her lips and tongue sent me into the stratosphere.

Sometimes I felt rushed at this point. Like I needed to hurry up and come before the woman I was with ran out of patience.

But with Sabrina...

God, there was nothing rushed about this. She was just as slow and decadent as I liked it, and I had this sense that I could enjoy the ride. That I could hover near that edge for a while, savoring the build instead of barreling through to the climax.

For long minutes, I indulged, blissed out on the magic she was working, all the while knowing my orgasm was well within my reach any time I wanted it.

Little by little, she pushed me closer to the edge. Close enough that I wouldn't be able to hold myself back if I tried.

I still tried... sort of. I loved the build. Loved the patient crescendo. Loved the feeling of being so close, so damn close, right on the edge, one breath away from letting go but not quite ready.

"Sabrina..." Her name rolled off my tongue like a curse and a plea in one. "God... Keep... Keep doing... Just like that." My hips bucked off the mattress like they had a mind of their own. "Oh, baby, I'm gonna come. Keep..." I bit my lip and arched my back as she slowly, gently, relentlessly took me higher.

Finally, I let myself fall, and I cried out things I didn't even understand as Sabrina kept me coming and coming until I breathlessly begged her to stop.

She brought me down as gently as she'd taken me up, easing off and relaxing her iron grip on my hips.

My head was just starting to clear when she moved up to kiss me, and I moaned as I wrapped my arms around her and searched her mouth for more of myself. Fuck. Her kiss had been amazing before. When her tongue tasted like my pussy and she was this turned on—this was heaven.

She pushed herself up and gazed down at me, a lopsided grin curling her kiss-swollen lips. "Maybe I'm not as bad at this as I thought."

I laughed, dizzy and delirious. "So humble."

"Meh. Humility is overrated."

"Uh-huh." I smoothed her hair. "Well, you've got every right to be smug and cocky, because your mouth is amazing."

She actually blushed, and it was ridiculously cute.

I wrapped my arms around her again, and this time I rolled her onto her back. Now that I was on top, I settled my hips between her parted thighs and kissed her, long and deep.

When I started down her neck, she whimpered, arching under me.

"Your mouth is *awesome*," I murmured against her skin. "But now it's my turn."

And I didn't stop until she came so hard she almost cried.

If landing naked in bed with Sabrina had been surreal, lying her beside her like this—still naked and now fully satisfied—was mind-blowing.

Faith was going to be insufferable once she found out. I could almost hear her chanting, "I told you so! I told you so!"

Eh. Worth it. Yeah, my roommate had been right, but I'd wound up having sex with Sabrina, so I couldn't complain.

I ran my fingertips down Sabrina's arm. "Are you going to be able to skate tomorrow?"

She laughed, sounding a little drunk as she curled next to me and slid a hand over my stomach. "I'll be fine. Long as I'm not this dizzy tomorrow."

I chuckled and stroked her hair. "Can't make any promises."

Her amusement was a soft, warm huff against my neck. "Eh. Worth it."

I just smiled, and we lay there in blissed-out silence for a while. After five orgasms between us—two for me, three for her—it was almost hilarious how worried she'd been about being good in bed. Her mouth, her fingers, how responsive she was—I had no complaints. And I was sure she'd have wrung a third orgasm out of me if that second one hadn't been so intense, it left me too sensitive to touch. Maybe later? In the morning? Something told me this wouldn't be our only opportunity to send each other to space.

Then she'd just gain even more experience. And probably kill me in the process, but—eh, what a way to go.

"So you really haven't been with a lot of women?" I asked

after a while.

"No." She shifted, lifting her head off my shoulder and propping herself up in her elbow. A few unruly strands of dark hair tumbled alongside her face as she met my gaze. "I hooked up with girls now and then when I was younger. Especially in major juniors, since I was far from home. But I didn't date a woman until after my divorce."

"Huh. So... you said you're not bi, right?"

She nodded. She studied me, brow pinched, but before I could ask my question, she beat me to it: "How did I end up married to a man?"

Face warm, I nodded. "I'm just curious. You don't have to answer."

"It's okay." She absently ran the backs of her fingers along my arm. "Like I said before, I spent years time telling people I wasn't a lesbian. So many people thought I was because I played hockey. Which is stupid—there's plenty of straight girls in hockey, you know?"

"Oh, I know." I groaned melodramatically. "The number of times I've had a crush on someone, and she turned out to be straight..."

Sabrina laughed. "Right? So I think I spent so much of my life saying, 'I'm not a lesbian,' that I never really gave myself a chance to consider if I was. And like, as a teenager, I experimented a little. But every time I fooled around with a girl, I'd go right back to boys because I was so afraid of being a lesbian." She rolled her eyes and sighed. "I think if I'd under-stood bisexuality, I'd have been a bit more open-minded about it. I'm not bi, but if I'd known that was an option, maybe I wouldn't have been so resistant to exploring things with women." She paused. "It... probably makes more sense in my head."

"No, it makes sense. So you dated men even though you weren't into them?"

"I *thought* I was into them. I thought some guys were good-looking, and the sex was all right. Sort of."

"Sort of?"

"Well..." She blushed again. "Ty really hated when I did anything for myself. Like if I played with my nipples while he went down on me, or touched myself while he was..." She rolled her eyes and shook her head. "At least he was good at what he did, because he sure hated me doing anything to help."

"What?" I scoffed. "Why would he be upset about that? It's hot as hell!"

"It is! But he was—I don't know. I had a boyfriend before him who was the same way. Like it made him all insecure or something."

I raised an eyebrow. "So, you helping yourself along meant he couldn't get you there or something?"

"Basically."

I snorted. "Wow. Fragile much?"

"Right? Anyway, *besides* that part, Ty was good in bed, so our sex life was... It *was* pretty satisfying. It just took me way too long to realize that what I felt when I looked at a woman"—she looked right in my eyes—"*that* was attraction."

"Huh." I thought about it. "I never had any illusions about being into guys, so I wouldn't know what that's like. But that must've been eye-opening when you figured it out."

"Like you wouldn't believe."

"How was being married, then? Wasn't he, um..."

"Kind of a dick?"

I laughed. "Well, you said it, not me." Turning serious, I asked, "Was he that much of an asshole? I mean, you married the guy. Did you two even like each other?"

"At first. But I think we both went into it with ulterior motives."

I raised my eyebrows. "Yeah?"

"Mmhmm. He wanted the prestige of being Doran McAvoy's son-in-law, and... I don't know, I think he had some weird thing about wanting to make a woman like me into his submissive housewife."

"Oh for fuck's sake." I huffed and rolled my eyes. "Seriously?"

"Yep. The girlfriend he had before me was absolutely his type—very submissive and meek. She was perfectly happy to just be a hockey wife and a mom. Which is fine, you know? If that's what makes someone happy, more power to them. But I think for Ty, he liked the challenge. He liked taking someone who had ambition and drive, and making her into what the woman before me would've willingly been."

"So he kind of screwed over both of you."

"Oh, big time. She was his girlfriend since major juniors, and everyone was sure they'd get married. Then he suddenly dumps her, and two months later, he's hitting me up."

"Sounds like a big red flag."

"In hindsight? Absolutely. But he fed me a bunch of bull-shit that she'd cheated on him, and he was laying on the charm with me."

I tilted my head. "You said you had an agenda, too."

Avoiding my gaze, Sabrina nodded. "Yeah. I wanted out of Buffalo, and I wanted to put some distance between me and the family. Then here comes this good-looking hockey player who's as passionate about the sport as I am, and he's playing in Texas." She grimaced. "I don't think he ever loved me—just my name. But I'd be a hypocrite to criticize him for that, because I think the only thing I really loved was the chance to go someplace else and start a new life." Sabrina looked in my eyes. "We both made a lot of mistakes. And we weren't good *for* each other or *to* each other. I can blame him for some things, but definitely not all of it."

"Sounds like it's good you got out when you did," I said. "For both of your sakes."

"Definitely."

I studied her for a moment. "At the risk of being way too personal..."

Sabrina ran her fingertips over my breast. "Pretty sure we're long past that."

I bit my lip as goose bumps rose all over my body from her touch. "Okay. Okay, fair point. But still, I'm just curious—if you weren't into men, how did that work with Ty? Like..." I gestured at her and myself.

"In bed?"

"Yeah."

She shifted onto her back, resting her hand behind her head on the pillow. As I settled on my elbow beside her, draping an arm across her flat stomach, she gazed up at the ceiling. "It wasn't as bad as you might think. Honestly, Ty was pretty good in bed. The sex was one of the few things I couldn't really complain about." She shook her head. "But that was just because it felt good. Physically. I... I mean, I made sure he was satisfied, but I was really never as *into* him as I am with women."

"Really?"

She nodded. "Like, the way I felt about him when he was making me come didn't hold a candle to the way I'd feel when I saw a woman I thought was hot. I don't know how I didn't make that connection for so long, but..." She chewed her lip. "This is going to sound bad, and it is bad, but Ty is part of the reason I figured out I wasn't bi or straight after all."

"How so?"

"Because he liked to put me in my place by letting me know how hot other women were. Like he wanted to remind me that he could do better or something."

I wrinkled my nose. "What a charmer."

"I know, right?" She rolled her eyes. "Anyway, we were watching a movie one night, and he's kind of been prickly all day. There's an actress on the screen who he's made comments about before, and in the movie, the guy just isn't into her character at all. Like he's totally oblivious to how hot she is and whatever. I guess Ty wanted to get under my skin, because he says, 'I don't know what this dude's problem is—I would put her on the counter and lick her until her soul left her body.'"

The laugh burst out of me before I could stop it, and I clapped a hand over my mouth. "Oh my God. Seriously?"

She was giggling too, and nodded. "Yep. I think he just wanted to get a rise out of me or something. But like, as soon as he said it, the only thing I could think was... 'yeah, me too'."

I straightened. "Oh, really?"

Her face was bright red, and she laughed as she nodded. "Yeah. I, um... The more he started making comments like that, the more I started realizing that I felt the same about women as he did. But I didn't feel that way about him. Or any other man."

"Whoa." I blinked. "That's a hell of a way to figure out your sexuality."

"Tell me about it. So after we separated, that's when I got involved with Kendra. Wasn't my first time with a woman, but it was the first time I went into it thinking, 'okay, I might actually *be* a lesbian and I'm okay with that.'"

"And then you dated her?"

"For a little while, yeah." Sabrina exhaled. "I was still working through my divorce, and I was also focusing hard on getting back into condition to play hockey, starting my PTO in Seattle—all of that. So I wasn't in a good place to be pursuing anything."

"That makes sense. Did it end on good terms?"

She shrugged. "I don't think she was happy about it." With a wince, she added, "I think, judging by some of the stuff she's said to reporters, she believes I was just in it to get a feel for being a lesbian."

"I've heard that," I admitted. "But that doesn't seem like something you'd do."

"No. It wasn't. It was just really, really bad timing in a lot of ways, and I wasn't as emotionally available as she deserved. I was over Ty, but I also wasn't, if that makes sense."

"It does," I whispered, covering her hand with mine. "But you're in a better place now?"

"I am." She looked at me through her lashes, and a small

smile came to life. "My divorce is over and done with. My career is on the rails. I know who I am now. So... yeah. I'm in a way better place." She swept her tongue across her lips. "That doesn't mean we have to date. This can just be—"

"It just started." I brought her hand up and kissed her palm. "It doesn't need a name or a definition tonight."

Uneasiness crept into her expression.

I released her hand, then curved mine behind her head and pressed a soft kiss to her lips. "I'm not going to show up outside your house with a U-Haul. We're teammates, and we had a bit of a rough start, and we're right in the middle of the chaos of the regular season. I'm fine with letting this evolve at its own speed."

That must've been the right answer, because tension I hadn't even noticed in her started to unwind. "Okay. Okay, that works. Because..."She bit her lip. "Whatever this is, I want to do it. But... one step at a time."

I smiled. "Sounds perfect to me. Especially because I'm really enjoying this first step."

She laughed, and the rest of that tension melted away. "I am too." She slid closer to me. "We should get up at some point. Maybe order room service or something. But..." Her lips brushed mine. "I'm not in any hurry if you aren't."

"Mmm, no." I tangled my fingers into her hair. "I'm not in any hurry at all."

"You know," Sabrina said, "if someone had told me when we first came to Pittsburgh that we'd end up like this? I'd have asked what they were on."

Feigning surprise as I picked up my wineglass, I said, "Whaaat? You didn't see all the romantic writing on the wall?"

She chuckled as she continued thumbing through the leatherbound menu. "Look, I've never been good at picking up the most blatant clues. If that was a reverse-psychology attempt at subtle flirting?" She shook her head. "You'd have been barking up this tree forever."

I laughed, almost choking on my wine. "Hmm, yeah, I'm oblivious too. Maybe that's why we had to start out the way we did." I winked. "So it was obvious when we started to like each other."

She grinned across the white-linen draped table for two. "I don't know how obvious it was. I'm not kidding—you probably wouldn't have been out of line to hold up a sign saying, 'Sabrina, I'm trying to flirt with you,' and even then I'd have missed it."

"Oh, me too. I am the worst at picking up clues." Grinning, I added, "But the contrast between how we started and how it's going—I mean, it does help, you know?"

Her laughter was seriously the cutest thing ever. I couldn't get enough of the way her eyes danced when she laughed, or the way her whole face lit up when she smiled.

God. We've been doing this for three days, and I have it so bad for you already.

Some part of me tried to be alarmed by that, but I just ignored it. I hadn't dated anyone in a while, and I liked these ridiculous fluttery feelings. If things fizzled in a couple of months or whatever—eh, I'd cross that bridge when I got to it.

Right now, I was completely stupid for Sabrina, and I didn't fight it. I straight up basked in it, because why not?

"So." Sabrina gestured with the menu. "Any thoughts on something to eat?"

Jesus, the innuendo was *right* there.

I shook myself and cleared my throat. "Um. I..." I looked down at my own menu. "Right. Food." I skimmed over the words. "The website said this place has amazing steak."

She made a sound that wouldn't have been out of place in bed. "Ooh, I could go for a steak. Especially after the tournament."

"Oh, come on," I teased as I brought up my glass for a drink. "Don't tell me you're tired. It was only three games of three-on-three.

She flipped me off, and I almost choked on my wine.

"You deserved that," she muttered.

I just rolled my eyes.

Truthfully, I wasn't surprised she was tired. In between the sex we'd been having at every opportunity, she'd had media availability, meet-and-greets with fans, and the tournament. Our division had ultimately lost the tournament, but it was a close game right up until the end, and Sabrina had scored two beautiful goals. Shame about that unfortunate penalty Hartford's player had taken in overtime, which had given the Western Conference the chance to win.

I was about to ask her what she thought about that penalty—if she thought the player was reckless or just made a bad decision on the fly—when a woman in a pantsuit approached our table.

"Hello, ladies." She smiled in that over-the-top way we

were trained to do in front of cameras. "You're Sabrina McAvoy, right?"

Sabrina returned the smile, though hers was more friendly than phony. "I am."

The woman turned to me. "And Lila Hamilton, correct?"

"Yes." Media smile, right on cue.

She shook hands with each of us. "It's lovely to meet both of you. Listen, I'm doing some interviews and stories with players who've come to the All-Stars. Especially those who've brought partners." Her eyes flicked toward me, then back to Sabrina. "I don't want to assume, but you two are teammates, and you also seem quite... friendly." She smiled. "So is this a night out for a couple of teammates?" The reporter inclined her head. "Or a night out for a couple?"

Heat instantly rushed into my face. Jesus. Reporters could be intrusive, but they usually had a *little* more tact than that. Before I could even look to Sabrina to get a bead on what she thought we should say, she laughed and said, "Just a couple of friends."

The reporter seemed vaguely skeptical, judging by the way she glanced back and forth between us, but she let the subject drop. Shifting gears, she asked us a few benign questions about the All-Stars and our season with the Bearcats. The whole time, my stomach wound itself in knots, but I kept my smile in place.

I understood that we were public people, but I wasn't entirely comfortable with reporters asking us such intensely personal questions. Some of them did because they were shock jock types who liked to stir shit up. Others—like this one—just seemed to think our personal lives were easy breezy conversation. Even though women's hockey was as accepting as they came about gay players, there was still nuance and caution about coming out.

Mostly, though, it was Sabrina's answer that left me squirming in my seat. Even after the reporter had left and we continued through dinner, I still couldn't relax.

"Hey." Sabrina nudged my foot under the table. "You okay?"

"Yeah. Yeah. I'm... I'm good."

The upward flick of her eyebrow called bullshit on that.

"Not here." I made a subtle gesture around us. "When we get back to the room. It's... I just don't like the way reporters pry, you know?"

Concern replaced the skepticism in her expression, but she nodded and let the subject go. I felt bad about that; no one liked the ominous feeling of "we need to talk about something in private," and it was especially uncomfortable early in a relationship.

But we were public people and I didn't want this conversation to be for public consumption. I just hoped Sabrina forgave me for the uneasiness.

I steered the conversation away from the subject until we'd left the restaurant. It was only a few blocks from our hotel, so we'd walked. I let her set the pace on the way back since she'd skated hard today, but she seemed comfortable with her usual brisk gait. Worked for me.

The distance between the restaurant and the hotel also meant we had some relative privacy. Now that we were out of anyone else's earshot, I cleared my throat. "So you, um... You don't want anyone to know we're together." I hoped it didn't sound like an accusation, though I was pretty sure my disappointment bled into the words. "I mean, if you don't want them to know, I get it. I'm out, so I don't care if..."

She smiled and put her hand on my back, a gesture that could easily be interpreted as platonic if someone cared enough to notice us. "I want people to know. Trust me—I do. But let's keep it to ourselves for a little while first. So we can enjoy it without the cameras in our faces for a bit, you know?"

I straightened. "Oh. Right. I..." I couldn't say I hadn't thought of that—it had been a reporter asking about us after all—but I also kind of *hadn't* thought of it. Even three seasons into my professional career, it was still surreal that anyone with cameras actually cared about women's hockey. We'd usually get some passing attention at the Olympics, and a week later, everyone would forget for another four years women played hockey at all. And like, female hockey players dating or even marrying each other was seriously common. The thought of anyone caring that two players were together —caring for more than the duration of the Olympics, anyway —was mind-blowing.

"I guess that makes sense," I whispered.

"It does suck, though," she admitted. "And there's also the issue that the tabloids still jump at every chance to be the first to out me with a new girlfriend," she said softly. "I had that one relationship after Ty, and they've been frothing at the mouth to write about me dating another woman. We're... This isn't going to go unnoticed."

"*Oh.*" I almost chafed my arms as my skin crawled. "I forgot about that."

"I've tried to," she muttered. "But every time anyone sees

me anywhere near another woman, I start getting emails and DMs from people who want to know if there's a 'story.'"

I cocked a brow. "Have you gotten any about us?"

With a somewhat sheepish expression, Sabrina nodded. "A few."

"Wait, really? You have?"

She avoided my gaze and nodded again. "Yeah. I guess people have noticed that there was some animosity between us, and now there isn't. Plus we've kind of been joined at the hip for a while, *especially* since we got to the All-Stars."

Warmth rose in my face. "Damn. And here I thought we were being subtle."

"We probably are," she said with a quiet laugh. "But when people are sniffing around for something..."

"Ugh." I groaned. "Why do they even have to care?"

Sabrina half-shrugged. "Because we're public people, so everyone assumes we're public property? And I don't care how accepting the League is—people still think queerness is scandalous."

At that, I laughed, and I slid my hand over hers as I offered a cheeky grin. "Are you suggesting there's something scandalous about us?"

She returned the grin. "We could be."

"Ooh, I like the way you think." I licked my lips. "Any chance you want to head back up to the room when we get to the hotel?"

Still grinning impishly, Sabrina arched an eyebrow. "So we can put on a game and watch hockey?"

I elbowed her gently. "Shut up, and let's get out of here."

CHAPTER 24

SABRINA

Good thing the All-Star tournament hadn't been as intense as a regular game. A lot of work, sure, but it wasn't exactly full-speed, make-it-count hockey. None of us put in a hundred percent during a game like that.

Which meant I could absolutely give a hundred percent to more interesting activities this evening.

As soon as we were in the room, I pressed Lila up against the door and kissed her hard. She gave as good as she got, tangling her fingers in my hair and moaning as she explored my mouth.

"Well, Miss Hamilton," I purred as I slid my hands beneath her blouse. "*Are* you and Miss McAvoy an item?" I traced the pad of my thumb over her clothed nipple. "Because you two seem... friendly."

"Hmm, I don't know where you'd get the idea we're more than friends." She nipped my lower lip. "Can't... Can't even imagine where you might think that."

I laughed, then claimed her mouth again. She was still grinning and so was I, but our lips quickly softened into a long, decadent kiss. I still couldn't get over how Lila kissed. How she could be so soft and gentle, but also firm and demanding—not quite aggressive, but nowhere near submissive.

Clothing put up a bit of a fight, but eventually, it was all scattered on the hotel room floor where it belonged. We tumbled onto the bed in a fit of laughter, which quickly turned into more kissing.

"You think..." She was out of breath, but she tried again, holding my gaze as she dragged her nails up my back. "You think they're on to something? That there's... some chemistry here?"

"Hmm, maybe?" I dipped my head to brush my lips across hers. "Might... Might need to do a bit more research."

"Yeah?" She arched under me, biting her lip. "Does that research involve orgasms?"

"Of course it does."

"*Fuck*, yeah."

I laughed, dizzy with arousal and playfulness and desire for this beautiful woman beneath me.

Lila parted her legs, and I settled over her, one thigh between hers and one of hers between mine. As I started rocking against her, she whimpered softly and dug her nails into my shoulders.

"That good?" I asked.

"Uh-huh." She arched under me, and then she was moving too, complementing my rhythm, just right. In no time, we found just the right angle and just the right rhythm, my clit rubbing on her thigh and hers rubbing on mine, and we made out as we moved together.

Every touch, every kiss, every ripple of electricity she sent through me—it was all-consuming, and I loved it. I couldn't get enough of her, and I wanted to make her come, and I wanted to come, and... God, yes, this was bliss.

Lila broke the kiss with a gasp, arching her back as she gripped my shoulders tighter. "Oh fuck, baby..."

"You almost there?"

She bit her lip and nodded.

I kept my rhythm exactly the same. Sometimes she liked to ride the edge for a while, sometimes she didn't. So I gave her what I knew would take her there, but let her decide when to let go.

Her fingers dug into my shoulders as she arched off the bed beneath me. "Fuck..."

Closing my eyes, I buried my face against her neck, and Lila made the most deliciously helpless sound as she fell apart beneath me. Her nails bit into my skin and her whole body trembled under me, her thighs clamping hard around mine as she whimpered into my hair.

As she started to relax, I slowed and stopped, not wanting to overstimulate her.

"Wow," she murmured. "Holy..."

I grinned and kissed beneath her jaw. "You're so hot when you come."

She squirmed under me. "So are you. So get on your back and let me make you come."

Laughing, I rolled onto my back, as soon as my shoulders met the bed, she was on top. She kissed me deep and hard, still breathless from her orgasm, and once she'd stolen *my* breath, she started working her way down my neck. Though I knew what she had in mind, she was in no hurry at all. She kissed all along my throat, then my collarbone. When she got to my nipples, she took her sweet time, teasing one with her mouth and the other between her fingers, then switching.

"I am getting so spoiled with you," I moaned.

"Why?" She ran the tip of her tongue around my nipple. "Because I can't keep my mouth off you?"

I bit my lip and squirmed beneath her. "Because you don't rush. Like... anything."

Lila huffed, her breath cool on my wet skin. "Who in their right mind would rush this?"

Before I could answer, her lips were around my nipple again, and the relentless attention from her tongue blanked my brain. Rush? Who said anything about rush? Nothing existed except Lila and all the incredible sensations she so effortlessly unleashed with her perfect touch.

She continued downward, kissing her way down my belly, and I whimpered as I parted my thighs. I knew exactly what was coming, and I swore I was halfway there from sheer anticipation alone.

Before she'd even reached my hip, I was playing with my nipples. I was still self-conscious about that at first, but one smoldering look from her—a glance at my fingers, then up at my eyes—told me just how sexy she found it.

So... I kept doing it.

And then Lila settled between my thighs, and...

Oh, my God.

The first time she'd gone down on me, she'd seemed...

explorative? Not tentative, but like she was testing the water. Seeing what I liked. What made me gasp and tremble.

This time?

Oh, fuck. Whatever cheat codes she'd been looking for the first time, she'd committed to memory. The way she'd swirl her tongue around my clit and send me almost to the edge, then back off and start over again, taking me just a little bit closer each time—she'd been incredible at edging me last time, but my God, it was like she knew exactly how to do it now. When I rocked my hips, searching for more of her talented lips and tongue, she moaned and gave me more.

I bit my lip and worked my nipples harder as she continued working her magic on my pussy, and it wasn't long at all before I was precariously close to that edge.

"Don't stop, baby," I whined. "Oh my God. Please... Just like..." I didn't even understand half of what I was saying, but she clearly understood the assignment: *keep doing exactly what you're doing, and you'll make me come.*

And she kept doing exactly what she was doing...

And I kept murmuring nonsense...

And...

She made me come.

Holy fuck, did she make me come. She held on to my hips and kept licking my clit just right to keep my climax rolling without making me too sensitive, and I was just... putty in her hands. Completely surrendered to the bliss Lila wrung out of me.

It was only as she came up and wrapped her arms around me that I realized how much I'd been crying out. As we sank into a breathless kiss that tasted like me, my throat was scratchy in that way that meant I'd been shouting.

I broke the kiss with a drunken laugh.

She tilted her head. "What's so funny?"

I combed my fingers through her hair. "Just... realized I might've just set us back on that whole 'let's keep this quiet' thing."

The laugh that burst out of her made my toes curl. This woman was just stunning. Eyes sparkling, she said, "Well, the people in the surrounding rooms definitely know *someone* just came like crazy. Doesn't mean they know *who*."

"Or who made her come like that." I lifted my head and kissed her again. "Can still be our little... screamy secret."

Lila snorted before claiming another kiss.

The truth was, I did want to shout this from the rooftops. I wanted everyone to know I was with Lila Hamilton (though maybe not the part where she was giving me earth-shaking orgasms).

And I would. We'd come out. We'd appear in public as a couple instead of just friends or teammates. Our team would know, and so would our fans, our friends, and—for better or worse—our families.

Eventually.

For now, though, I was more than happy to keep all this bliss between us.

<hr />

In the three weeks following the All-Star weekend, I really shouldn't have been surprised that, despite our best efforts...

people knew. Either Lila and I weren't being very subtle, or the hockey community was just completely used to the idea of teammates dating.

There were plenty of straight women in the League, as well as bisexual women who were with men, but lesbians like us were definitely well-represented, too. And unlike the men's league, there hadn't been any need for slow and steady acceptance of queer players in their ranks. It had taken literally over a century before one of the men had come out, and that was after he'd retired. It was almost three years later before an active player came out, and another decade on before two players became a couple. Every step of the way, there'd been controversy and people screaming about wokeness and other bullshit, but eventually, the men's league had reached a point where a handful of gay and bi men played and not many people cared.

In women's hockey, it just... wasn't an issue. Never had been.

Which was why it didn't really surprise me when our teammates started gently teasing us about "date nights," or when the team's travel coordinator had come right out and asked if we wanted to room together on road trips. We'd gone from despising each other to being friendly to... well. This.

No one had any issue with it because why should they? And anyway, they were probably just happy that we weren't butting heads anymore. If we were getting along well enough to spark rumors about dating—great.

"Whatever you're doing," Coach Reilly had told us a week or so after the All-Stars, "just make sure it's not on the ice. As long as it doesn't cause any disruptions on the team, I really don't care."

She probably gave that talk to any teammates who dated, but I imagined there was a little extra emphasis where we were concerned because of our past animosity. I could live with that.

Beyond our team, though, we weren't out, per se. We weren't going to any great lengths to hide it, but we weren't broadcasting it or strolling off the bus holding hands. We hadn't posted any couple photos on social media. We hadn't changed our relationship status.

I could live with that. I wasn't about to come out to a nosy reporter, but letting our teammates and coaches figure it out was hardly the end of the world. The rest would shake itself out over time.

Besides, Coach Reilly was right about not letting it cause any disruptions on the team. With the All-Star break behind us, the playoffs were coming up fast. We needed to be focused as a team, especially in our division where every point counted. We'd been comfortably in third place since before the All-Stars, but Detroit was creeping up fast again. They were only four points behind us now, and they were on a winning streak. If we fell apart now, they'd knock us into the wild card slot before we knew it.

We'd lost to Chicago last night, and now we were up against Seattle. We *had* to win this one, especially since Detroit was playing Albuquerque, which had fallen apart after their strong start in the League; they were now dead last in the Western Conference.

Fortunately, I knew how Seattle played, so I was ready for

them, but holy crap, they were putting up one hell of a fight tonight.

Halfway through the game, neither team had scored. Both sides were making drive after drive, but not getting past the other's defense. When they did get far enough for a scoring chance, the goalies played lights out. Seattle only had seven shots on goal. We only had nine.

Both sides were playing clean, too—there hadn't been any penalties so far, and it wasn't because the officials were letting things slide. Seattle always played a very disciplined game, as did Pittsburgh, so that was no surprise.

It was a grind, but we were determined, damn it. I didn't want to lose to my old team, and Pittsburgh didn't want to lose at all.

Seattle didn't want to either, though, so we all continued fighting for every millimeter of ice.

They kept us hemmed into our end long enough to wear down both our offensive and defensive lines. Finally, though, Euli got the puck away and into the neutral zone, and our exhausted skaters sprinted for the bench. My line went over the boards. Lila and Sims joined us.

Seattle managed to get some fresh bodies on the ice, too, but they still had a pair of forwards who hadn't been able to get off. They were tired, and we took full advantage.

Anastasia slapped the puck into the offensive zone. Laws, Lila, and I all zipped over the blue line, and after a brief battle against the boards, Lila had the puck. She sent it to me, and I fired it at the net. It didn't go in, but the rebound got away from the netminder. Anastasia seized it before a Seattle forward could get on it, and she passed it to Sims at the point.

I turned, ready to call for the puck, but something else caught my attention.

I wasn't usually dialed in to what the crowd was doing. I'd distantly notice if they were cheering or booing, and certain chants sometimes made it to my ears.

But every once in a while, there'd be a collective gasp and a ripple of concern. Even panic. Sometimes, if I was close enough to whatever had happened, I'd notice people banging on the glass, usually to get the refs' attention.

It was that collective gasp coming from our defensive zone, followed by a whistle, that spun me around so fast I almost lost an edge.

Instantly, I zeroed in on one of my teammates who'd gone down by the boards. One of Seattle's players stood over her, waving for the officials, who were hurrying that way. Connie, our trainer, was already on the ice and heading in the same direction.

Panic zipped through me, and I started in that direction as I quickly took stock of who was still standing, trying to figure out who'd gone down.

Sims... Laws... Anastasia...

Oh no.

Blood pounded in my ears as I crossed the ice toward the fallen player, and my stomach lurched up my throat as I confirmed what I'd already suspected:

Lila.

She was curled on her side, her face was contorted with pain. Connie was holding Lila's leg still, but the other moved, dragging Lila's boot along the ice as she writhed as much as Connie's grip allowed.

My heart slammed against my ribs. The leg Connie was pinning was Lila's bad leg.

Oh God. Please don't let it be her knee...

Not that any injury was ideal, but her knee could only take so much more before hockey was no longer an option.

The way Connie was holding Lila's leg, though, it had to be her knee. Maybe a hamstring or a quad? Something muscular instead of another tendon or ligament? At this point, a broken bone was probably more ideal than the alternative.

There was a little room beside Lila's shoulder, and after I'd tossed my stick and gloves away, I crouched next her. "Hey. Hey, take it easy. Don't move too much."

Still grimacing, she managed to open her eyes and meet mine. She reached for my hand, then paused as if she'd realized she still had on her glove. She tossed it away and grabbed on to my hand. I returned her tight grasp, not sure if she needed reassurance or a distraction. Maybe both.

Connie peered up at Lila. "What did you feel when you went down?"

Lila swallowed like she was trying desperately not to get sick. "It... like something gave?"

"Did anything pop? Crack?"

Lila shook her head slowly. "No. Not like last time."

That was a relief. Sort of. There were any number of things that could go wrong in someone's knee, and even the same injury didn't always feel or sound the same twice.

I squeezed her hand, and she gazed up at me, fresh tears in her eyes and her expression full of fear. Rubbing my thumb alongside hers, I shakily said, "You're going to be okay. You're in good hands."

She grimaced and nodded slightly. She was gripping my hand so tight it was almost painful, but I didn't complain.

Beside her, Connie, our team doctor, and one of the EMTs had a brief but animated conversation. Then the EMT gestured at his partner, who said something into his radio that I didn't understand.

The Zamboni gates opened, and my heart sank. The rattle of stretcher wheels on ice made my skin crawl.

"I'm going to get out of their way," I told her. "I'll be there as soon as I can, all right?"

Lila nodded. I gave her hand one more squeeze, then got up and skated a few feet away so the EMTs could do their job.

Deep down, I knew the decision to use a stretcher didn't mean the damage to Lila's knee was catastrophic. Sometimes we'd skate off the ice with help from our teammates. Even with lower body injuries. I'd skated off with a fractured tibia; hurt like hell, and I'd had to lean hard on two teammates, but I'd made it.

Sometimes, though, the people with letters behind their names decided it was more prudent to use a stretcher. Even if the player wasn't going to the hospital, it was best to get them off the ice without potentially making the injury worse.

That was what I told myself as the EMTs and trainers carefully moved Lila onto the stretcher.

It was what I told myself again as I gave her hand one last squeeze before letting go, and at least a dozen times as I watched them roll the stretcher out of sight. I wanted to follow. Cry. Puke. The last thing in the world I wanted to do was stay out here and play hockey.

But Lila was going to be an emotional wreck tonight no matter what. If the rest of the team fell apart over this, the guilt would be insult to very literal injury.

The Bearcats *had* to keep playing. *I* had to keep playing. I was the captain of this team, and everyone on it knew I was Lila's girlfriend. I had to be the one to lead us, keep my head together, and show everyone—my teammates, our fans, and my girlfriend—that we could play through this and anything else that came our way.

I called on the determination I'd had the day one of my teammates in major juniors had fractured her femur. She'd been rushed off to the hospital, and we'd all rallied as best we could, still managing to win that game even if it had been by the skin of our teeth. I'd managed to score even after I'd watched my linemate and close friend screaming in pain before they'd carted her off the ice.

I'd done it then. I could do it now.

I took a deep breath to pull myself together. When I turned to my shell-shocked linemates and Lila's rattled D partner, I could see the same determination in their eyes.

"We've got this," I told them. "Let's do it for Hams."

Nods all around.

I skated to the bench and conferred quickly with Coach Reilly. She kept my line out—we'd more than caught our breath from our intense shift—but she pulled Sims back and sent out the second defensive pair. We were down a blue liner now, and Coach wanted Sims to take a moment to strategize with the defensive coach. Sims probably didn't mind a few minutes to get her bearings; I sure didn't blame her.

Everyone was rattled. Everyone was worried about Lila.

And when we hit the ice again, we played our hearts out because we weren't losing our best defender *and* the game in the same night.

CHAPTER 25

LILA

My knee didn't swell up as much as it had last time. That was probably the one silver lining of this whole shitshow. Maybe I hadn't torn my ACL as bad. Maybe I hadn't torn it at all.

Except I was pretty sure I'd torn *something*. It hadn't felt quite the same as last time, but I'd had enough injuries to know they were all a little different. I'd sprained my left elbow three times, and though there'd been consistencies, they hadn't felt exactly the same.

Something had popped this time and last time. The pain was worse last time. Maybe because my knee had already been such a mess back then? Maybe because this tear wasn't as bad? Was that why it wasn't swelling like before?

The trainers had X-rayed it at the arena, and nothing was broken, but the EMTs had taken me to the ER for an MRI and a more thorough evaluation. Now I was just waiting for the results and pleading with the pain relievers to do something. I had no idea how bad I'd messed up my knee, and I was too afraid to check my phone and see how the game was going. Had the team been able to keep it together? I wouldn't have blamed them if they couldn't—I'd been in that position before myself—but I'd feel terrible. We needed points, especially against division opponents. We couldn't afford to lose tonight.

I didn't look. I just waited for someone to tell me. About the game. About my knee. About my career.

The only thing I knew for sure in that moment was that something was wrong, and I'd already been playing hockey on borrowed time. Lying in this hospital bed, I wiped a hand over my face. I wanted to believe this wasn't a career ender. I'd come way too far, damn it.

But when I was in this much pain—when it hurt to move my knee at all—it was hard to imagine ever lacing up my skates again. Just the thought of putting weight on it made me want to start crying again.

And God, I hated that I'd cried on the ice. One reporter had written a scathing article a couple of years ago about how women weren't suited for hockey, and their tears over injuries were exactly why. He'd waxed poetic about players in the men's league gritting their teeth through all kinds of awful pain, still remaining stoic even when they had to leave the game or go to the hospital. Then he'd included pictures of a few players from the WHPL, as well as one from the Olympics and one from major juniors (which was a *kid*, for Christ's sake), each showing a player in tears after an injury.

Never mind that there were *reams* of videos and images of male hockey players crying. Anything from a serious injury to an emotional retirement speech to a devastating loss or emotional win. Hell, one of the guys had choked up during a press conference when he found out—in front of the cameras —that his best friend had just been traded. Toxic masculinity was definitely present and accounted for in men's hockey, but there was no hockey without emotion, and sometimes emotion included tears. Nobody even cared. I mean, there was no faster way to reduce an entire arena of fans to sobbing than for a legendary player to tear up while making his final lap around the ice before retiring.

But yeah, we girls were too weak and emotional because Lisa Brewer cried after breaking her shoulder, Kolleen Gray shed some tears after a puck fractured her cheekbone, and Elsa Karlsson—who was *fifteen*—cried after a collision left her with three cracked ribs.

Whatever.

It was stupid, but it stuck with me, and all I could think now was that the video and images of me wiping away tears were filtering their way onto the social media of that reporter and his fans. That there were already posts about how I was evidence that women were too soft and delicate for this sport.

I didn't know why that was bothering me so much tonight. Maybe it was because fixating on whether or not someone cared about me crying was a lot less scary than wondering if I'd played my last game of hockey tonight.

I closed my eyes and rubbed them. This was hell. Couldn't they just come give me the prognosis? Like... now?

Except I also didn't want to know. I was afraid to know.

So I just focused on how much I didn't want to start crying again. Because in that moment... Fuck. I felt like breaking.

There was a knock at the door, and then a nurse peeked in. "Ms. Hamilton? You have a visitor."

Clearing my throat, I sat up a little. "I do?"

"Yes. Sabrina?"

That was the first good news I'd heard all night. "Send her in. Please."

The nurse disappeared, and then Sabrina stepped in, dressed in the suit she'd worn to the game.

"Hey." Her eyes were wide with concern. "How are you feeling? Have they said how bad it is?"

She reached out to me, but I put up a hand.

"I... still smell like the game."

Sabrina rolled her eyes and gently knocked my hand out of the way. "I don't care." Then she hugged me, and suddenly I didn't care either. I buried my face against her neck and held on for a moment, eyes squeezed shut as relief came my way for the first time since I'd gone down. Hot tears came too, but I just didn't care. Sabrina was here. She wouldn't give me grief for being emotional right now.

I was so damn glad she was here. So damn relieved. Especially since—

My brain caught up, and I drew back. "Wait, shouldn't you be at the airport?" The team had to be on their way there right now.

Sabrina grimaced. "I've got a flight first thing in the morning. I told Coach I wanted to be here with you, at least for tonight."

My stomach knotted with guilt. "But you need to sleep. You'll be exhausted and jetlagged when you get to—"

Her soft lips stopped mine. "I'm not going anywhere. It's a short flight. I'll be fine."

I let my shoulders slump. "I guess it's good I didn't do this right before a West Coast road trip."

Sabrina kissed my forehead, then eased down on the edge of the bed, sitting beside my uninjured leg. She gripped my hand tight. "I just wish I could stay beyond tomorrow morning."

Shaking my head, I whispered, "No. The team needs you."

"But I need to be with you."

I didn't know what to say to that. And as much as I didn't want the team to be without her—without their captain—I was so relieved she was here with me.

It did give me pause, though, and I squeezed her hand. "People will figure us out, you know. The public, I mean. That we're..."

Her soft, tired smile shut me up. Rubbing her thumb along mine, she said, "I'm not worried about it."

"You're not?"

She shook her head. "No. I wasn't going to broadcast it on social media or tell that weird reporter five minutes after we got together, but I mean, the team knows. If other people find out..." She trailed off and shrugged. "I'm more concerned about being here for you than about keeping us a secret."

At that, I relaxed a little. "Thank you for coming." I moistened my lips. "How, um... How did the rest of the game go?"

"It was a hell of a grind, but we pulled it off."

My spirits brightened minutely. "Yeah? What was the final score?"

"2-0." She smiled. "Sims got a gorgeous empty netter."

I managed a laugh. "Good. She's been losing her mind that she hadn't scored a goal yet."

"She has a truckload of assists, though."

"Yeah, but you know how it is."

Pursing her lips, she nodded. "Yeah. Well, she's got one now. And she got a primary assist on my goal."

I laughed. "Why am I not surprised you scored?"

She just smiled, leaned down, and kissed my forehead.

I was glad the team had held it together, and that my defensive partner had rallied too. I knew from experience how easy it was to shake apart after my D partner had been carted off to the hospital. That she'd managed a primary assist and a goal—empty net or otherwise—meant she hadn't spiraled like I'd done in the past. I could definitely breathe easier now knowing I hadn't thrown her off her game.

Sabrina continued filling me in on the game, which lifted my spirits a lot. It was good for the soul, listening to her tell me about Laws chirping at one of the opposing players until she goaded her into throwing a punch, and how Anya had made two highlight-reel saves during the third period.

"I'm not surprised the officials reviewed that second one." Sabrina shook her head. "We *all* thought the puck went in. I mean, most of *Anya* went in! But when they showed the video review..." She whistled. "I don't know how, but she kept that puck from crossing the line."

"Wow," I said with a laugh. "Where was it?"

"Caught between her skate and her pad. She said afterward she wasn't even sure if she'd felt it, but she was pretty sure that was where it was. Sure enough..."

"Jesus." The goalies had almost no peripheral vision and could barely feel anything through their gear. "I'll bet Seattle wasn't happy about that."

Sabrina laughed and shook her head. "I'm surprised their coach didn't get ejected, honestly. She's about as chill as any head coach, but oh my God..."

"What did she expect the officials to do, though? Make an exception when the puck didn't cross the line?"

"I think she was convinced it *did* cross the line, but Anya nudged it back over."

"Oh for God's sake."

"I know, right? So the refs threatened to eject her, and we got a power play because of the bench penalty for unsports-manlike. Kind of tilted the ice in our favor after that, but they still made us work for it."

"Those assholes."

"Seriously." She scowled playfully, then laughed. Sober-ing, she reached into her suit jacket and took out her phone. "Oh, and Detroit was losing last time I checked." She peered at the screen and tapped it a few times. Then her face lit up as she showed me the phone. "Looks like the hockey gods are working in our favor tonight."

I looked at the screen.

Detroit: 2

Albuquerque: 5

Time remaining: 0:32

I laughed as I relaxed back against the pillows. "I mean, stranger things *have* happened, but down by three with thirty-two seconds left? Looks like that winning streak is probably over."

"Let's hope. They've been—oh, they just scored." She frowned at the screen. "They'd better not turn that around..."

"Oh crap. Did I just jinx us?"

"Probably."

I rolled my eyes and laughed. Then she leaned closer and turned the screen so we could both watch. We couldn't see the game play out, but the League's app showed the timer, who had possession, and the score, so we could at least keep up.

The acronym EN appeared beside Detroit, indicating they now had an empty net.

"Ooh, they pulled their goalie," I murmured. "Think it'll help?"

"Maybe." We watched the time tick down.

Then Albuquerque's score changed to 6. A second later, the player's name popped up with ENG, indicating she'd scored an empty net goal.

With four seconds left on the clock.

We watched the last four tick down, then cheered quietly (we were in a hospital, after all). Our team still wasn't out of the woods yet—there were still plenty of games left, and it was still statistically possible for us to get knocked out of the playoffs—but we had a little more breathing room than we had earlier.

We. As if I'd be playing alongside the Pittsburgh Bearcats again this season.

"Hey." Sabrina took my hand. "What's wrong?"

I sighed and met her gaze. "It's probably a safe bet that

the Bearcats are going to the playoffs. But..." I gestured at my leg. "Somehow I don't think I am."

Sabrina frowned. "The important thing for you is to get better. We can take it from here."

"I know you can. But I don't want to leave the team in a lurch."

She was already shaking her head. "You're not. You played a key part in getting us this far. We wouldn't be where we are in the standings without you." She squeezed my hand and softly said, "We'll hold down the fort while you get better."

I smiled even as a lump rose in my throat. "You better. I did all that work, so..."

That made her laugh and roll her eyes, which helped to soothe that lump.

Right then, there was a knock at the door, and a second later, the doctor came in. My humor vanished along with the threat of tears, and I was suddenly in semi-panicked mode. This was it, and the doctor's grim expression wasn't promising.

"Well, we've got your results back, Ms. Hamilton." She turned on a flatscreen monitor and pulled up a few black-and-white images. I was more or less familiar with what a knee MRI looked like, but hell if I could actually decipher them.

"The good news," she said, "is that you didn't tear your ACL."

I released some of my breath. Not all of it, though, because I could hear the "but..." hanging in the air. "What's the bad news?"

The doctor gestured at one of the images. "You're looking at a grade three tear of the medial collateral ligament."

"The—" My brain caught up, and my heart sank. A torn MCL. Just what I needed. "Grade three? How bad is that?"

Her expression remained grim. "It's a complete tear. Honestly, I'm surprised your ACL didn't tear along with it— you don't usually see an MCL tear like this without additional tearing elsewhere."

I swallowed. "Oh. Guess I should... Guess I should buy a lottery ticket, then."

"I would."

Oh. Hell. I'd been joking, but... okay.

As much as I wasn't sure I could stomach the answer, I asked anyway: "Am I going to be able to play hockey again?"

The doctor was quiet long enough that I could already feel the crushing devastation setting in. This was it, wasn't it? My career was over. I'd finally done enough damage that there was no going back.

What do I do now?

I'd spent a lot of time last season wondering what post-hockey life would look like, and I still hadn't figured it out. Now I had to do it all the fuck over again. With the playoffs so close I could taste it.

I swept my tongue across my lips. "Am I still going to be able to play hockey?"

Her expression stayed grim. "You're looking at a lengthy recovery. At *least* six weeks after surgery before I would recommend even thinking about skating. Most likely longer."

"But I'll recover?" I asked. "Enough to play hockey?"

She pursed her lips. "I don't want to make promises based

on future predictions. We won't know the full extent of the damage until we're operating, and there's always the possibility of setbacks and complications. It is absolutely possible you will recover enough to return to playing professional hockey. It's also possible that you won't." Shaking her head, she softly added, "We just won't know until you get there."

I closed my eyes and pushed out a breath through my nose. I'd been around this block enough times that I knew her answers were the best she could offer. There were no guarantees in medicine. I knew players who'd come back from injuries that should've had them permanently sidelined, and others who'd had their careers ended by things that should've been easy to bounce back from. The human body was a mystery sometimes. A mystery and a shitshow.

"I'll write you a referral to an orthopedic surgeon," she went on. "The sooner you have surgery, the better your chances of a full recovery."

"Thanks," I said numbly.

She answered a few more questions for me, then left, and for the first time, I wished Sabrina hadn't come to the hospital. I wanted to crash and burn and wallow in self-pity and the possibility that the life I'd worked so hard to build was over. I wanted to be angry and devastated without anyone telling me things would be okay. Because there was a very good chance things *wouldn't* be okay, and I deserved to be pissed off about that for a while.

Sabrina got up and eased herself down on the edge of the bed. "Come here," she whispered, and wrapped her arms around me, drawing me in to lean against her.

I squeezed my stinging eyes shut.

"I'm sorry," she whispered as she stroked my hair. "This really sucks."

That hit me harder than a bullshit platitude would have, and I couldn't hold back the tears. The whole time I cried, she just held on. She didn't tell me it would be okay. She didn't tell me to stay strong or to think positive. She just kept stroking my hair and holding me together while I fell apart.

And despite wishing momentarily that she didn't see me like this...

I was grateful beyond words that she was here.

I should've been used to watching my own team's games on TV while I was home with my knee in a brace. That was how I'd spent most of last season.

It was different this time, though. Harder. I missed the game, but I missed my teammates even more. Especially Sabrina.

She stayed with me as much as she could. When the team was in town, I had both her and Faith helping me out. When they were on the road, I was on my own, though Euli's wife was amazing about helping me get to and from doctor appointments.

My surgery had gone well. The orthopedist was optimistic that they'd repaired my MCL, and they hadn't discovered any additional damage in the process. I'd have another post op appointment in a week, and depending on how that went, I'd start steadily rehabbing.

I wasn't going to play again this season, though. I'd known

that as soon as I'd gone down, and every medical professional in a fifty-mile radius had been sure to drive the point home. I *might* be ready for training camp, but that was far from a guarantee.

Fuck my life.

It was like watching my career going on without me. I'd had that feeling last season, too, but this time it had the added sting of watching my girlfriend from a million miles away.

In the beginning, I'd been so bitter and irritated that we were on the same team, constantly in each other's vicinity. Now I was a mess watching her on TV. I wanted her *here*.

No, that wasn't it. I wanted to be *there*. With her. Playing hockey alongside her. Sharing fist bumps on the bench and psyching each other up in the locker room, and then sitting together on the plane or curling up together in the hotel.

Now we were days away from the playoffs. Detroit had made a hell of a push to snatch the third place spot in the standings, but Pittsburgh had also rallied and jumped up to second, with both teams knocking Cleveland clear down to the first wild card spot.

Tomorrow night was the final regular season game. Next week, the playoffs would start.

And I wouldn't be there.

Well, I would be. I'd be in the owners' box along with some of the other injured players, sitting high up above the action and cheering helplessly while the game went on without me.

I'd get to see Sabrina before and after games, but only briefly. She'd be flying back and forth between Pittsburgh and Detroit for alternating games. If Pittsburgh won that series, then it would be another week or more of the same with another city. It could be a solid month before the season ended.

I wanted Pittsburgh to go all the way. If we could—if *they* could hoist the Cup in our first season, that would be amazing.

But I wouldn't lie—I would miss my girlfriend.

Worse... a month or so of barely seeing each other when we'd only been dating for a few weeks? Would she even still be interested in me after that?

Fuck. That was just what I needed. Lose my career and my girlfriend all at once.

The thing was, hockey was Sabrina's life. And professional hockey kind of made itself *every* player's life anyhow. The schedule was intense. The travel was constant. It was well-known throughout both the men's league and ours that being a hockey spouse was hard because of that. Some people thought, *oh boohoo, you're the wife of a millionaire pro athlete —cry me a river.* Not that anyone was a millionaire in our league, but even the spouses of the highest paid players in the men's league had to sleep alone more often than not for most of the year. Giant rocks, enormous houses, and piles of money only made up for so much of that.

Most of them made it work. I didn't know how happy they were, but they usually stuck it out one way or the other.

It probably helped that a lot of them had been together since high school. They had history. They'd made it through the U16 and major junior and college years. The pro hockey life had all the bullshit of those years with a sweet paycheck to make it all worthwhile.

Sabrina and I... we didn't have history. Not as girlfriends, anyway. Not even friends.

Burrowing deep in my gut was a cold fear and a miserable resignation that Sabrina wasn't coming back.

Oh, she'd be back in Pittsburgh. When the team came back, so would she.

But how much time would she spend with me?

She could be training. Skating. Working out. Running. Flying out. Flying back. Living her damn life.

Where was there room for the prickly asshole who'd thought the worst of her, grudgingly let her in, and given her a few short weeks of sex and togetherness before being laid up?

"Okay, someone's getting up in her own head." Faith's voice pulled me back into the present, and I peered up at her as she stepped into the living room. "What's wrong?"

"Besides everything?" I replied testily. Then I felt bad for snapping at her. "Just... this all sucks. My leg. Not playing hockey." I sighed. "Being away from Sabrina."

Faith watched me sympathetically as she eased herself down on the couch beside me. "Yeah. It does suck." She inclined her head. "And isn't it time for you to take another painkiller?"

I made an admittedly pathetic noise. My leg *was* aching, as were all the other muscles that didn't like sitting still this long. "I hate what they do to my head."

"I know you do. But you need to stay ahead of the pain."

"It isn't that bad." Not entirely a lie. "I'm good."

"Don't try to power through it. It'll just make your recovery longer." She paused. "Take half a pill now? See how you feel?"

I chewed the inside of my cheek, then nodded. "Okay. Half a pill."

She picked up my pill bottle off the coffee table and disappeared into the kitchen.

Rubbing my forehead, I exhaled. She was right and I knew it, but I still didn't like taking these stupid things. I was also scared to death of getting hooked on them. Nobody wanted to talk about how often that happened in hockey, but I'd watched it play out with my own eyes before. I didn't want to go down that road.

The cushions shifted beside me. "Lila. Look at me."

I turned to Faith, eyebrows up.

She reached over and squeezed my arm. "I know why you don't like taking them. But you should manage your pain."

"It's fine," I said. "I think I just overdid it a little yesterday."

"That's on-brand."

I managed a laugh, if a halfhearted one. Truth was, I hadn't done much yesterday, but I was supposed to be doing a lot *less*. Getting up and walking around on my crutches was good, especially to avoid blood clots and other unwelcome things like that, but I'd probably done more moving around than I should have. I couldn't help it—I was restless. I was a hockey player. I didn't *do* sitting around waiting for something to heal.

I dutifully took the pill she'd broken in half, though, washing it down with my water bottle. Then I blurted out one of the things that had been bothering me the most: "What if my career is over?"

Faith, like Sabrina, wasn't one for platitudes about how

positive thinking and all that bullshit would get me back on my skates. "It could be over," she admitted. "But you won't know that for a while. Don't start grieving your career when you still might have it."

"But I want to be ready if I don't have it," I said.

"Fair enough." She studied me. "You know, a career-ending injury isn't the same as a life-ending one."

I chewed my lip and nodded. She knew of what she spoke —her own career had ended abruptly thanks to a neck injury. She could still skate, and she still did great as a skills coach, but full-contact and full-speed play was off the table for her.

"I know it isn't," I said quietly. "I just... don't know what to do next."

"It's a tough thing to figure out," she admitted. "And I won't lie—I still miss being able to play. The adjustment period sucked. I won't blow smoke up your ass and tell you you'll magically be okay with not being okay enough to play hockey."

Closing my eyes, I exhaled. That was surprisingly liberating. Sometimes all I needed to hear was that I didn't have to be happy with the cards life dealt me. After a moment, I faced her. "I'm also worried about what this is going to do to me and Sabrina."

Faith's eyes widened. "What do you mean?"

"I mean..." I told her everything I'd thought about earlier, with Sabrina's demanding schedule and being separated as much as we were. "Even when she's home, there's no guarantee we'll see each other. Sometimes she just needs to sleep, you know?"

Faith nodded.

"I'm just... I'm afraid she'll... I don't know if saying she'll forget about me is the right way to describe it, but that's what it feels like."

It sounded so stupid when I said it out loud, and I cringed, expecting Faith to roll her eyes and tell me what a dumbass I was.

Instead, my friend regarded me silently for a long moment. Then she reached over and clasped my hand in hers. "Don't take this as me telling you this all in your mind or you're imagining things, okay? But one thing I learned when I hurt my neck was that sometimes, when you're dealing with a crisis"—she tipped her head toward my leg—"it can seem a lot bigger than it is. Like it's going to last forever and never get better and everyone around you is going to leave you behind."

I swallowed hard. It did feel like that—like this was never going to end, and I was always going to be in post-op limbo.

"It also makes everything else seem bigger," she went on, keeping her voice as gentle as her grasp on my hand. "It isn't because you're being dramatic or projecting or whatever—it's because you already have so much on your plate, even adding some minor stress is overwhelming."

"So... straws and camels' backs."

"Exactly. So I suspect that while you're here worrying that Sabrina is going to forget about you, or that a few weeks of not seeing much of each other will be something you can't come back from..." Faith offered a soft smile. "Your girlfriend is probably just counting the hours until she can be with you again."

My throat tightened around my breath, and I avoided my friend's gaze.

She gave my hand another squeeze. "Remember, there's two people in this relationship. It's not just you. If Sabrina is worth being your girlfriend, then she also understands that she has to pull her weight too. I mean, if she was injured, would you expect her to be putting a hundred percent into the relationship?"

"I..." Some warmth rushed into my face as I sheepishly admitted, "No. Of course not."

"Right. And right now, you're in a position where you have to focus a lot of energy on recovering while she's focusing her energy on the playoffs. Neither of those things a forever. You give her space and understanding while she concentrates on hockey for a few weeks. If she's the kind of girlfriend I think she is, she'll do the same while you're recovering."

"God, I hope you're right."

"Pfft. I'm always right."

That brought a laugh out of me that gave me more relief than anything this pain pill could. "I'm going to ask your wife about that."

"Don't you dare." She let go of my hand and huffed melo-dramatically.

I snickered, but as I sobered, I said, "Maybe I should suggest we go somewhere after the playoffs. Like take a vaca-tion. You know, so we have something to look forward to together?"

Faith's smile was gentle and sincere. "That sounds like an excellent idea."

I released a relieved sigh. "Okay. Okay, I'll do that." My

head was getting a little foggy, though, so I added, "Maybe after this pill wears off."

Faith patted my arm. "Good idea. Get some rest."

I nodded.

And a few minutes later, tugged under by Percocet and not so wound up over my future with Sabrina, I was out cold.

CHAPTER 26

SABRINA

That was a hell of a game! Lila had written. *Nice goal!*

I smiled as I wrote back, *Thanks. We could've used your grit out there. They've got some forwards who need a defender to put them in their place.*

Lying in the hotel bed, I read and reread my message. For a moment, I was worried that wasn't the right thing to say. I knew she was struggling with not being out here, and that she felt like she was letting the team down, but I also wanted her to know she was missed. Though we were holding our own in the playoffs, we were definitely feeling her absence both on the ice and in the locker room.

When she replied, I felt a little better: *The girls from the minors are holding their own. And you all looked good out there. It sucks not being able to play, but it's fun to watch everyone.*

Would be a lot more fun with you, I told her honestly. *Especially before and after games.*

The next game is at home. Can't promise a lot of fun, but I'll do my best. (winking emoji)

Just being able to see you will be amazing. BTW how is your knee?

Eh. Sore. Would be better if these jerks didn't make me do exercises and crap.

I laughed as I wrote out, *Those bastards, doing their job to make sure you recover.*

I know, right? I'm going to speak to their manager.

Giggling into the silence of my room, I rolled my eyes. I could perfectly envision her smirking as she wrote those words. *You're not the easiest patient in the world, are you?*

What makes you say that?

I was halfway through typing a response when the screen suddenly switched to an incoming call.

Dad.

My pleasant mood instantly evaporated, and I indulged in a muttered, "Fuck!" before I sighed and accepted the call. "Hi, Dad."

"Hey, kiddo. That was quite a game tonight."

I tensed. Lila had said as much, but I expected that from her. Dad didn't watch my games, never mind compliment them. This *had* to be baited. A backhanded comment, like calling someone's performance "remarkable" when he actually meant "remarkably terrible."

Instead of taking the bait, I cautiously asked, "Did you watch it?"

"I missed the first period, but I caught the last two."

My lips parted, and I had no idea what to say. My dad

had... watched my game? Not just the highlights so he could pick apart my performance?

Before I could find my breath or my voice again, he added, "Your stepmother and I will be at your game on Tuesday."

I blinked. "You... You will?"

"We will. How about we take you to dinner after?"

"I..." It took a full ten seconds for me to remember how to speak. "There's—we'll be flying out right after the game."

"Ah, they don't let the grass grow, do they?"

"They never do." And he knew that. How many times in his career had he gone straight from an arena to an airport? That was pretty much life as a hockey player. And it would be my life on Tuesday night unless—

Unless we lost.

Because Tuesday was an elimination game. We were down 3-2 in the series. A win on Tuesday would force a game seven. A loss...

A loss would mean I was available to have dinner with my dad.

I swallowed. "Well, I'm sure we can do something after the playoffs are over." Which could be Tuesday. It could be Thursday. It could be two, three, four weeks away. There was no telling.

But holy shit, I was suddenly determined as hell to make sure I *couldn't* have dinner with him on Tuesday. The Bearcats had come too far to give up now, and my father's presence would just drive me on.

"Well," he said. "You played well tonight, Sabrina. I'm sure you will on Tuesday, too."

I was again brought up short. That didn't... It didn't *sound* backhanded. "I did?"

He laughed, and it actually sounded genuine. "You came away with four points. In a playoff game." He paused. "Though you could've had a hat trick if you'd shot instead of passing to Lawson."

Holy shit. He *had* watched.

"Oh. I..." I cleared my throat. "That goalie's blocker side is a lot weaker than her stick side. Lawson had much better odds of finding the back of the net."

He chuckled a little condescendingly, but to my surprise, he said, "Better for the team to get the goal by any means necessary, I suppose. Especially in a tight playoff game."

"Yeah. Yeah, that's what I was thinking."

"All right, well, I'll let you go. Good luck on Tuesday."

"Thanks, Dad."

We ended the call, and I stared at my phone as my stomach roiled. All my damn life, I'd wanted my father's support. I'd wanted him to come to my games and cheer for me. I'd wanted him to pay attention to how I played and see that I really was a good hockey player.

Now that he was maybe doing all that...

I didn't know how to feel.

This was something I'd wanted my whole damn life, and now that it was quite possibly here...

Fuck. Was I just being ungrateful? He'd finally seen the light and realized I was good at a sport that was worth playing. Why was I looking this gift horse in the mouth?

Sighing, I picked up my phone again and started typing a message to Lila.

Hey, sorry for the slow reply. My dad called. (skull emoji)

Uh-oh. What did he say?

I chewed the inside of my cheek. *That he's coming to Tuesday's game. And he watched tonight. And he thought I was good?*

Oh wow. That's new, isn't it?

Very.

Now that you mention it, the network showed an interview with him during the game. He was more positive about it than I thought he would be.

I stared at her message before thumbing back, *They did what now?*

Yeah. It was kind of weird, honestly. He's acting like he's supported you all along.

Which network?

She did me one better and sent a link to the interview. I tapped it and hit play.

Dad was on a Zoom call opposite the commentator, sitting in his familiar office with trophies and accolades in the background.

"This must be an incredibly proud moment for you," the commentator said. "Having a son *and* a daughter competing in their professional hockey leagues' postseasons."

"I'm very proud of both of them," Dad said with a bright smile. "Mark has played some of his best hockey this season. And Sabrina—well, what can I say?" He chuckled. "Those McAvoy genes are strong."

I gritted my teeth. Of course he was taking some credit for it. But... he was also acknowledging my hockey ability. This *was* progress.

"Now, Doran," the reporter went on, "there have been rumors that you're not supportive of the Women's Hockey Professional League. Can you speak to those, especially with your daughter's impressive season?"

Rumors. Was that what kids were calling it these days? But I supposed a reporter had to be a little careful how he approached the subject if he didn't want Dad to lose his mind or end the interview.

Dad's lips tightened, but only for a second. "Obviously there is a demand for women's hockey, and this league has been meeting that demand. The players are exceptional—can't deny that."

I actually had to pause the video and replay that bit just to make sure I heard him right. I even put on closed captioning. Had he really...

Holy shit.

Dad continued, "These girls worked very hard to get where they are, and they had to work to build a professional league at the same time." He shrugged. "My league was in place for a century before I was even drafted. We didn't need to develop it while we also played in it." He gave a soft laugh. "Trust the women to be able to multitask better than us."

My jaw went slack and I wavered a little. Good thing I was leaning against the padded headboard; even then I almost toppled off the mattress. He'd *finally* figured that out? Had my stepmother talked some sense into him? Had three ghosts visited him in the middle of the night or something? Because... whoa.

And why didn't I feel anything?

Shock, yes. But all the other emotions I'd have expected—

they were absent. If anything, I just felt... empty? Numb? Those didn't make sense, but I couldn't figure out how else to describe it.

I closed the video and reopened the text window with Lila. *Is it weird that I'm not as excited about this as I thought I'd be?*

After all the shit he's said to you and how he's acted about women's hockey? Of course not.

But what if he's really changing his tune? What if he's finally supporting me for real?

Lila started and stopped typing a few times.

Then the screen lit up with a FaceTime request from her. Of course, I accepted it.

"Hey." She smiled at me on the screen, but then turned serious. "Figured this would be easier than typing it all out."

"Yeah, probably." I ran a hand through my hair and sighed. "What is wrong with me?"

"Nothing. There's nothing wrong with you." She seemed to study me. "Do you think he's sincere about it?"

I gnawed my lip. Was that the problem? "I don't know. Part of me feels kind of meh about it whether he's serious or not. Part of me really, really *wants* him to be serious about it. Like I'm so afraid he's going to yank the rug out from under me."

Lila's brows knitted together. "Do you think he'd try to be a dick to you like Ty was at the All-Stars?"

I considered that. "Maybe? Because they both do shit like that. Wait until I'm on some kind of pedestal, and then make sure to bring me down a peg. Especially in front of people."

Lila rolled her eyes. "Jesus."

"I know, right? And I... I mean, I do want this to be real. I really want my dad to finally accept me playing hockey and be proud of me. I'm just..."

"Afraid it's a bait-and-switch?"

I nodded.

"That's valid. It really is. He's done it enough times, anyone would be."

"Exactly. And I also..." I sighed, pressing back harder against the headboard. "Even if he *is* sincere, I still feel weird about it. Like it's not *just* because I'm afraid he's bullshitting me—there's a part of me that thinks he might actually mean it, and I don't feel as good about that as I should." I grimaced. "Does that even make sense?"

"Do feelings ever make sense?"

"Okay, that's fair."

"You've also got a lot of years of bullshit behind you," she went on. "He's built up a lot of resentment in you. Even if he does a complete one-eighty, you're not required to drop all that resentment overnight, you know?"

I pushed out a breath. "You're right. You're—yeah. That's definitely it. Maybe I'll warm up to it when I've had a chance to process things. And see if he really means it."

Lila nodded. "Give yourself time. If he's actually seen the light and come around, he should probably also apologize to you and accept that you need some time, you know?"

I wanted to laugh. My father? Apologizing for his behavior? That would be the day. But after tonight, hell—stranger things had happened. "I guess we'll see how it goes."

She smiled. "That's about all you can do."

"Yeah. It is." I rolled my shoulders, wondering when

they'd started getting so tense (as if I didn't know). "Well, I should probably get some sleep. We're heading to the airport first thing in the morning."

"Good idea. But, um... before we go..." Lila flicked her eyes away and chewed her lip.

My heart jumped. "Hmm? What's up?"

"I, um..." It could've just been the light, but I thought some color bloomed in her cheeks as she looked at the camera again. "I was just thinking—do you want to go somewhere after the playoffs are over?"

Another jump in my chest, but this time a much more pleasant one. "Like where?"

"I don't know." She shrugged. "A vacation? Maybe someplace with beaches?"

"Ooh, that sounds nice. And it would be great to have some time with just you."

The blush might've been the light, but the obvious relief on her face had to be real. "It would. It's been—I love watching you play, but it's been hard, being apart all the time."

"It has. It won't be that much longer, though."

"It better be!" she said. "The team needs to get to the finals!"

I laughed. "Hey, we're still in the first round. One thing at a time."

"Pfft. To hell with that. If you win, I'll still get my name on the Cup, so *win*, damn it."

"Okay, okay!" I said, still laughing. "All right, let me get some sleep. When I get back, we can talk vacation plans."

Oh, her smile was so pretty. Couldn't I be home right now?

Unfortunately no, and we ended the call so we could both crash for the night. I got ready for bed, and then I lay there in the darkness, thinking about my calls with my girlfriend and my father. Thinking about the playoffs. The Cup my team and I were pursuing.

I hoped we won for a lot of reasons. Getting Lila's name on there along with mine? Oh, that was on my list.

And maybe Dad will finally be proud of me.

My mood darkened at that thought. Yes, Dad *seemed* to be coming around. He *seemed* to be changing his attitude about the WHPL. About me.

Maybe with time, I'd finally be as happy about that as I'd always thought I would be.

"Oh my God, I'm wiped." I leaned into Lila on her couch. "Playoffs are no joke."

She laughed softly and kissed my temple. "See, that's my secret—get hurt right before they start so I can just chill while you all do the work."

I snorted and gave her a playful nudge.

She chuckled again. "Hey, at least you've got a few days off."

There was that.

Playoffs were always intense. I remembered that from my dad's playing days, my youth days, and major juniors, not to mention my first season with the WHPL (not that Seattle had made it past the first round). But it always seemed new. Every time, it was like I'd never experienced this chaos and pressure before, even though it was as familiar as my gear.

We'd narrowly held on in the first round. We'd gone 3-1 against Detroit, but we managed to rally, force a game seven, and win in double overtime. Compared to that uphill comeback, the second round was a breeze—we'd swept Toronto, absolutely stomping them in two of the games. Even with my dad in the crowd for some of the games—*especially* with him there?—I'd played my heart out, and the Bearcats were killing it.

Since we'd only had to go to game four, we had a nice little break until the third round started. We were still practicing daily, but at least we could have some downtime and sleep in our own beds. I'd enjoy that while it lasted, because we were about to go up against Hartford, who everyone was *betting* on to win not only the Eastern Conference Championship, but the Cup.

No pressure, or anything.

"I still can't believe we made it this far," I mused softly. "Not just into the playoffs, but... all of this. Having our own pro league. The works."

"Yeah. It's pretty amazing, isn't it?"

"It really is." I shifted a little, trying to get comfortable without jostling her leg. "They interviewed Calgary's goalie before their game last night. She talked about how much her family had to sacrifice to get her there."

"I think that's true for a lot of us," Lila said softly. "More of us than I realized, that's for sure."

I nodded. "I don't know how some of the families do it."

"Especially the ones with goalies."

"Right?" Hockey was expensive under the best of circum-stances; goalie gear rocketed right past expensive into *absurd*.

How many exceptional players out there had incredible potential, but were held back by the financial burden? Lila herself could've missed out on reaching this level because of that, and she had parents who'd been willing and able to sacrifice enough to keep her on the ice. Even that hadn't been enough, and she'd had to work in between hockey and school. How many other kids could be on a pro hockey trajectory if money wasn't a barrier?

I absently played with the hem of Lila's shirt. "You know what we should do?"

"Hmm?"

I shifted a little so I could look at her. "We should start an organization. One that helps girls get their hands on hockey gear." I paused. "Maybe low-income kids in general, since boys have a hard time with it too, but with a lot of outreach to girls, you know?"

Lila's eyes widened. "So like... providing gear to young players who want to give the sport a try?"

I nodded. "I mean, you told me what you were up against coming up, and I remember so many kids from my youth days who had to give it up because their families just couldn't afford the gear." There was also travel, registration, lessons— but gear seemed like a good place to start.

"That would be an awesome idea," she said softly. "Maybe we should see if some players from the men's league want to get involved."

I tilted my head. "Go on."

"Well, I mean, we're all getting paid a lot more than we were a few years ago, but none of us are raking in millions like the men. They've got all the big endorsements and the huge salaries. And the big platforms—we can't deny their support was a major reason why our league got off the ground."

"That's true." I thought about it. "You know, we could probably talk to my brother. He'd be all over something like this, and I bet his wife would want to get involved."

"Yeah?"

I nodded. "Imani is an absolute boss when it comes to running charitable organizations. She's been doing them for as long as she and Mark have been married, and I swear she's got a magic touch with them."

"Well, hell," Lila said. "I don't know the first thing about that stuff, so if she's game..." She waved her hand.

"Same," I said with a laugh. "Sometimes I think the reason I fought so hard to play hockey is I know damn well I'd fall on my face in any other job."

Lila smirked. "To be fair, you sometimes fall on your face in this one."

Rolling my eyes, I gave her a playful shove. "Shut up."

She giggled and reeled me in close.

Sighing happily, I draped my arm over her and cuddled close. "You know, I can't tell you how amazing it is to finally be with someone who encourages me to play hockey."

Lila combed her fingers through my hair. "It's hard to imagine anyone not encouraging you. You're an amazing player. You *should* be playing hockey."

My face burned, and I smiled. "Well, there were people in my life who definitely disagreed with you."

"Good thing their opinions don't matter." She flashed a toothy grin. "Sucks to be them."

I laughed. When I'd made myself available for the WHPL, it was half about playing hockey and half about escaping a miserably oppressive marriage.

Who knew it would land me in the arms of the last person I'd ever imagined connecting with like this?

CHAPTER 27

LILA

Hockey fans would be talking about these playoffs for *decades* to come, I just knew it.

Even after Pittsburgh swept Toronto, everyone had expected them to lose the Eastern Conference title to Hartford. Pittsburgh was good, but Hartford had dominated the League all season long. And anyway, no expansion team had made it to the Cup finals in their first season.

During the second intermission of the first game of the Eastern Conference finals, a commentator mused, "If I were the Cup engravers, I'd go ahead and start setting up the machine with all the names of the Hartford players."

Now Hartford fans were pissed, saying he'd jinxed them. That, or he'd lit a fire under Pittsburgh's ass. Knowing my team, I'd say it was a little of both, especially after hearing how my teammates reacted to that comment.

"Screw him," Anya said. "It's only game one!"

"We're only down by two," Euli had declared. "We've come back from worse."

Whatever the case, Pittsburgh came out in the third period, clawed their way back from a 4-2 deficit, and won with a buzzer beater. The next three games were absolute bloodbaths, with neither team willing to give an inch and Pittsburgh clearly playing with a chip on their collective shoulders.

In the end, Pittsburgh committed the upset of the century, eliminating Hartford in a 7-2 blowout in game six. The photo of Sabrina hoisting the Eastern Conference trophy and shouting with triumph was Pulitzer material as far as I was concerned.

Of course, I might've been a *little* biased.

Now Pittsburgh was the first expansion team to make it into the finals in their inaugural season, and after six games, it came down to this: game seven. Someone was taking the Cup home tonight. It was either us or the reigning champions, the Calgary Blizzard.

From the energy in the locker room, every member of our roster was more than ready to hoist the Cup.

"Let's do this!" Coach Reilly cried over raucous cheers from the team.

Everyone was pumped. Everyone was *ready*.

Almost everyone.

Jamie Tucker looked absolutely shell-shocked. She was a young defender who'd been brought up from the minors during the Eastern Conference Championships to fill in for Nora, who was out with a concussion. Coming up to the majors was intimidating enough—being called up during the playoffs? That had to be terrifying.

"Hey." I nudged her arm. "You okay?"

She looked up at me with wide eyes. "I think so? I only played two games in the regular season. Now I'm..." She gestured with her glove at a Cup finals banner, and she gulped.

I eased myself down on the bench beside her and leaned my crutches against my leg. "It's a lot of pressure. Believe me, I get it. But you're not out there alone, you know? And you wouldn't be here at all if you hadn't earned a place."

The fear held fast in her expression. "I know. I... On some level, I know that. But it's still..." She swallowed again, and she looked like she was on the verge of tears.

"Take a breath, okay?" I rested my hand on her padded shoulder and looked right in her eyes. "At most, you're going to play seven or eight minutes the whole game. If all you do out there is keep the puck out of our zone and out of our net while the other defenders catch their breath, then you're doing just fine. No one's expecting you to go out there and score the game-winning goal."

She laughed nervously. "That's good, I guess."

"It is. And you're going to be paired with Euli." I nodded toward her D partner. "She's an offensive defender, so she might go into the offensive zone sometimes, which means all you have to do is stay back in case someone tries to break away. If they do, Euli is fast as hell—she won't leave you hanging."

Jamie exhaled slowly.

"You've got this, okay?" I gave her shoulder a firm pat. "This isn't all on you—I promise."

A smile finally formed, and she nodded. "I'll keep that in mind. Thanks."

The team was getting ready to head out for warmups, so I said a quick goodbye to my teammates—plus a slightly longer one to my girlfriend—and hobbled toward the elevator. With a couple of badge swipes, I got to the second level and into the owners' box where I settled my aching carcass into a cushy leather seat.

"Are you comfortable?" Dad asked. "Do you want me to see if we can get you some ice for—"

"I'm good." I offered a reassuring smile.

He didn't look convinced and neither did my mom. They'd been fawning all over me at home and at every game, and I doubted that would stop any time soon.

I elbowed him gently. "Trust me—I'm fine."

"Okay. But just say so if you're not, you hear me?"

I smiled. "I will."

Below us, the game kicked off again. I hated watching from up here. I wanted to be in on the action, damn it. The last couple of weeks, though, I'd settled into it to some extent. Especially since Sadie—the defensive coach—and I would text throughout the game; I'd tell her things that were more visible to me up here than they were down at ice level.

They're angling for Anya's stick side, I said early in the first period. *Someone needs to protect that side.*

Shortly after that, I noticed a defender stuck closer to that side of the net. Good thing, too—that one shot absolutely would've gone in if Sims hadn't been there to block it. She'd stopped the puck with her boot and limped off the ice, but she'd been back out for her next shift, so I suspected the impact had just stung. Given that she hadn't let the player score, I didn't imagine she complained about it too much.

Not long after that, there was a commercial break. The Zamboni gates opened and the ice crew came out to clean the ice.

A roar of applause went up, and I looked to the Jumbotron to figure out why.

As soon as my gaze landed on the screen, my heart dropped into my stomach.

A gray-haired man in a suit stood from his chair in one of the other suite level boxes, beaming as he waved to the cheering crowd.

Below that:

Doran McAvoy. 4-time Cup Champion.

Sabrina McAvoy's father.

Beside me, my own father bristled. My mother glowered, shaking her head. Neither said anything—they didn't have to.

The camera changed to Sabrina, who was looking up at the screen as well. When she saw herself, she smiled and waved, and I hoped no one else could see what I did—the hurt behind the smile. The frustration.

Don't let him get to you, baby, I silently begged. *Don't let him get into your head.*

He'd been at most of the games in Pittsburgh since the playoffs started. He and his daughter hadn't interacted much because there simply hadn't been time; either she was being dragged away for media availability or a flight, or he was too busy holding court with fans and reporters. All told, over the past four weeks, they'd probably spent an hour in each other's company.

Sabrina still didn't know how to feel about his presence. Sometimes she looked up at where he was sitting and she seemed to get choked up. Other times, she'd grit her teeth while his face was on the Jumbotron.

"I'm glad he's here," she'd told me in bed the other night. "I'm glad he finally supports me. But I'm so focused on the playoffs, I haven't had the time or energy to process any of this and figure out what I feel. Or what I should feel."

I'd wrapped her in my arms and kissed her temple. "He's a hockey player. He of all people should understand where your focus is right now."

That had seemed to do the trick, and she'd relaxed and drifted off a moment later. I'd stayed awake, listening to her breathe and mentally threatening Doran McAvoy if he stepped out of line.

I wanted to tell her she had every right to reject his ass. Yeah, he was coming around to her career and her sport, but at what point was it too little too late? If the Olympics and Junior Worlds hadn't been enough to get his attention, wasn't she within her rights to say he'd waited too long?

But that wasn't my place. She had to decide how to deal with him. All I could do was support her and gently encourage her to be kind to herself.

I had suggested a counselor during one of our FaceTime calls a couple of weeks ago. Even if her father's intentions were good and everything with him was the best-case scenario going forward, there was no shame in talking to a disinterested third party who could help her sort out her emotions. I'd always listen and offer my thoughts, of course, but I wasn't a trained professional who actually knew how to navigate these murky waters.

"Whatever you need," I'd told her. "You know you have my support."

On my screen, she'd smiled. "I know. I don't know how I'd handle any of this without you."

I doubted that; she was stronger than most people I knew. But I was still glad to help.

Far below me on the ice, the game continued, the screen having shifted away from Doran.

Sabrina's line was the first out after the commercial break, and she lost the faceoff. Then she was able to get the puck, but promptly turned it over.

"C'mon, baby," I murmured. "Get it together."

She didn't. Not that shift, anyway. She was a mess. Two more turnovers, one of which resulted in a scoring chance, and then she fanned a shot on goal.

Mercifully, her shift ended, and I craned my neck to peer at her on the bench. Coach Reilly was bent over beside her, a hand on her shoulder, and Sabrina was nodding along. Coach didn't seem angry; knowing her, she was asking if Sabrina was okay.

And knowing Sabrina, she was insisting she was even though she clearly wasn't.

It couldn't be a coincidence that she fell apart right after the fans had cheered for her dad. Right after his face had been plastered up on the giant screen so she couldn't forget he was here. That had happened at a couple of other games, too, and it threw her off every time.

Shit. Was this part of his plan? Fuck with her head just by being here? Even if he didn't respect women's hockey or his own daughter, he wasn't *that* malevolent, was he?

Fortunately, Sabrina's next shift was better. She wasn't completely herself, but she protected the puck, her passes were crisp, and that shot she fired at the net was just *barely* deflected by the crossbar. If the problem was her dad or she was just getting into her own head, she seemed to be pulling herself back out of it.

I didn't wait for the period to end before I headed down the locker room. With two minutes left to go before the buzzer, I told my parents I'd be right back, then picked up my crutches and hobbled out of the suite to the elevator.

As I was coming into the locker room, the horn sounded, and a moment later, my teammates clomped in.

Sabrina gave me a weak smile, but then she dropped her gaze and focused on taking off her gloves.

"Hey." I touched her face and kissed her lightly. "You okay?"

She pressed her lips together and nodded. "Yeah. I just..." She glared upward as if she could see her father through the ceilings and floors between them. "It's driving me nuts that he's here."

I scoffed. "He probably just wants to be seen as Father of the Year."

"Yeah, right." She dropped her gloves on the bench beside her helmet. "I keep avoiding him. I won't be able to avoid him after this game, though."

That caught me by surprise. "You've been avoiding him?"

She nodded without meeting my gaze. "Sometimes it's

easy—gotta talk to reporters, catch a plane, whatever. But a lot of times..." She sighed, shoulders sinking under her pads. "I *could* see him. I just don't."

"Why not?"

Sabrina shook her head. She picked up her water bottle from her locker stall and took a deep swig, then poured a little down the back of her neck. "I can't decide if I'm afraid he's being insincere... or that he *is* sincere."

My heart ached for her. I could only imagine that kind of turmoil—wanting her dad's love and approval for so long that when it finally came, she couldn't enjoy it *or* trust it.

"Hey." I cupped her face in both hands. "Look at me."

She did, and the hurt, anger, and frustration in her eyes were heartbreaking.

"He doesn't matter," I told her. "There are almost twenty thousand people out there and God knows how many watching at home who *do* think our sport and our players matter. Your mom and siblings are here and cheering for you. *My* parents are here and cheering for you. Him?" I scowled. "He's already taken way too much away from you." I lifted her chin and kissed her softly. "Whether he's being sincere or not, don't let him ruin all this for you."

Sabrina's eyes welled up, but she smiled. "Yeah. You're right."

"And..." I hesitated.

She arched an eyebrow. "Hmm?"

"Just..." I bit my lip. "Look, take this or leave it, okay? But after the game—you don't *have* to see him."

She blinked. "What?"

"You're not obligated to see him," I said gently. "Even if

he's moving in a good direction for real, and even if you two are going to have a better relationship going forward—it's okay if you focus on you and the team tonight. Give yourself some time to figure out how you feel about him before you're face to face with him, you know?"

She studied me, then slowly relaxed. "That's... I hadn't thought of that. You're right, though." She rolled her shoulders and offered a small smile. "I'll keep it in mind. Hopefully I'll be too busy celebrating with the team to care about him."

I grinned. "That's the spirit."

Sabrina's smile broadened, and she kissed me softly. Then she looked past me, and her brow pinched. Voice so low I barely heard her, she said, "You might want to have a chat with your protégé. I think she's getting up in her head again."

I glanced over my shoulder and found Jamie sitting on the bench on the verge of crying. "Oh. Crap. Yeah, I'll go talk to her." I turned to Sabrina again. "You good?"

"I'm fine." She gave me a little nudge. "Go."

We exchanged smiles. Then I crossed the locker room to Jamie.

She was jittery and off-balance, and now that I was close enough to see her well, there were definitely tears in her eyes this time.

"Hey," I said. "You okay?"

She glanced up at me, and then her face crumpled. "I suck."

"No, you don't." I eased myself down on the bench beside her, biting back a wince when my knee protested. "You're great out there."

Jamie shook her head. "They almost scored on us *because of me*."

"It's okay. Anya made the save."

"But she shouldn't have had to." She buried her face in her gloves and groaned. "I can't believe I turned over the puck and—"

"Jamie. Look at me."

She lifted her head, her eyes red and wet.

"We *all* turn over the puck. The team had like eight turnovers that period, and only one of those was yours." I gestured toward Anastasia and lowered my voice. "Hers *did* result in a goal against. Yours gave them a scoring chance, but they didn't score. That's what matters."

"Still. It was..." She wiped her eyes. "I don't belong here."

"Yeah, you do." I put a hand on her shoulder. "I promise. I've been watching the whole game and texting Sadie the whole time about any issues I see with defense. Your name hasn't been in any of those texts."

She looked up at me, her eyes begging me to mean that.

"Take a deep breath," I told her. "Have some water. Go out there and play like you did last period, and you'll be fine. I promise."

"But what if I screw up again?"

"It's hockey." I nudged her gently. "We all screw up. All the time. I know it's a ton of pressure, but you wouldn't be here if you hadn't impressed a lot of people along the way."

At that, she smiled weakly, still nervous but rallying. "Thanks. How do you handle the pressure playing at this level all the time?"

I laughed. "Well, fortunately, it's not *always* the Cup finals."

"Thank God for that," Anya muttered from two seats over.

"Right?" Euli shook her head as she retaped her stick. "I'd be a walking ulcer if we played like this all the time."

Jamie stared at them with wide eyes, but something finally seemed to settle in her, as if she realized at last that she wasn't the only one feeling the pressure.

I clapped her shoulder. "You going to be all right out there?"

Her smile was brighter this time, and she nodded. "Yeah. I'll be fine."

"Okay. Good luck. And don't forget to enjoy it, you know?"

She laughed. "I won't. I promise."

I left her to continue putting her gear back on, and I stopped by Sabrina to wish her luck as well. She seemed to be in better spirits, which was a relief. The last thing a team ever needed—but especially during a playoff elimination game— was their captain out of sorts.

While the team headed back out to the ice, I made my way back up to the owners' box and settled into one of the plush seats again.

Dad leaned over. "How is Sabrina?"

"She's stressed because they keep showing her dad on the screen." I rolled my eyes. "And there's nothing anyone can do about it."

He scowled, but didn't say anything. He didn't have to; I'd told him and Mom all about Doran, and they'd already decided they *did not* like him. My parents liked everyone, but Doran McAvoy didn't make the cut.

Moments later, the game kicked off again.

It was a hell of a battle. Neither team wanted to give an inch. Defense was strong on both sides, but there were still shots on goal piling up as players fired puck after puck at each net.

By the end of the second, the score was 2-2. With four minutes left in the third, it was 3-2 in Calgary's favor.

I was on the edge of my seat, barely noticing the ache in my leg as I tried to will the puck away from our goal and into Calgary's. At the very least, we had to tie it up; that would keep us alive enough for overtime.

Jamie and Euli relieved Sims and her temporary D partner, joining Sabrina's line in our zone. Sabrina and one of Calgary's skaters battled it out for the puck, and the other skater ended up winning. She spun around to head for our net, but then out of nowhere, Jamie did a viper fast pokecheck and stole the puck off her blade.

Before the player even knew what had happened, Jamie whipped around and started barreling toward the neutral zone with Laws and Sabrina on her heels.

A defender got in Jamie's way, hindering her progress across the zone. Sabrina got into the offensive zone before she'd realized Jamie was tied up, and I cringed, afraid that Jamie—who'd untangled herself from the other defender— would cross the blue line and render the play offside.

Should've known she was too smart for that.

Jamie fired the puck across the blue line and right onto

Sabrina's tape. Sabrina bodied her way around a defender, then shot the puck at Euli, who tipped it right into the goal.

Everyone roared to their feet as the stadium lit up red. I had to lean on my crutches, but I got up too, screaming my voice raw alongside my parents as my teammates celebrated.

We were still alive. Still a chance to win.

"The Pittsburgh goal!" the announcer's voice boomed over the roaring crowd. "Scored by number forty-three, Euli Eskola. Assisted by number five, Sabrina McAvoy, and number nineteen, Jamie Tucker!"

I pumped my fist and shouted as our teammates piled on the gobsmacked young defender. Jamie's first ever point in the WHPL, and it had come not only in the playoffs, but in the Cup finals. On a decisive goal, too.

This was definitely a night she wouldn't forget.

CHAPTER 28

SABRINA

Jamie's drive had led to Euli's goal, which tied up the game. Two minutes remained on the clock, and I could see my own thought in all my teammates' eyes:

Forget overtime. Let's win this in regulation.

I agreed. Especially since Calgary was dangerous in OT —of their twelve regular season games to go into overtime, they'd lost two. In the postseason, they were 3-0 after regulation.

Yeah, forget overtime. We're winning this now.

My line was gassed, so we went to the bench. The second line went out, and right about the time the announcer called out that there was one minute left to play, Coach sent my line back onto the ice.

I was ready. So were my linemates.

Sims and Caldwell were fresh, too, and I glanced from player to player. Nothing but fierce determination.

We could do this.

They weren't going to make it easy, though. It was a battle to get possession after the faceoff. One of Calgary's defenders had the puck, but Sims checked her hard, knocking her off the puck and stealing it away.

All the action quickly moved into our offensive zone, where it was cycle after cycle, battle after battle, until finally —fucking finally—we were set up. Caldwell passed me the puck. Our defenders situated themselves in front of the net to block the goalie's sightlines.

I had the puck. Shoot? Pass?

In the space of nanoseconds, I analyzed the situation.

I had the shot, but the goalie was poised and ready. Even with a screen of three players—one of hers and two of mine— between us, she could still catch glimpses of me. Still anticipate what I was going to do.

Laws, however, was off to the side. Wide open. With a much better shooting lane than I had.

I wound back for a one-timer, and the goalie and screening players all moved around to try to either block me or the goalie.

Just before my blade hit the puck, though, I stopped, then snapped it toward Laws.

No one was expecting it. No one but her.

And before anyone could course correct, Laws fired it on net.

I didn't even hear the goal horn over the crowd. We almost toppled Laws in hugs, and when we skated back to the bench for fist bumps, everyone was on their feet and practically jumping up and down.

Nineteen seconds left on the clock. We had the lead.

We could... We might fucking *win this thing.*

We set up again. This time, we weren't going to make a drive for the goal—just take possession, and hold on to the puck. Cycle it. Skate around with it.

Unfortunately, Calgary won the faceoff, and the puck holder skated for all she was worth toward our defensive zone.

We were on her heels, but she was fast. Too fast.

Panic surged through me as she neared the goal.

Anya was ready. Low. Glove and stick both ready.

The player shot.

Anya batted it away with her stick. Rebounds were never ideal, but—

The buzzer went off.

The game was over.

The playoffs were over.

We'd...

We'd won.

This didn't feel real. Even after I'd almost suffocated in the pile of hugs after my teammates cleared the bench... even after they'd wheeled out the Cup... even after I'd hoisted it above my head and skated around the ice to the deafening roar of fans and teammates...

It just didn't feel real.

The ice crew rolled out rugs, and family members poured onto the sheet to celebrate with us. I looked around for Lila, but she wasn't out here yet. Probably waiting out the biggest crush so she could move more slowly on her crutches. I could wait; I wanted her to be safe more than anything.

My brother shouldered his way through the crowd

wearing a *Pittsburgh Bearcats, WHPL Cup Champions* base-ball cap like the one I had on. He threw his arms around me and damn near knocked me onto the ice. "Holy crap, Beans! You won the Cup!"

I almost started crying again, hugging him back fiercely. "We did! I can't believe it!"

"Pfft. I can." He gave my back a slap and let me go. "I've watched almost every game—you've all been killing it!"

"Yeah, but they gave us a run for our money."

"Well. Yeah." He rolled his eyes as if I were still his dumb little sister. "It wouldn't be worthwhile if it was easy."

"Eh." I shrugged. "If I wanted easy, I'd play against your team."

"Oh. Oh." He touched his chest. "That's cold, Beans. *Cold.*"

I snickered and hugged him again. "You deserved it and you know it."

He just chuckled and smacked my back. He'd made the same comment to me when we were teenagers, and I'd been waiting a damn decade to toss it back at him. "Seriously, though," he said. "Congrats. This is amazing."

"Thanks." I pulled back. "Maybe next year will be your year."

With a quiet, self-deprecating laugh, he said, "Yeah. We'll see."

His team had been eliminated during the men's league's second round. It hadn't been a blowout, but it hadn't been their greatest performance, either. To be fair, they'd been plagued with injuries as most teams were this time of year, and they'd been down three of their top six. His coaches didn't seem to think depth was all that important, so they hadn't done much to shore up their bottom six; losing an entire line's worth of their best forwards had been a *disaster*.

Next year? Maybe if they replaced all their coaches.

My mom and sister came down too, and we shared hugs.

And then...

Oh, God.

I knew it was coming, but I still wasn't ready when my father's face emerged from the crowd.

And I didn't know what to make of the way he was beaming. Or the fact that he wore a cap that matched the one my brother and I wore.

He was... celebrating my team's win?

Oh my God.

This *was* real. He really was here and celebrating.

I glanced at my mom, who nodded.

Then I skated to the edge of the carpet where he was standing. "Dad?"

He beamed. "Well done, kiddo." He smacked my padded shoulder. "Turns out you've really got it."

I had to blink past the sting in my eyes. All my damn life, I'd waited to hear him say that. To hear him tell me I was good at hockey, and that the hockey I played actually mattered. Now that I had Olympic medals, World Junior Women's medals, *and* a Cup, he finally saw what I'd been *begging* him to see all along.

The little girl watching him at training camp couldn't have even dreamed of this moment.

But the woman standing here now...

Pulling in a deep breath, I skated back, getting out from

under his hand and out of his reach. "No, Dad. We're not doing this."

He blinked, hand still hovering in the air where my shoulder had been. "Not doing—what are you talking about?"

I let go of a caustic laugh. "You did everything you could to stop me from playing hockey. Everyone says you opened doors for me, but you and I both know you put up nothing but walls." I sensed people watching, including some with cameras. All my media training told me to stop. That I would get into trouble. But goddammit, I wasn't about to let this be Dad's moment of fatherly glory. And I *owed* this to that little girl who'd been hurt so badly by her father's cruel dismissiveness. "Don't tell me you've suddenly decided women's hockey is worthwhile now that you can take credit for your daughter, because all you ever did was try to stop me from playing." I gestured around us. "You had nothing to do with this."

"That isn't true," he growled. "You had access to—"

"I had all the lessons and coaching Mom could sign me up for behind your back," I snapped, and people definitely heard that. I should've stopped. I really should've. But I looked him right in the eye and snarled, "You don't get to take credit for any of this, Dad. You don't get to celebrate it with us. Not after you told me time and time again that there was nothing more useless than being an expert at something worthless."

The gasps around us told me my words had carried farther than I'd expected. My father's eyes flicked from side to side, as if he'd realized the same. The rising panic in his expression told me he knew his entire reputation was as vulnerable as an empty net—one well-placed shot away from game over.

"Sabrina," he said in a low voice. "This isn't the time or place for—"

"It isn't the time or place for you to pretend you care about me or about this sport," I threw back. He narrowed his eyes, taking on that expression I knew well from when teenage me had pushed him too far. I could let him snap now. Let him eviscerate his own reputation right here in front of cameras and hot mics. Let him finally show the hockey world who he'd been all along.

But winning via the other team's own goal was never as satisfying as potting that decisive point myself, so I started talking before he could.

"You can't spend my whole life trying to pull me back down the mountain, then think you can celebrate with me when I reach the summit. This is *my* moment. My *team's* moment. You've made it clear for years that you wanted no part of it." I shrugged with all the defiance I'd been culti-vating for my entire life. "You're not welcome here."

And then I skated back to join my teammates, keeping my head high and pretending I wasn't shaky all over from standing up to him like that. In *public*. In front of *cameras*.

Lila caught up with me, leaning on her crutches at the edge of a carpet. "Hey. You okay?"

I exhaled. "Yeah, I'm..." I glanced back to where my dad and I had faced off. He was gone now, several people—including reporters—looking around with startled and puzzled expressions. We definitely hadn't gone unnoticed. My shoulders dropped beneath my pads. "Fuck." I rubbed my hand over my face. "Now all the coverage is going to get hijacked to be about me and my dad instead of the team and the—"

"Sabrina." Lila gathered me in her arms. "That's not your fault. The commentators and reporters fed that monster, and so did your dad."

"But I made a scene with him *here*." I gestured around us. "*Now*. This is supposed to be about us winning the Cup, not..." I exhaled hard.

"It's not about him." Lila kissed my temple, then let me go and took my hand. "It's all about us and the team." As she herded me toward our teammates, she added, "We're not going to waste any more time on what he did, because we're going to celebrate what *we* did."

I tried to smile, but it was tough. Yes, we could focus on our team's achievement, but I'd spent my whole life around the highest levels of this sport. I knew how an exchange like the one we'd just had would become a huge scandal, overshadowing everything the Bearcats had done. As it was, no media outlet could mention my name without trotting out my pedigree. I wasn't naïve enough to think *"Bearcats win Cup in Inaugural Season"* would be the headline when *"Doran McAvoy, Daughter Square Off After Cup Win"* would be so much juicier.

I was proud of myself for finally standing up to my father and for refusing to let him act like he'd always been the supportive dad. But I also hated myself for tarnishing this moment for our team. This should've been about us, the Bearcats. Not us, Doran and Sabrina McAvoy.

"Come here." Lila pulled me in closer, and she kissed my

cheek. "You're amazing. You played through his bullshit your whole life, and then you didn't let him come in at the last second and act like he deserved to be here. You're a lot stronger than you think."

I exhaled. Then I met her gaze, and I smiled. "Do you care if anyone knows we're together?"

She laughed. "You mean the five or six people who haven't already figured it out after I've kissed you like three times?" She shook her head. "Not at all."

I grinned. Then I kissed her. Not deeply or inappropriately, but long and tender. I thought I heard some camera snaps, but I didn't care.

She drew back and grinned up at me. "I'm going to go congratulate Jamie. She's probably beside herself right now."

"Good idea. And you made a big difference for her tonight." I caressed Lila's cheek. "Don't think for a second that you didn't contribute to us winning."

"Oh, I know," she said with a cocky grin. "I'm just glad *you* all know that."

I laughed and rolled my eyes. "Shut up."

She giggled, then hobbled along the crowded carpet to find our rookie teammate.

A moment later, my mom appeared beside me again, and she reeled me into a tight hug. I almost cried as I enveloped her in my sweaty gear and jersey. We'd already celebrated together, but suddenly I was overwhelmed by how much she'd done to get me to this level. By how much she'd fought against to help me lived my dream. At least one of my parents deserved to be out here with me. "Thank you for everything."

"You're welcome, sweetheart." As she pulled back, there

was an unusually wicked little glint in her eyes. "And good job, putting your father in his place."

"You saw that?"

She smiled. "I'm pretty sure everyone saw it."

I groaned.

"It's okay." Mom put a hand on my arm and squeezed just hard enough for me to feel it through my pads. "It was long overdue for everyone to see who he really was."

"But did it have to be *now*?" I gestured at my teammates, who were celebrating with their families as they continued passing the Cup around. "Today should be about us. Not him."

"It won't be about him."

I shot her a dubious look.

She gave me one of those *"Mom knows best, just wait and see"* looks. "All the sports networks have been ignoring the bad things about him for years, and they know it. Now that he's made an ass out of himself in a way they can't ignore, they're not going to want to touch it with a ten-foot pole because they all helped make him into the monster he is."

I scowled. "They'll just act all shocked and scandalized like they had no idea he was this way."

"They can try." Mom smiled knowingly. "And even if they do try to crap on him, everyone knows your father will sic his lawyers on them. Some of the tabloid sites might try to make a big stink out of it, but the sports networks that want to stay relevant and solvent aren't going to take that risk."

I considered it, then sighed. "I hope you're right." I wanted to believe her. I really did. I just wasn't sure if I could.

Mom patted my arm again. "Either way, don't let him

steal your night." She pointed with her chin at my teammates. "Go celebrate. You've earned it."

I chewed my lip. Yeah, I'd earned it. But had I also blown it?

Right then, Val skated up beside me. "Hey, Mac. You okay?"

"Yeah. Yeah, I'm..." I turned around and realized about half a dozen of my teammates had joined her, and they were all looking at me with concern written all over their faces.

When they should've been celebrating the biggest moment of their careers.

Goddammit.

"I'm sorry about..." I gestured to where my dad and I had had it out.

Val shook her head. "No, don't be."

"Definitely," Sims agreed. "He was all ready to make tonight about himself." She nodded in the same direction I'd pointed. "But now he's gone."

I looked, and... she was right. He was still MIA. Scanning the ice, I couldn't find him anywhere, and he was not an easy man to lose in a crowd. He'd quite possibly left the building by now.

I exhaled, letting my shoulders drop.

"Come on." Anya wrapped her arm around me. "Let's go celebrate."

I hesitated, worried I didn't deserve to take part in something I'd almost ruined.

Lila appeared beside my mom, and she gave me a gentle nudge. "Go. You've earned this. He doesn't deserve to take it away from anyone, including you."

I held her gaze, then smiled and tipped my head in the direction our teammates had gone. "You coming?"

"Of course." She beamed. "They're going to do the group photo by one of the carpets so I can join in."

That had joy bubbling up in me. She was part of this. We'd all done this together, including me and Lila. Both of us would be in that group photo with the Cup. Both of our names would be engraved on it. Though there would be articles and commentary, I was sure, the pall of my dad's presence was gone. There was nothing left but joy and celebration.

So I joined my team. I posed, smiling beside the Cup. I drank from it just like everyone else did, and my God, champagne had never tasted so good.

As far as I knew, my father had left. I didn't see him for the rest of the night, and no one—not even the nosiest and most obnoxious reporters—mentioned his name to me.

Tonight was about the Pittsburgh Bearcats.

We'd all made it. Into our own professional league. To the top of our game. To the playoffs.

And tonight, we'd won the Cup.

No one could take that away from any of us.

EPILOGUE

Pittsburgh Bearcats beat Reigning Champions in Cup Final; First WHPL Expansion Team to Win Title in Inaugural Season

PITTSBURGH – In a shocking upset, the Pittsburgh Bearcats have won the WHPL Cup Final, ousting the Calgary Blizzard—the reigning champions—in a wild Game 7.

No other expansion team has earned the title in its first season in the League; only Chicago, one of the Original 10, has won in its inaugural season.

Captain Sabrina McAvoy led the team with 5 goals and 9 assists, including the game-winning goal in Game 2.

Of the victory, head coach Hannah Reilly said, "They fought hard, and Calgary didn't make it easy.

Every inch of that ice was a battle. These women should be very proud of what they accomplished out there. I'm certainly proud of them."

Calgary head coach Emily Corbin told reporters, "It's impressive, what the Bearcats did this season. It's always hard when the whole team is new to each other, and getting to this from scratch—I won't tell you it's fun to lose to them, but I have a ton of respect for these women."

Normally, the losing team leaves the ice after the postgame handshakes, but a few Calgary players stuck around for the Bearcats' celebration. Vanessa Tucker-Crowe stayed out to congratulate her younger sister, Bearcat blue liner Jamie Tucker. Goalie Amber Grayson brought her twin sons out to celebrate with her partner and their mother, Pittsburgh forward Jennifer Valentine. And three players lingered for a short time to share some hugs with previous Olympic teammates Sabrina McAvoy, Lila Hamilton, and Simone Yates.

"During the game," Grayson said to reporters, "we're all out for blood. We want to win, no matter what it takes. But when the buzzer goes off, these are our friends and teammates. Maybe someday I'll get to raise the Cup myself. Tonight it's Jenny's turn, and I'm over the moon for her."

SUPPORTIVE FATHER OR UNREPENTANT SEXIST? – "SHE HAD THE POTENTIAL TO BE BETTER THAN HIM"

Confrontation between Sabrina McAvoy, Father, Leads to Accusations of Misogyny

PITTSBURGH – A tense conversation played out between Pittsburgh Bearcats captain Sabrina McAvoy and her father after the team's victory in the Cup Finals.

McAvoy accused her father, likely future Hall of Famer Doran McAvoy, of criticizing the existence of the women's league, and of keeping her back in her journey through the sport.

"You can't spend my whole life trying to pull me back down the mountain," Sabrina was overheard telling her father, "then think you can celebrate with me when I reach the summit."

She then dismissed him from the ice and returned to celebrating with her team. Doran exited the arena shortly after, refusing to answer questions about his daughter's comments or her team's victory.

St. Louis forward Mark McAvoy—Doran's son and Sabrina's brother—was present for the postgame celebration. He did not leave with his father but also dodged questions about anything except the Bearcats' championship win.

The father-daughter confrontation was brief but

raised questions about the senior McAvoy's thoughts on the existence of the Women's Hockey Professional League and his own daughter's participation in the same. Most former teammates and coaching staff have not returned phone calls, but not all.

Ollie Gray, who famously requested a trade out of Buffalo after clashing with his superstar teammate, told reporters, "Everyone knows Doran McAvoy is a sexist [expletive]. They won't admit it to a camera, but everyone knows."

Another former teammate, speaking on condition of anonymity, said that he found McAvoy's comments about other players' wives and daughters to be inappropriate. "They weren't sexual or anything, but he clearly didn't have any respect for them." He went on to add, "Doran *always* had something to say if someone brought their little girl to a family skate in hockey gear. Even if we were just knocking some pucks around for fun—it wasn't something girls had any business doing,"

Doran's longtime linemate, Cary Olson, admitted, "No one was surprised when he and Nancy (McAvoy's ex-wife) broke up. We were just glad it happened before Doran found out she was letting Sabrina play hockey." When pressed to explain this comment, Olson simply said, "Everybody knew he didn't want Sabrina playing hockey. We could all see that she had the same talent has her dad and brother, but he wasn't having it." He then paused before adding, "Maybe that was why Doran didn't want her to play. He knew she had the potential to be better than him."

Reporters reached out to Sabrina McAvoy for her perspective, but the only response was a message from her agent, Meryl Sheary: "Sabrina is taking a well-deserved vacation after her Cup win. Upon her return, she will not be commenting publicly on private family matters."

"THEY'VE WORKED HARD TO GET WHERE THEY ARE—THEY DESERVE BETTER THAN THIS."

Companies distance themselves from Doran McAvoy over accusations of misogyny, disrespect toward WHPL

NEW YORK – Doran McAvoy has taken the next step in falling from grace: losing lucrative endorsement contracts.

Following the confrontation between McAvoy and his daughter, Pittsburgh Bearcats captain and recent Cup champion Sabrina, the player once certainly destined for the Hall of Fame has soured in the public eye. After a leaked video surfaced of him telling former teammates that "women playing hockey is a joke, and not even a funny one," fans of both leagues are outraged.

Fueling this fire, McAvoy responded to criticism

over his comments, stating on his social media accounts: "No one objects to keeping professional football and baseball as men's domains. It shouldn't be controversial to say that ice hockey is and always will be a men's sport."

While McAvoy's stats may still ensure him a place in the Hall of Fame one day, speculation that he'd be inducted within the next five years have gone all but silent.

"The Hall of Fame recognizes players for their hockey skill," a Hall representative told reporters, "but they are also expected to be ambassadors for the sport. To be so publicly disrespectful toward women's hockey is to not embody the values of the Hockey Hall of Fame."

In the weeks following the leaked video, BladeWorks and Karbon Stixx, manufacturers of ice skates and hockey sticks, respectively, each announced they were "moving on" from McAvoy's endorsement. On Wednesday of this week, sporting goods giant Bob's Athletic Gear, a massive corporate sponsor of the WHPL since the League's inception, announced they were ending their $5 million/year contract with McAvoy. CEO Mike Thorson said to shareholders, "They've (WHPL players) worked hard to get to where they are—they deserve better than this."

McAvoy is still contracted to endorse Colson Tires, Western Canada Fuel, and BioSurge Energy Drinks. Representatives from these companies did not respond to requests for comment, though there are unsubstantiated reports that BioSurge is holding a previously unscheduled vote among shareholders. The reason for this vote is unclear, though an insider believes it is regarding the McAvoy endorsement.

McAvoy did not respond to requests for comment, and his social media has not been updated for over a week.

PITTSBURGH BEARCATS SIGN MERCY NELSON
Agree to Terms with McAvoy, Austin

PITTSBURGH – With summer trades and free agency in full swing, the Pittsburgh Bearcats front office has been busy.

Unrestricted free agent Mercy Nelson (D), one of the hottest assets on the market this off season, just signed a four-year deal with the Bearcats. The two-time Cup champion with Calgary says she is "excited to play for Pittsburgh" and looks forward to joining the team in next season's campaign for a repeat victory.

Team captain Sabrina McAvoy (F) has agreed to terms for a five-year extension beginning next season at the end of her current two-year deal. She led the Eastern Conference in assists and points last season, and was second in the entire WHPL for power play goals.

Finally, Maryann Austin (G) has also agreed to

terms and is expected to sign a five-year deal as well. This past season, she was narrowly eked out for the Hale MVP Goalie Trophy by Hartford's Marta Lane. Austin ended the regular season with a 1.99 goals against average and 0.93 save percentage, close behind Lane's 1.93 GAA and 0.922 SV%.

Bearcats General Manager Chloe Morin told reporters there are other trades and deals in the works which will be announced soon.

Lila

Eighteen months after winning the Cup.

When I'd worn a suit instead of my gear for last season's home opener, I'd been miserable and restless. I'd hated being relegated to the bench for the introductions, then up to the owners' box to watch the game.

I'd wanted to *play hockey*, damn it.

Tonight, as the Pittsburgh Bearcats put on their gear for warmups at our third home opener, it was a little bittersweet. Yes, there would always be a part of me that wanted to play hockey. Always. It had been in my blood for as long as I could remember, and the ice would never stop calling to me. And I would play hockey for as long as my body would hold out—just not at this professional level. Not anymore.

Letting go had been heartbreaking, but once I'd made the decision, I'd quickly made peace with it. Taking that pressure off myself—both mental and physical—had been a bigger relief than I'd anticipated, and despite some second thoughts early on, I knew I'd made the right choice.

Things had worked out, too. I was happy with my new role with the Bearcats and with how my life had shaken out both professionally and personally. There would always be a part of me that missed the roar of the crowd and the push to win the Cup or the medal or whatever was at stake. I suspected most hockey players, even those long retired and into their twilight years, would always miss that.

But this? I could live with this.

The team started to head out for warmups. On her way to the tunnel, Sabrina paused. She smiled down at me—in her skates, she towered over me, especially since I could only wear flats—and she was sexy as hell.

"Ready for another season of chaos and pressure?" I asked with a grin.

"Absolutely." She kissed me lightly, returned my grin, and then continued out with the rest of the team.

Once the players had made their way to the ice, I followed along with the rest of the coaching staff.

It was still a little weird, walking down this long, familiar hallway in shoes instead of skates, but I felt all right. Even standing behind the bench and watching my former teammates warm up, I wasn't too bad, if a bit melancholy about the chapter of my life that had closed.

I'd tried. I really had. My knee had mostly recovered from that last injury and the subsequent surgery, but reality had started to make itself known when I'd returned to on-ice conditioning halfway through last season. It had been undeniable once I'd started practicing with the team.

My leg had been fine. Mostly pain-free. Mostly steady beneath me.

The problem was in my head.

I couldn't help treating my knee like it was made of glass. I was afraid to check or be checked. Every time I raced for a puck, I held back out of fear of losing an edge or ramming into the boards. Even board battles made me nervous because all it would take was getting tangled up in someone's stick or skates, and I could be back to square one. Every twinge sent panic through me. Every morning I woke up with an ache or some stiffness in that joint, I went through that cascade of *oh God what if I can't get past it this time?*

It was more mental than physical, and the therapist I'd started seeing had said it was something I could work through. A lot of people—athletes and otherwise—struggled to get past the fear of reinjury long after the injury itself had healed. That fear was no more insurmountable than the torn MCL had been.

Over time, I'd realized I didn't want to keep fighting against myself like that. I loved hockey, and I missed hockey, but there was no going back fully to the fearless, physical player I'd been before. More than I wanted to return to the ice, I wanted to let go of the stress and pressure.

So, about two weeks before I'd been expected to come off LTIR and be reactivated, I'd instead announced my retirement from professional hockey.

In the weeks between my decision and my announcement, I'd lost plenty of sleep, worrying I was about to make a huge mistake. The moment I'd made my retirement public, though, I'd been hit with more relief than I'd felt in a long, long time. As hard as it was to let hockey go, it was the right decision at the right time.

And it wasn't like I was completely disengaging from the sport. When I'd told Chloe I was retiring, she'd immediately asked if I was interested in a coaching position. I'd left her office with an offer in hand, which I'd accepted the next day.

Before the ink was even dry on my retirement, I was officially the new defensive coach for the Pittsburgh Bearcats.

I was officially in love with my new job, too. Training camp had been a blast, especially working with the prospects. We had some incredible young talent on the blue line, and I was excited to be helping them develop their amazing potential. Plus we'd acquired Mercy Nelson over the summer; a generational talent for our top defensive pair? Hell, yeah. She was also a great leader, and I loved working alongside her to make the Bearcats' defense into a force to be reckoned with.

Jamie Tucker, the terrified defender who'd been there for our Cup win, had come into her own last season. She'd been brought up a few times to fill in for injured players, and after this year's training camp, she was firmly ensconced on the third D pair. Her lack of confidence was a distant memory now—her future definitely looked bright, as did the team's future.

It looked pretty bright for me, too, even if it wasn't how I'd envisioned things not too long ago.

In addition to making changes to my career, Sabrina and I had made good on our plan to start an organization outfitting kids whose families couldn't afford hockey gear. Her brother was all over the idea, and he'd donated half a million dollars to get things off the ground. His wife—already a champ at running non-profit organizations—had offered to take the helm so Sabrina, Mark, and I could focus on hockey, and she was turning it into something amazing. Imani was making deals with everyone from stick manufacturers to corporate sponsors. Several teams, not to mention individual players and coaches, from both the WHPL and the men's league were donating money, time, and facilities so kids had access to not only gear, but ice time and instruction from professionals.

Sabrina and her brother had vowed to make sure every kid who signed up had the equipment and training that she'd desperately wanted and he'd had since he could walk. I was determined to keep as many kids as possible from facing the uphill battle that both Sabrina and I had, for different reasons, faced in our journey to the big leagues.

With Imani working her magic, money coming in from all directions, and kids signing up in droves... I was confident we were going to pull this off for real.

And while Imani turned our dream into reality, Sabrina and I were still living our other dream. The one we hoped some of these kids would eventually live as well.

Warmups ended and the Bearcats trooped back into the locker room. Since this was the home opener, the next step was the introductions of everyone on our roster.

That started with the coaches and front office, and one by one, we stepped out to our introductions.

"Your defensive coach," the announcer's voice boomed, "from Bethesda, Maryland, Lila Hamilton!"

The applause and cheering made my face warm, and I waved at the crowd as I joined the other coaches behind the bench. They roared when Coach Reilly was introduced as our head coach for yet another season, not to mention Andi Carter, the newly signed power play coach and of course, Faith, our skills coach.

After us, it was the players. The announcer read through the roster, and each player skated out to salute the crowd. Then came the alternate captains, followed by:

"From Buffalo, New York, number five, your captain, Sabrina Hamilton!"

My face hurt from smiling as the roar of applause went up. I was proud of my wife—who wouldn't be?—but there was also a little surge of triumph at the sound of her name and the sight of the letters beneath her number as she skated out to the circle.

Hamilton.

For all the hockey world had convinced itself Sabrina had ridden her father's name to the top, she was wearing *my* name now. *Our* name.

The press still referred to her as Sabrina McAvoy sometimes, or they hyphenated her name, but we figured that was something that would get better with time. I did notice they were mentioning her father, brother, and ex-husband far less often in articles these days, and sometimes they didn't mention them at all, so that was promising. Ever since Doran had opened his big mouth on social media and started shedding endorsements as a result, everyone had been hesitant to mention him at all unless they were discussing his plummet from grace.

In fact, the last time I'd seen his name come up in an article about Sabrina had been in the one announcing that we had gotten married over the summer. There was one line indicating that Doran had not come to the wedding, and the rest was about how happy we were and how supportive our families had been as we'd celebrated our marriage. I'd been a little salty that his name had come up at all, but Sabrina had made a good point about it.

"They basically said we were all having an amazing

time," she'd noted. "But he wasn't there. It makes him sound pathetic and alone." With a grin, she'd added, "He probably wishes they hadn't mentioned him either, because it just reminds him that we're all happy without him."

Couldn't really argue with that, could I?

Time and therapy had done a lot to help her come to terms with cutting off her dad. It probably also didn't hurt that she'd hit the father-in-law jackpot. I was biased, of course—I'd always known my dad was amazing—but he treated Sabrina better than Doran had ever aspired to. He texted her after games to either tell her she'd kicked ass or to her a little pep talk about how the next one would be better. He cracked her up with dad jokes, and she loved the way both my parents would goof around at family barbecues or holidays. The speech he'd given at our wedding—talking about how proud he was of both of us and how happy he was that we'd found each other—had made us both cry.

My mom adored Sabrina too, and she'd also become good friends with my mother-in-law. It wasn't unusual at all for the camera to find my parents and Sabrina's mom sitting together at games, especially on theme nights when they could all dress up.

If Doran wanted to be miserable, he was welcome to it—this family was doing just fine without him.

The player introductions had finished, and the team saluted the crowd. Then they skated back to the bench, and it was time to kick off the game.

I stood behind where the blue liners sat, while Sabrina would be sitting on the other end of the bench with the forwards. Right now, though, she was going to stay on the ice for the anthem and then puck drop.

Before she took her place for the anthem, she came up to the bench, took off her helmet, and grinned at me as she leaned over the boards. I recognized that sparkle in her eye, so I stepped over the bench and up close to her, and we shared a quick kiss.

"Good luck tonight," I said.

"Thanks." Holding my gaze, she smiled. "The name really has a nice ring to it when the announcer says it, doesn't it?"

I laughed. "It really does."

We exchanged smiles, and then she leaned in to kiss me again.

Our lips hadn't even met before the entire arena erupted with applause and cheers. Sabrina twisted around and we both looked up, and… surprise, surprise: there we were on the Jumbotron with the words KISS CAM underneath.

We both laughed, and I wondered if her face was as hot as mine.

Then she met my gaze again and gave a questioning half-shrug, raising her eyebrows. I just laughed, touched her face, and kissed her, prompting more cheers.

"All right." I playfully nudged her toward center ice. "Time to get to work."

She nodded. "Think we can get our names on the Cup again?"

"Pfft. Of course we can. Now get to work."

She winked. "Yes, Coach."

As she skated away my heart fluttered once more at the sight of *Hamilton* beneath her number.

Yeah, we could get our names on the Cup again. Hell yes, we could.

And this time, there wouldn't be a single trace of Doran McAvoy's legacy.

Just hers. Mine.

And ours.

ALSO BY LAUREN GALLAGHER

For more books by Lauren Gallagher, please visit
http://www.gallagherwitt.com

Contemporary Romance

Heterosexual * Sapphic * Bisexual

ALSO BY LAUREN GALLAGHER

Sapphic Romances:

BCC

Razor Wire

Stuck Landing

M/F & M/F/M Romances:

All the King's Horses

The Best Laid Plans

Who's Your Daddy?

Kneel, Mr. President

World Enough and Time

Light Switch

Reconstructing Meredith

Damaged Goods

The Virgin Cowboy Billionaire's Secret Baby

...and more!

ABOUT THE AUTHOR

Lauren Gallagher has finally settled in Pittsburgh along with her husband, two cats, a harem of concubines, and a phosphorescent porcupine, she remains, as always, in hiding from the Polynesian Mafia. For the moment, she seems to have eluded her nemesis, M/M romance author L.A. Witt, but she figures L.A. will eventually become bored with the Pittsburgh Penguins and come looking for her.

And when that time comes, Lauren will be ready. Assuming she doesn't have her hands full keeping track of Lori A. Witt and Ann Gallagher, which she probably will.

Website: http://www.gallagherwitt.com
    E-mail: gallagherwitt@gmail.com
    Twitter, Instagram, & Threads: @GallagherWitt

www.ingramcontent.com/pod-product-compliance
Lightning Source LLC
Chambersburg PA
CBHW031314280626
47169CB00019B/1614